G. Allen Wilbanks

DEAD TOWN

BOOKS BY G. ALLEN WILBANKS

DEAD TOWN SERIES

Dead Town

The Assassin's Spell

Coven Wars

ON DANGEROUS GROUNDS SERIES

Testing Grounds

Proving Grounds

Hunting Grounds

NOVELS

A Life of Adventure

When Darkness Comes

Deadly Seven

SHORT STORY COLLECTIONS

Thirteen Rooms

Not for Bedtime Stories

Deep Dark Thoughts Publications LLC

Dead Town

Visit my website at www.gallenwilbanks.com

This is a work of fiction. All characters and events in this publication, other than those clearly in the public domain, are fictitious, and any resemblance to real persons, living or dead, is purely coincidental.

Paperback: ISBN 978-1-952630-12-5

E-book: ISBN 978-1-952630-13-2

Cover design: MoorBooks Design

G. Allen Wilbanks

DEAD TOWN

Deep Dark Thoughts Publications LLC

For Jen, Allison, and Samantha

CHAPTER 1

Mitch Loman sprawled on his tattered brown couch. With his head resting on a pillow propped up on an arm of the sofa, he watched *It's a Wonderful Life* for the third time that day; reciting lines along with Jimmy Stewart as characters in black and white ran and cavorted on the television set in front of him.

He grabbed his whiskey tumbler from the coffee table. There was no coaster under the glass and condensation had left a wet ring on the polished, wooden tabletop. He didn't care. It wasn't as if Linda was still around to nag him about damaging the furniture, or anything else for that matter. He raised his head and brought the drink to his lips, finishing the last half swallow of alcohol remaining.

As soon as the glass was empty, he swung his feet to the floor and sat up. A green bottle of Glenfiddich was the only other item on the coffee table and Mitch scooped it up to pour another two fingers of amber liquid into the tumbler.

"Hmm," he mused, swirling the scotch around in the glass. "No ice."

He had started with two ice cubes, but they disappeared somewhere along with his second drink. Frowning, he pushed himself to his feet with an audible groan, then wandered into the kitchen to replenish. As he opened the freezer and plopped two more ice cubes into his scotch, Mitch glanced at the cheap, plastic clock on the wall over the kitchen window. The hands indicated it was 9:38 PM.

He took a long, deep breath and released it slowly. It was time.

Returning to the living room, Mitch settled back onto the couch, propped his sock-covered feet on the coffee table, and resumed watching his movie.

"Daddy?" a voice called from the stairs behind him. He turned to find a four-year old boy in blue, footed pajamas peering at him through the wooden railing. The child's fine, blond hair was mussed and damp, and one small fist was pressed to his eyes trying to wipe away the sleep. "Did Santa come?"

"Hey, there's my big guy," said Mitch, setting his glass on the table. "No, buddy, he hasn't come, yet. It's only nine-forty. He won't come for a little while."

"Oh, okay." The boy turned to climb back up the stairs.

"Hey, Denny," Mitch called out. "Why don't you come sit with me and watch a movie for a little bit? We can hang out for five minutes. It's your favorite. It's the one with the silly guy that ties strings all over his fingers."

The child stared at his father for a moment in surprised disbelief, then with a grin, he toddled quickly down the steps. With one hand held high, he balanced himself against the banister as he navigated the last few stairs. The moment his pajama clad feet hit the floor, he ran for the couch as if the carpet were hot and he might burn his toes if he touched it too long. Denny flopped into his father's lap and curled up, sticking a thumb into his mouth while settling in to watch the movie on tv. Mitch wrapped his arms around the boy and hugged him tightly, resting his cheek against the top of his son's head and inhaling the musty scent of his sweaty hair.

"Where's Mommy?" asked Denny, pulling his thumb from his mouth only long enough to ask the question.

"Sorry, buddy. Mommy isn't here right now. But don't worry, she'll be back before you get up tomorrow morning."

"I love Christmas," Denny said, squirming with nervous energy in his father's lap and bobbing his head to the rhythm of some far-off music that only he could hear.

"I do, too," said Mitch. He sniffed and wiped at a sudden wetness in his left eye.

The two sat in contented silence, watching an angel named Clarence try to earn his wings. Denny suddenly turned to look at his father, a concerned, serious expression clouding his face. "Did you remember to tell Santa what I wanted?"

"I did, buddy. But just to be sure, why don't you tell me again? You know, in case Santa's listening right now. That way, you can be sure he gets it right."

Denny looked up toward the ceiling and peered around the living room as though trying to figure out where Santa Claus might be hiding. He announced in a loud, deliberate voice, "I want a new teddy bear. The brown one with a yellow tummy that Daddy and me saw at the store."

Mitch squeezed Denny again and leaned close to whisper in his ear. "I think he heard you. I think you're going to get that teddy bear."

Denny squealed with pleasure at the news. "It'll be under the tree in the morning?" he asked.

"You bet," Mitch assured the boy before pausing to swallow a sharp lump that had formed in this throat. He wiped at his eyes again. "I would love to sit here and hang out with you, bud, but you know Santa won't come until you go to sleep. Maybe it's time for you to head back up to bed."

"You said I could watch the movie with you," the child complained.

"I did, but our five minutes are up."

Denny did not argue further. He twisted enough to hug his father around the neck before sliding off his lap and scampering up the stairs on all fours. Mitch watched the boy until he disappeared from view at the second-floor landing.

Not bothering with the glass this time, Mitch picked up the Glenfiddich and drank directly from the bottle. The alcohol burned his throat going down, just as he hoped that it would. It was going to be a long night, and sober was no way for him to get through it.

Mitch slumped into the couch cushions with his chest and stomach pleasantly on fire and tried to make himself concentrate on the ending of the movie. They had reached his favorite part. Jimmy Stewart was alive and running maniacally around the town annoying anyone who paused long enough to listen. Mitch couldn't focus, though. His thoughts wandered back to his fight with Linda.

She had wanted him to sell this house and move two-thousand miles to live closer to her parents. She said she couldn't stand being here any longer and didn't understand why he wanted to stay. He told her there was no way in hell he was moving, but if she really wanted to leave, she was free to go. Mitch regretted saying that last part. He took another long drink from the bottle in his effort to get drunk enough to pass out.

He was unsuccessful.

Forty-five minutes crawled by as he wrapped his head in the haze of hard alcohol. The damned movie started over again for the fourth time. Mitch thought he might have dozed for a moment but was unsure if it was actually sleep or the alcohol that had turned his brain off. He was startled fully awake by a high-pitched scream coming from upstairs. The sound lasted barely a second before it suddenly cut off.

Mitch did not go upstairs. There was no point. He knew he probably shouldn't go outside either, but he did not have the strength to sit on the couch and do nothing. Still clutching the whiskey bottle in one hand, he exited the sliding door at the rear of the house and staggered out onto the back patio.

A small, crumpled, blue form heaped on the concrete patio drew his eyes immediately. Denny lay face down and unmoving no more than ten feet from where Mitch stood. He froze, swaying drunkenly, unsure how to react as he stared at the broken shape of his child. A million half-formed responses swam through his booze-soaked mind, none of them able to completely resolve into a coherent thought. Anger, loss, regret, and self-recrimination all fought for dominance in the soup of emotion filling his head.

A slight twitch of the boy's left hand finally broke his paralysis.

Mitch glanced upward and noted the open, second-story window of his son's room. He had closed and locked it earlier this evening but, of course, that had been futile. He lurched a few unsteady steps forward and collapsed gracelessly to sit next to the boy. Setting the whiskey bottle down carefully so it would not tip over, he gathered Denny into his arms and cradled him in his lap, just as he had done an hour ago on the couch.

The boy remained motionless, but Mitchell could feel his labored heartbeat against his own chest and the intermittent rise and fall of Denny's ribcage as his son struggled to breathe. He pressed his cheek against the back of Denny's head, feeling the dampness there and knowing this time it was not the child's sweat wetting his hair.

Denny would not wake up again. His injuries were too severe for him to regain consciousness. Still, it would be thirty-eight minutes before his body completely failed, his heart would cease beating, and this ordeal could finally end.

Mitchell fumbled out a hand and found the bottle resting beside him. He upended it into his mouth, taking another long drink.

Nine hours later, the moment the front gates were unlocked in the morning, Mitchell wandered into Dasan's Terrace Memorial Park and Cemetery a few miles from his home. Nauseated, cotton-mouthed, and still slightly drunk from his binging the night before, he staggered among the headstones carrying a brown grocery bag tightly clutched in his arms. His feet led him unerringly to where he wanted to be, though he paid little attention to where he was going. Rows of neat, orderly headstones and polished marble markers filed past him, almost unnoticed. He stopped when he arrived at the correct location and dropped onto his knees next to one of the grave sites, still hugging the bag to his chest.

Waiting patiently in the grass and dirt, leaning against the headstone, a faded and moldy teddy bear sat vigil over the grave. Despite the weather and sun damage from twelve months of silent guard duty, the stuffed toy still had a few thick patches of fur that had maintained their original soft, brown color. Shiny, black plastic eyes gazed unblinkingly at Mitch, as if to ask, "Is it time?"

Mitch picked up the bear and set it aside in the grass next to him. Reaching into the paper bag, he removed a brand-new version of the same bear. It was identical to its tired, faded brother, but it glistened in the sunlight with the sheen of undampened, store-bought perfection. A fresh soldier to relieve the old, exhausted sentry.

Mitch lovingly settled the new bear at its post at the base of the arched headstone, brushing at the grass to level a spot for the toy to sit. When the bear was secure in its new home, he laid his hand against the cool, damp stone marker behind it. His breathing caught and hitched as he ran his fingertips along the letters and numbers etched into the gray marble slab.

DENNIS CHRISTOPHER LOMAN

FEBRUARY 12, 2016 - DECEMBER 24, 2019

"Merry Christmas, buddy," Mitch whispered. "Santa brought you a new bear, just like you asked. Just like you always ask."

Tears flowed freely down Mitchell's cheeks as he picked up the faded old bear next to his thigh and rose to his feet. Its time here was finished at last, and it would soon join its predecessors in the toybox at the rear of Denny's closet. Mitch could not bring himself to throw it away, to throw any of them away. The very idea of discarding the Christmas gift felt wrong. No, he would keep it with the others.

He sniffed and swiped the sleeve of his shirt across his face.

"I really miss you, Denny. But I'll see you again next Christmas Eve."

CHAPTER 2

Professor Solomon Schick opened his eyes. Inhaling and releasing slow, shallow breaths, and staring off into the nighttime gloom of his bedroom, he wondered why he was awake. At 68 years old, Solomon was no stranger to sleepless nights. Various aches in his joints and muscles frequently roused him from slumber, and his losing battle with his own bladder typically drove him from the shelter of his bed two or three times each night, but this was different. This time, something outside of his own physical ailments and bodily needs had brought him awake.

Curled on his side under thick, warm blankets, he was comfortable, neither too hot nor too cold. Nothing hurt, and his bladder was not at the moment uncomfortably full. The house was silent, and he had not been having a bad dream. Quite the opposite, in fact. So, what had disturbed his peaceful rest?

Solomon closed his eyes and tried to will himself back to sleep, back to the quickly dissipating fragments of the pleasant dream he had been enjoying before being so rudely pulled from its embrace. After only a few seconds, his eyes popped back open. He puffed out a frustrated breath and decided that since he was already awake, he might as well take the opportunity to urinate. It was probably better to take care of the task now than to fall back asleep only to be awakened in thirty minutes time by a more urgent need to do so.

Before he could move, he heard a distant creak from somewhere downstairs. He froze, and his heart stuttered in his chest. Solomon lived in an old house, and it was prone to groans and moans as the aged foundation occasionally resettled itself. That was nothing new. This sound, however, was not a random shift of the home's framework; this sound was more familiar than that.

He knew this sound.

It was the high-pitched squeak created by a particular loose board in his library only a few paces inside the doorway. It was the sound of a person's weight settling onto the warped floorboard and causing it to flex just the tiniest fraction of an inch. Solomon was intimately familiar with the wood's keening complaint as it greeted him several times each day. Every time he stepped into the library to find a book to read, or to admire the various contents of his small collection of antiquities, the board's creak welcomed him into the room.

If Solomon was upstairs in bed, wrapped warmly in his covers, then whose weight was on that board?

His hands grew cold, and they began to shake slightly. Solomon lived alone and there were very few people in this world that he trusted with a key to his front door. He could imagine no reason why any of those who had a key would suddenly find a need to secretly visit him at this early hour of the morning. Somebody was in his house, and it was not someone he wished to be there.

He held his breath so as to better hear any further noises from downstairs. The house remained quiet, but Solomon did not try to fool himself into believing it had been his imagination. He was awake and the sound had not been merely a part of his dream pulled into consciousness. There was a prowler in his home. He was absolutely certain of that fact.

His home had an alarm system that Solomon used without fail whenever he went out, but it was currently turned off. In order to use it at night when he was home, he had to disable several of the motion sensors so he did not set off the alarm himself during one of his numerous trips to the bathroom. It was only a couple of extra buttons to push. Still, he had gotten tired of the additional steps and now opted to leave the damned thing off during the night. Solomon cursed himself silently for his laziness.

With his right hand, Solomon pushed the covers down. An uncomfortable rush of cold air swept away the warmth trapped under his blanket causing him to shiver. Or perhaps the shiver was from more than just the cold. He swung one leg forward, preparing to place his foot on the floor and rise from the bed, when a section of the box-spring supporting his mattress cried out with its own rusty complaint to match that of the floorboard downstairs. Solomon froze again, eyes squeezed shut and teeth clenched as he willed the bed to remain quiet.

He held the awkward pose for several seconds, balanced on his hip with one leg extended, hoping he had not been heard, yet fearing that he had. The world seemed to pause with him. Solomon was reminded of nature programs where predator and prey became aware of one another, but each held their ground, unsure as to what their next move should be. Solomon was similarly unsure as to what his next move should be. He was not even certain which side of the coin he represented in this situation. Was he predator? Or prey?

The house felt unnaturally silent as both current occupants remained motionless, waiting on the other to make the next move. They had entered the eye of a storm, knowing the calm surrounding them was merely an illusion, and the false peace would be swept away when the tempest inevitably returned.

Solomon had almost decided to climb from his bed, regardless of how much noise he might make, when the crash of breaking glass echoed through his home. The intruder had also decided that stealth was no longer an option and moved on to direct action. The shattering glass was followed by the pounding of soft-soled shoes slapping the hardwood floors as his uninvited guest ran out of the library, through the living room and into the kitchen. There was no sound from the back door, so Solomon assumed it was already opened and the intruder had not bothered to close it behind himself – herself? – as they fled into the yard.

Tossing the blankets aside, the professor scrambled to his feet, pausing only long enough to step into the slippers he kept at the foot of his bed. He rushed from the bedroom toward the stairs. There was always a risk the burglar was still downstairs, or perhaps there had been more than one intruder and, although one had fled, the second was waiting for Solomon to come stumbling downstairs into his waiting arms.

He did not think so, however. He felt quite certain whoever had broken into his house had taken flight and was now as far away from the home as he or she could get in the time it took Solomon to get down the stairs. When he reached the landing on the first floor, he discovered he was correct in his assumption. The rear door to the house was standing wide open into the waiting dark of night, and there was no sign of anyone remaining inside his home.

Ignoring the opened kitchen door, Solomon hurried into the library to determine the source of the breaking glass sounds. There were four glass covered display cases in the library, each holding artifacts he had collected during his travels as a young man throughout Europe and northern Africa. Three of those cases held items that were extremely valuable to the right collectors, while the fourth contained something highly dangerous if it ever fell into the wrong hands. He prayed it was only a financial loss he had suffered.

Solomon felt his heart drop into his stomach, his guts knotting painfully as he surveyed the damage. It was the fourth case that had been shattered. Two small pedestals stood prominently inside the destroyed glass box, one to either side of the display space. They were both empty.

"Oh, no. No, no, no, no, no."

Solomon approached the case and dropped to his knees, heedless of the shards of glass littering the floor. He ran his hands through the broken pieces, hoping to find the objects inside the case had merely been displaced and fallen to the floor. It was only through a minor miracle that he was not cut by the jagged fragments.

When there was no remaining doubt the contents were indeed gone, he pushed himself back to his feet. He stared at the two empty pedestals. Their round, bare surfaces seemed to glare back at him accusingly, like two flat, mahogany eyes. Solomon had assured the old rabbi, his mentor, that he would keep the objects safe. He had promised.

He had failed.

"This is very bad," he muttered. "Very, very bad."

CHAPTER 3

"Good morning, Dot. You're in early, today."

At the unexpected greeting, Dorothy Kristiansen paused in her typing and peered over the computer monitor on her desk to see who had wandered into the front office. She smiled at the familiar face grinning down at her then turned her attention back to the display in front of her, disappearing behind the wide, rectangular screen and all the other various clutter gathered across her workspace. A long, triangular placard perched on the front of her desk read: DOT KRISTIANSEN, ADMINISTRATIVE ASSISTANT.

"Good morning, Chief. Yeah, I guess so. I didn't sleep very well last night, so I thought I might as well get up and come in to work."

Simon Jefferson, Chief of Police for the Dasan's Terrace Police Department, frowned slightly at his secretary's pronouncement. "Couldn't sleep? Bad dreams, or anything I should know about?"

Dot waved a hand dismissively. "No. Nothing like that. Just your average bout of insomnia. So, how was your night? Sleep well?"

"I did," Simon agreed. "I slept very well. Better than I have in a while, as a matter of fact."

The chief stepped around the desk and behind Dot's chair to peer over her shoulder at what she had been typing when he walked in. With the chief standing directly behind her, the two appeared as physically different as any pair of people could be. Dot was tiny - a perfect example of her nickname – with a porcelain complexion, long blond hair, and bright green eyes. She appeared delicate, almost birdlike, as she sat at the edge of her chair. Simon, in contrast was a stocky man with dark skin, black hair that he kept cropped close to his scalp, and light, smokey gray eyes. He was broad through the chest, with wide shoulders and long arms, and though he was growing a bit soft in the middle, his physique was still more muscle than fat.

At five feet, eight inches tall, Simon was only of average height, though he still appeared to tower over Dot. But then, so did most people. Standing upright, Dot failed to reach five feet tall without the aid of heels.

Their personalities were equally disparate. At only twenty-six years old, Dot's tiny frame and bubbly personality made her appear younger still, and many people upon first meeting her quickly dismissed her as a child. Simon had never been taken for anything but an overly serious man, grown old before his time. He had never been perceived as a child, even when he had actually been one.

Despite all the physical and character differences, they were alike where it mattered. Both were smart, dedicated, and worked well together. As a team, they had been running the DTPD like a well-oiled machine for the past five years.

"What are you working on?" Simon asked.

"The Board of Supervisors is voting on those emergency budget cuts next week. Supervisor Sommers has been talking about taking a bite out of the Sheriff's funding. I just thought I – although I suppose I should say 'we' since it's your name on the email – should remind him that the DTPD is still part of the Sheriff's Office."

Simon leaned closer and read over Dot's shoulder. "'In closing, I would like to say thank you for the recent invitation to your home. It was a pleasure to have the opportunity to meet with you and your lovely family.' That was subtle."

"It's a public email address. Other people are going to see it, so I figured that was better than saying, 'Hey, remember when we took that poltergeist out of your house?'"

Simon laughed appreciatively. "True. Do you think we should threaten to return the antique chair it was attached to?"

"I thought about it," Dot muttered seriously, "but it would be an empty threat. Violet already came by and exorcised it. Remember? It's just an old rocking chair, now."

"Too bad." Simon straightened. "Go ahead and send the email. Consider it reviewed and approved."

A few quick taps on her keyboard and Dot sent the message on its way. She spun her chair to face the Chief.

"Done. So, what do we have on the agenda for today?"

"For me? Not much," said Simon. "I have a few phone calls to return this morning, and I'm meeting Captain Butler for lunch. The rest of my calendar is clear. You, on the other hand, are going to be running some errands."

The Chief disappeared into his office as Dot sat patiently waiting for the other shoe to drop. She had a suspicion already as to what these unspecified errands were going to be, and when Simon returned holding three slender Manilla folders, she nodded to herself in confirmation.

"Assuming our budget remains intact, we have an open position we need to fill. Out of the lateral transfer requests we received when we posted the position, these three are the only ones that I am considering." He handed Dot the files and she began to leaf through them. "I'd like you to go meet with each candidate and size them up before we schedule interviews."

"The informal interview before the formal one?" Dot said.

"Exactly. I figure why bring them in and make them sit through an hour of interrogation if you already know in the first thirty seconds that they aren't going to fit in here. Two of the candidates are working this morning and I've arranged with their lieutenants to make them available to you when you arrive. The third deputy doesn't come in until two o'clock this afternoon, so I figured you can go out and have a nice lunch before you meet with her."

Dot rolled her eyes. "I can have lunch? How sweet of you. You're always thinking about your employees, aren't you, Chief?"

"What can I say?" Simon concurred. "I'm a giver."

"Fine. I'll check them out. Do me a favor, though. Can you give me a couple of blank application forms? You never can tell. I have a good feeling I might stumble across someone interesting."

Mitch sat on the damp grass with his back pressed against the side of his son's headstone. The surrounding cold and the wetness soaking into his pants left him chilled and shivering slightly despite the heavy coat he wore to fight off the January weather. He didn't mind the discomfort. In a way, he felt it was appropriate, that he deserved whatever punishment his surroundings had to offer. He had failed his only child because of his negligence. What was a little cold in the face of that colossal sin?

He had failed a lot of people, he realized. He lost his son, then his wife, and most of his friends. They hadn't simply abandoned him, either. He had worked very hard over the past few years to drive them away. His own father barely spoke to him these days. On top of all that, he was now facing the loss of his job.

"Your old man really messed up this time, Denny. I might not be with the Sheriff's department much longer. I think they want to fire me this time."

Mitch picked a few shoots of grass from between his feet and tossed them away, watching them drift to the left with the steady wind blowing through the cemetery.

"Remember last year? I told you I went in to work right after you … after you came to visit me. Somebody smelled booze on my breath while I was working and reported me. They gave me a week off without pay and sent me to that rehab center for a few weeks. I didn't need it. I'm not an alcoholic. I only drink around Christmas when I know you're coming."

A stricken look crossed Mitch's features, and he spun to face the gravesite. He reached out and stroked a hand across the fur of the teddy bear sitting sentry in front of the headstone.

"That's not your fault, buddy. You know that, right? That's my fault for not knowing how to handle my own emotions. You haven't done anything wrong. I don't want you to feel bad about visiting and I want you to know it's okay that you come see Daddy on Christmas."

He paused for a moment as if expecting a reply from either the teddy bear or the grave. When both remained silent, Mitch settled back against the stone marker.

"Anyway, that doesn't matter. This year, I thought I was being a little smarter. I stopped going to work until I could sober up. I stayed home for three weeks. They can't write me up for drinking on the job if I'm not there, right? And I have the leave balances on the books, so why not?"

Mitch shook his head ruefully.

"Turns out, you can't take that much time without a note from a doctor, and no doctor is going to write me a note saying, 'Mitch can't come to work because he can't stop drinking.' My boss asked Internal Affairs to open an investigation on me. I'm being accused of job abandonment, neglection of duty, and drinking on the job." He laughed, a short bark of noise that had no real humor to it.

"Drinking on the job," Mitch snorted. "My lieutenant said because I had no excuse for not coming into work, that he considers me technically to have been at work while I was home drinking. It's a bullshit charge. Sorry about the language, buddy."

Mitch patted the bear again.

"I shouldn't talk like that around you, but Daddy's a little upset. The fact they're charging me with drinking on the job again means they want to use the progressive discipline clause against me. If they can prove I violated the same policy twice, they can hand down a larger punishment than if I only did it once. That's why the lieutenant is trying to get the drinking on duty accusation to stick. He doesn't like me, and he wants me gone. I think he's going to be able to do it, too."

He lowered his head until his chin rested on one knee.

"He wants to fire me. He'll probably get what he wants. He usually does. He already got me suspended until the investigation is finished. At least I'm still getting paid for now."

Sniffing, Mitch wiped a hand under his nose. He told himself it was just the cold making his nose run, ignoring the wetness that had formed in his eyes.

"I'm not sure what I'm going to do if I lose this job. I don't have a lot of extra cash lying around. I'll figure something out, though. Don't you worry, Denny. I promise you I will find a way to keep making the house payments. As long as you need a place to come back to every Christmas, I am going to make sure you have a home with me to do it. I won't abandon you. Not like…"

He shook his head. He was being unfair to Linda, and he knew it. She couldn't be blamed for needing to leave. Mitch dealt with Denny's visits by drinking himself into oblivion every December, so who was he to throw stones?

"Never mind. Mommy and I both love you, and we will find a way to keep the house."

Mitch fell silent. He peered up at the gray skies overhead and tried to guess the likelihood of rain in the next few hours. Although clouds covered the world all the way to the horizon, they did not look particularly threatening. Not yet. His gaze fell back to the grass between his feet. He spent the next half hour in that position, letting his mind loop over and over on how he might be able to keep his job, or what else he might be qualified to do if he got fired.

Being a cop was all he had ever known. He went to college and earned a degree in criminal justice, then hired on with the Sacramento County Sheriff's Office right out of school. He didn't know how to do anything else.

Mitch finally stood up. He wiped at the back of his pants, but the damp had soaked through the material all the way to his skin by this time and the gesture was pointless. He tapped the top of Denny's headstone with a gentle finger. "I love you, buddy. I'm going to go now, but I'll be back to see you again soon. I don't have a job to go to, so I have a lot of free time on my hands. We'll talk some more later."

Stuffing his hands into his coat pockets, Mitch started walking. The Dasan's Terrace cemetery grounds were massive, covering over 600 acres of land. Much of it was designated as a historical landmark, with grave markers and stones dating back almost two hundred and fifty years. There were older, unmarked graves as well, believed to contain the bones and artifacts of several Native American tribes that had lived in the area. These areas were fenced in, unvisited, with old growth trees, rock outcroppings, and some protected wildlands interspersed among the burial plots. In contrast, the more recently used areas, including Denny's grave, were green and flat and perfectly manicured by a team of gardeners. There were even concrete paths and lighting fixtures for evening visitors.

The newer property was also closer to the cemetery parking lot, so Mitch did not have far to walk to get to his car.

Mitch stepped off the curb from the main cemetery grounds into the narrow, paved, parking strip. Pulling keys from his pocket as he approached his blue Ford sedan, he noticed a girl standing at the far end of the lot watching him. She was blond and slender, and appeared to be no more than twelve or thirteen years old. The girl had a stack of papers tucked under one arm and a hand buried in her purse as though she had been searching for her own keys when she spotted Mitch. Her head tilted a little as she observed him.

He glanced around the parking area and then toward the office buildings directly behind the girl, looking for her parents. Was she lost, he wondered, or had they sent her out to get something from their car?

The girl laughed.

"No," she called out to him. "My mother isn't here. She's actually been dead for quite a while. And, no, I'm not lost either."

"I'm sorry?" Mitch replied, startled by her comments. Could she hear his thoughts? "Can I help you?"

"I'm twenty-six, but I know that, *'are-you-lost-little-girl?'* look when I see it."

Mitch felt color rising in his face, and the girl laughed again.

"It's okay. You're not the first person to assume my age, and you won't be the last, I'm sure. My name's Dot, by the way."

"Mitch," Mitch replied.

The girl, Dot, strode purposefully through the parking lot toward him. Mitch simply stood beside his car and waited as she approached. When she was only a few steps away, she paused.

"You work for the Sheriff's department?" she asked.

"Um, I do," stammered Mitch, surprised by the question. "I'm a detective. How did you…?"

In answer, Dot pointed toward Mitch's waist. His coat was partially open, revealing his badge clipped onto his belt. "Lucky guess," she teased. "Me, too. I'm the Chief's secretary at Dasan's Terrace Police Department."

"The cemetery has police officers?" asked Mitch, surprised. "I thought it was just security guards here."

"No. We're real cops. The cemetery contracts deputies from the Sheriff's office. In fact, while I have your attention, we need a new officer. Would you be interested in transferring to our department?"

Mitch smiled and waved a hand in the negative. "That's nice of you to ask, but no, thanks. Your chief wouldn't want me even if I did put in an application."

"I think you're wrong, there," said Dot, seriously. "I think he would very much want you. In fact, I think you are exactly what we need. I also think you and I were supposed to meet today."

Dot pulled open her purse and rummaged around the contents until she found what she wanted. She removed a sheet of paper folded in half. Opening it, she held it out toward him. Mitch read the top line of the form. It stated: "Inter-agency Transfer Request."

Mitch stepped back a pace. "Look. Not that it's any of your business, but I'm probably going to be out of a job in the next couple weeks, so this is a really bad time for you to be trying to recruit me."

He turned his back on the tiny woman and held up his car keys. He pushed a button on the black plastic fob, and the Ford chirped twice as it unlocked.

"Wait!" interjected Dot. "What if I told you that I could help you keep your job? We really do need a new officer, and I believe you may be exactly the person we want to bring in. If Chief Jefferson likes you, and I think he will, he can make whatever problems you're having go away."

She paused, pensively, then asked, "You didn't kill anyone, did you?"

Mitch turned back toward Dot. "No, I didn't kill anyone."

"Then give us a chance. What could it hurt?"

She held out the paper again.

"Fill it out and give it back to me. See what happens."

"You had better not be fucking with me," Mitch warned.

Dot did not flinch at the language. *Maybe she really does work around cops,* he thought.

Mitch accepted the paper this time. He glanced at it to give himself something to do as he considered the offer. He currently did not have a lot of options, and if this crazy woman really was presenting him with a chance to save his job, who was he to turn it down? After a moment, he sighed.

"I suppose it can't make things any worse than they already are. Okay, I'll fill it out."

"Good!" said Dot. She reached back in her purse and retrieved a pen. She held it out toward Mitch.

"Oh, you want me to fill it out right now."

Dot nodded firmly. "I want you to fill it out and hand it back to me before you leave my sight. I'm not letting you get away."

CHAPTER 4

Dot had not been lying when she said she could help Mitch with his current difficulties, and she wasted no time in proving it. The following morning, Mitch awoke to the sound of his cell phone ringtone. He picked up the phone and blearily peeked through one half-opened eye to read the display screen. It was his lieutenant from the detective's bureau.

Groaning, Mitch tapped the accept button on his screen and held the phone to his ear.

"Detective Loman here," he said. There was a long, empty pause before the lieutenant responded.

"Detective," said Mitch's boss, sounding unhappy about something. That was nothing new. The Lieutenant frequently sounded displeased around Mitch. The two had never been the best of friends before the Internal Affairs complaint, and their relationship had only gotten worse from there. "This is Lieutenant Hostler."

Yeah. I know who it is, you asshole. What do you want? Mitch did not say the words out loud, but instead waited patiently for the lieutenant to continue.

"I don't know what you did, or how you did it, but your complaint investigation has been put on temporary hold. I can only guess that you went and cried to one of the captains or chiefs and they bought your story. It won't last, though. I'll make sure of that."

"Sir?" said Mitch, growing angry at the accusations leveled at him by his supervisor. It was bad enough the man wanted him fired, now he was waking him up in the morning to attack his character? What a prick. This was still his boss, however, so he had to be careful how he responded. "Are you calling me for a reason, or is this social?"

He heard Hostler sigh in frustration on the other end of the line. "You have been reinstated until further notice. This was not my idea, but I'm ordering you back to work, effective immediately."

"Oh. Okay. Um, I need to shower, then I'll be at the office as soon as I can…" Mitch trailed off as he realized he was talking to empty air. The lieutenant had already hung up.

Mitch set his phone aside and stared at the ceiling. He thought about the transfer papers he signed for Dot and wondered what exactly he had gotten himself into. Whatever it was, Lieutenant Hostler clearly didn't like it. Which was fine. Mitch generally enjoyed anything that made the lieutenant unhappy. If the whole deal fell through, however, this was only going to make things worse in the long run. Whatever steps Dot had taken in the past twenty-four hours had bought him some breathing room, but as soon as the temporary hold on Mitch's investigation ended, the lieutenant would come after him with all guns blazing.

Mitch soon discovered that Dot was not yet finished working her magic. The following morning, he received an email from the Human Resources Department. He was directed to report to Chief Simon Jefferson's office at the Dasan's Terrace Police Department for a formal interview to determine fitness for permanent reassignment. The interview was scheduled for the following week.

Transfer requests generally took weeks or even months to process and finalize. It seemed Chief Jefferson's bubbly little office assistant was determined to have everything completed in a matter of days. More shocking still, Human Resources had jumped to accommodate her.

Mitch closed the email. He sat back in his office chair and stared at the now blank computer monitor. The desk in front of him was bare except for a lime green blotter, a ceramic mug full of pens, a desk calendar, and a completely empty, black plastic inbox. Although Mitch had been ordered back to work, Lieutenant Hostler had not seen fit to assign him any actual cases. It was a subtle reminder that his boss did not think this return to the office was going to last for very long.

With nothing else constructive to do, Mitch opened a window on his computer with his internet browser. He had an interview to prepare for. Maybe it was time to do a little research on Dasan's Terrace and this odd little police department that he had never previously heard of.

Mitch paused in the cemetery parking lot, studying the police administrative building. Standing in almost the same spot where he had first met Dot Kristiansen a week ago, he straightened his tie with one hand and pulled the coat of his suit together before buttoning the front closed.

The structure in front of him was two stories tall, but three stories in all, with two levels above ground and one below. The bottom floor was officer locker rooms, an armory, two supply closets, and a massive property storage room. The ground floor was a reception area, patrol briefing room, a computer room for report writing, and officer and sergeant work desks. It also held a bare-bones dispatch center including one computer, a phone, a radio, and not much else. The dispatch room didn't need much since it was only used for special operations or large events on the cemetery property. The rest of the time, the officers simply used person to person radio channels for communication.

The top floor held offices for the Chief, Assistant Chief, administrative assistants, and any other brass temporarily assigned to the DTPD. There were also several conference rooms and smaller meeting spaces. It was to this floor that he was headed today.

He was about to meet the chief for the first time. A great deal was hanging on this interview for Mitch. If it went badly, he had no doubt the suspension would be reinstated, and his Internal Affairs investigation would immediately start again. Lieutenant Hostler would be breathing down his neck the second after that happened. He had to impress Chief Jefferson or he would be unemployed, and very soon.

He took a deep breath and straightened his tie once more, though it remained smooth and flat against his shirt. Mitch could not recall being this nervous in a long time. Of course, it had been a long time since he had so much riding on a single interview.

Striding through the parking lot like a death row inmate on his final march to oblivion, he approached the front doors of the building. By the end of this day, his fate would be decided.

He would have a new job, or he would be days away from no job at all. Mitch felt a sudden urge to run, to dash back to his car and drive away. He squashed the impulse and forced his feet to keep moving forward. When he reached the entry doors, he congratulated himself on his courage as he grasped the handle after only a brief hesitation.

To his surprise, as he pulled one of the paired front doors open, he found Dot in the lobby, chatting amiably with an elderly gentleman in a pale blue uniform, seated at the reception desk.

"There he is," she exclaimed, when she spotted Mitch in the doorway. "Right on time. Mitchell, this is D.J. He's one of the volunteers that help out around here. D.J., this is Mitchell Loman. I'm hoping he is going to be our newest officer."

The old man smiled and nodded a greeting. "Good morning, Mitchell. Nice to meet you."

Mitch nodded awkwardly back. "Uh, you too, D.J."

"Don't stand there like a lost puppy. The Chief is eager to meet you. Come on." Dot waved a beckoning arm, indicating Mitch should follow her into the building.

He raised a hand in farewell to D.J. as he passed the desk, then positioned himself beside Dot, who was waiting at an interior door. D.J. reached under his desk and pressed a button, buzzing them both into the secure areas of the main building.

Dot led Mitch to a stairwell and guided him upstairs to the second floor.

"We can do the whole tour thing later if you like. There isn't a lot to see, though. The entire department functions out of this one building. The other buildings on the property are all part of the cemetery and dedicated to their business operations, so unless there is a problem, the officers rarely go into any of them. Before you ask, there is an elevator in our building, but I find it takes longer to wait for it than simply using the stairs. Hope you don't mind a little exercise."

"No. Not at all," he said.

Dot continued with a lively banter during the trek up to the second floor. At the head of the stairwell, they stepped into an open landing area with three doors leading north, south, and west. Mitch was pointed toward the west door and ushered through.

"These are our offices. Mine is the first desk you pass from here, and the chief's office is directly behind me. We are going left into the breakroom for command staff. The chief thought it would be a little more informal and comfortable for you than bringing you into his office. That, and we have easy access to water, coffee and snacks."

Mitch followed Dot's directions and walked past her desk, down a short hallway, and into the breakroom. The chief's secretary followed him in, tugging the door handle so the door swung closed behind them. The room was already occupied when he stepped inside. A stocky, black man wearing a class-A police uniform was seated at a long, cafeteria-style table, balanced on a flimsy plastic and metal chair. The man was clean shaven, and his dark hair was cut very close to the scalp. He peered up at Mitch with gray eyes the color of a thundercloud. An almost full, steaming mug of coffee rested on the table in front of him. The two, tiny gold stars on his lapel informed Mitch this was Chief Jefferson.

The man rose as Mitch entered the breakroom, a broad smile on his face. The chief was almost half a foot shorter than Mitch's own six feet, but the ease in which he moved and his sense of control over his surroundings filled the entire room, making Mitch feel dwarfed in his presence. He looked to be only in his mid-thirties, though he carried himself like someone much older.

"Hello, Mitch. Dot has told me so much about you I feel like we've already met." He extended a hand.

Mitch glanced back toward Dot, confused. He had only spoken with her one time in a parking lot for all of five minutes. How much did she have to tell?

"It's a pleasure to meet you, Chief Jefferson. Thank you for the opportunity to interview."

Mitch accepted the outstretched hand. As their palms met, Mitch felt momentarily dizzy. His vision blurred. The outline of the man in front of him shimmered, fuzzy around the edges, and he thought for a moment he saw a young boy of about 17 years standing in front of him. He blinked to clear away the fog in his head and the chief's features resolved back to the man he had seen a moment before.

"Are you okay?" asked Chief Jefferson "You look disoriented."

Mitch mentally shook himself and forced a smile back on his face. "I'm fine, thank you, sir. It's a pleasure to meet you."

"You already said that," the chief told him. "Take a seat and relax for a second."

"Would you like some coffee?" asked Dot still hovering behind him.

"Um, water would be nice. Thanks."

Dot hustled across the room to a full-sized, two-door refrigerator and pulled out a couple of cold bottles of water. She set one bottle down on the table next to where Mitch had seated himself, then walked around to the opposite side and settled herself in the chair beside Chief Jefferson. Apparently, she was remaining for the interview. That suited Mitch fine. He felt more comfortable with Dot present. She seemed so happy to have him here, and her overt confidence that he was going to be an asset at the PD made this interview much less intimidating.

Mitch snapped open the plastic cap and sipped at his water.

The interview started as he had expected it to. He talked about his time working for the Sacramento County Sheriff's Office and his current assignment as a detective investigating property crimes. He was asked about his education and training, as well as a few more personal questions about his home life. The subject of his Internal Affairs investigation was not brought up, but then, Mitch figured the chief had already read the entire file. There wasn't much more to say on the topic.

After a while, the chief asked, "So tell me, what do you know about us? What do you know about Dasan's Terrace?"

"Not much," Mitch admitted. "I did some research before coming here today, of course. I know the cemetery has been here almost two hundred and fifty years, long before California was a state. I know it's one of the largest cemeteries in the world as far as acres and numbers of people interred here. As much as I looked, though, I wasn't able to discover who Dasan was. I assume it was the name of the person who originally owned the land, or perhaps the first one buried here."

The chief glanced toward Dot and grinned. His secretary gave him a knowing eye roll and shook her head.

"No," Chief Jefferson corrected. "Dasan isn't a person. Or rather, it isn't one person in particular. Dasan is an ancient Native American term for chief. And the cemetery is much older than a couple hundred years. Thousands of years ago, the native tribes here believed that this land was sacred, special. Perhaps even magical. Several tribes went to war over hundreds of years trying to take control of it, but none succeeded, or if they did, it wasn't long before someone else took it away from them. Thousands of people died during those wars. Tribes were decimated.

"The formal name of this place was 'land upon which the chief's tears fall.' After a while, the people here stopped believing it was sacred and began to think it was cursed, which it sort of was. They abandoned it, but the name 'land of chief's tears' stuck. When the Spaniards came to California, they learned about this place from the native peoples, and they also called it Dasan's Tears. In the 1850's or 1860's, when this became a cemetery for the new settlers, they changed the name to Dasan's Terrace. Maybe they figured that was a more pleasant name. It didn't evoke such dismal imagery."

The chief paused. Mitch took another sip of his water, then shook his head, impressed.

"Wow. I had no idea this place was so … old. Or that it had such history. I grew up around here and I had no idea."

"Most people don't," Chief Jefferson agreed. "Maybe it's better that way."

"Do you believe in ghosts?" asked Dot.

"I, uh… What?"

Chief Jefferson chuckled. "That was a bit abrupt, don't you think, Dot? But still, since you asked the question, I'm curious to hear Mitch's answer."

Mitch fiddled with the cap of his water bottle as he digested the question and tried to come up with an answer that wouldn't make him sound like a lunatic. He wasn't about to tell the man that could save or end his career that his dead son came to visit him once a year on Christmas Eve. He might as well hand in his badge and gun right now before admitting that little tidbit.

"I believe there are things in this world that are extremely difficult to understand or put a label on," he began, choosing his words carefully. "In all honesty, as far as the supernatural goes, I'm not sure what I believe."

"A very politically phrased response," said the chief. "We'll let that go for now."

"I'm going to take your answer as a yes," said Dot, using her finger to scratch an obvious checkmark on the table. "If I'm wrong, please correct me now."

Mitch opened his mouth, but when he realized he didn't know what he was about to say, he closed it again. Dot nodded as if he had delivered an enthusiastic confirmation. Chief Jefferson glared toward Dot, trying to quiet her, but the smile on her face showed how little she cared about her boss's current displeasure.

"I suppose I only have one more question before we wrap this up," said the chief, turning back to face Mitch.

Here it is, thought Mitch. He had hoped the topic was going to be ignored completely, but of course, that was impossible. It was the 800-pound gorilla in the room. Although the chief had most likely read the Internal Affairs file on him, it was only natural that he address the situation before offering to hire an unknown candidate. He needed to know this was a one-time (or two time?) incident that was not likely to repeat and cause future issues for his department.

Before the chief could ask the question, Mitch spoke up preemptively.

"I'm not an alcoholic," he said.

"I was not going to suggest you were," the chief responded calmly.

"I… I thought I should say that. Thought you should know if you hire me, I won't cause problems for you."

"Simon! I found something I think you should see right away!"

Mitch jumped. He had been so fixated on the interview he hadn't noticed somebody else entering the break room. He twisted in his seat to find a tall, older man in a brown suit urgently beckoning the chief to stand up and follow him.

The man had curly brown hair that drooped down low enough to cover the tops of his ears, a pallid face burned ruddy from too much time in the sun, and a burly gray mustache that reminded Mitch of every cop show he had ever watched from the 1970's and 80's.

"Tim. This is a bad time," said the chief, rising from his chair. "We're right in the middle of an interview with a potential new transfer."

Watery blue eyes shifted to peer at Mitch as the intruder looked him over.

"Mitch, this is Timothy Delaney. He's … the assistant chief here at DTPD. Tim, this is Detective Mitch Loman."

Mitch leapt out of his seat and extended his hand to the newcomer. Remaining seated while both his prospective bosses were standing in the room was out of the question. "It's a pleasure to meet you, sir."

Delaney hesitated, examining Mitch from his carefully combed hair down to his polished dress shoes and back, then unenthusiastically reached out to take the offered hand. As they touched, Mitch half expected another bout of vertigo and to see Assistant Chief Delaney's face change as the chief's had earlier. He exhaled a quiet sigh of relief when nothing happened. The man's features remained unblurred, although his hand did feel disturbingly cold and clammy. The experience made Mitch think of squeezing a dead fish in his fist, and he suddenly realized he did not like the assistant chief very much.

From the unpleasant look on Delaney's face, it appeared the feeling was mutual.

Mitch shook the assistant chief's hand as briefly as possible while still remaining polite, released it, and took a step backwards. He forced a smile on his face to be friendly. He did not need to make an enemy of the assistant chief of the department moments before this interview ended. It could spell disaster.

Dot was on her feet by this time. Whatever she had intended to do was unclear as she had paused shortly after standing up, frozen in an awkward stance with one hand still on the back of her chair. Her mouth had popped slightly open, and her eyebrows raised in mild surprise.

"Tim, why don't you head back to your office, and I'll come talk to you when we're finished here." Chief Jefferson stepped over to the breakroom door, pulled it open and ushered the assistant chief out of the room. "Go on. I'll see you in a bit."

When Delaney was gone and the chief had let the door swing closed, Mitch settled back into his chair. Dot and Chief Jefferson returned to their seats across from him.

Mitch cleared his throat and prepared for the interrogation on his actions over the past month. "You said you had one more question, sir?"

The chief glanced at Dot who nodded in response.

"Yes, I guess I do. Tell me, Mitch, when can you start?"

CHAPTER

5

Mitch accepted the position as soon as it was offered. Refusing would have been career suicide as his only alternative was returning to the Detective's Bureau, temporarily, then waiting for Internal Affairs to eventually fire him. The moment he said yes, Dot went back to work.

The next day he received another e-mail from Human Resources notifying him that his job transfer request had been approved and would become effective the following Wednesday. He was directed in the notice to requisition a new badge and identification as soon as possible from the Administrative Assistant to the Chief of Police. Although Dasan's Terrace P.D. was still part of the Sacramento County Sheriff's Office, and they wore the same uniform and patches as the other Deputies in the department, each DTPD officer wore a Dasan's Terrace badge and carried I.D. unique to their assignment.

That part should be easy, Mitch figured. Dot was the Administrative Assistant, and since she was the one who had recruited him, it shouldn't be difficult to get in touch with her. Requesting a new badge should be as simple as a phone call.

Uniforms would be easier still. Fortunately, even though he had been working in plain clothes for a couple of years, he still fit into his old patrol gear. He would not need to buy anything new.

The best part, in Mitch's opinion, was that he did not need to return to work in the detective's bureau. He did not even need to speak with Lieutenant Hostler as a copy of the email Mitch received had been forwarded to his boss already. The break was fast and clean, and there was nothing Hostler could do to get in the way.

Mitch's new assignment with Dasan's Terrace consisted of twelve-hour shifts, from 1900 hours to 0700 hours. He would work the second half of the week, Wednesdays through Saturdays. Since the work period was twelve hours, he would have every other Saturday off so the department could avoid paying him overtime. Mitch was familiar with the schedule as he had worked an identical routine early in his career while stationed in the Sacramento County jails. The shift was referred to as B-Nights. A-Nights worked Sunday through Tuesday, also coming in to work every other Saturday night to make sure all days of the week were covered.

Although he was familiar with the schedule, he didn't love it. Mitch grimaced at the news that he would be going back to working nights. He hadn't worked a night shift since promoting to detective two years ago. Still, if he was being honest, night shift was preferable to unemployment.

The next few days were the most peaceful Mitch had experienced in months. With Internal Affairs on pause, and a new assignment on the horizon, Mitch finally began to feel like a normal person again. At least, as normal as anyone whose dead child continued to return for brief visits every year. His appetite returned, and he actually managed to sleep through the night on a couple occasions.

The following Monday, two days before beginning his new job, he received a phone call from Chief Jefferson.

"Mitch, I wanted to call you personally and let you know the results of your Internal Affairs investigation. I didn't want you to hear it in a letter, or worse, from that self-important, wet rag running your bureau."

Mitch inhaled sharply at the chief's reference to his old lieutenant. While he shared his new boss' sentiment, he had never expected to hear the comment from the mouth of a senior officer.

Chief Jefferson must have heard the soft gasp, because he said, "Yes, Hostler and I go back a while. I never cared for the man much when I first met him, and he hasn't done anything over the years to improve my opinion of him."

"Thank you, sir, and I appreciate the phone call. I thought the investigation was on hold for now."

"It was, but I figured there's no reason for it to remain there, hanging over your head like the sword of Damocles. They finished the investigation during the weekend and the charge that you misused your sick leave has been sustained. The other charges were clearly garbage, and you are cleared of any further wrongdoing."

"What discipline did the investigator recommend?"

"You are to be immediately stripped of your position as a detective and reassigned to the Dasan's Terrace Police Department."

Mitch paused to let the news sink in. "But that was already happening," he said, confused.

"Yes, it was," the chief agreed. "Rather convenient, I thought. Oh, and your pay will remain the same. You lose the five percent pay you were receiving as a detective, but placement with the DTPD comes with a five percent pay hike. So, it's a wash overall."

"Chief Jefferson, I don't know what to say. How can I thank you?"

"There's nothing to thank me for. I was looking for an officer and you were a perfect fit for what I wanted. This isn't a favor, Mitch. We need you as much as you needed us."

"I don't see how that could be true, but thank you anyway, sir."

"There's one more thing I should tell you."

"Yes, sir?"

"I'm not big on formalities. The men and women who work for me call me Simon. Do you think you can do that?"

Mitch laughed, perhaps the first genuine laugh to come out of him in too long to remember. "That will probably take a little time to get used to, but I think I can do that … uh, Simon."

Wednesday evening arrived, and per his transfer orders, Mitch arrived thirty minutes before his assigned shift to change and prepare for his first briefing. Sergeant Jorge Smythe would call roll at seven P.M sharp and Mitch had no intention of showing up late for his first day. Employees were permitted to park behind the police building inside a gated parking lot, but as the cemetery facility itself was already fenced away from outside passersby at night, most used the public lot at the front of the property. The walk to the doors of the police department was shorter from that side. Out of habit and ingrained paranoia, Mitch opted for the gated lot behind the building.

The front doors were locked when Mitch reached them, the volunteer working the front desk having secured the building and left for home at five o'clock. Fortunately, along with his new badge and identification card, Dot had issued him a set of keys that would allow him into every building on the cemetery grounds. The only doors he could not unlock without assistance were the bosses' offices upstairs and the property room located on the bottom floor of the police building. Mitch let himself in, checking to be sure the door relocked behind him after he closed it, then headed downstairs to find the locker rooms.

He found his locker – number 12 – without too much difficulty. There were only a dozen metal storage cabinets in the men's changing room, so locating the correct one was a simple matter of going to the middle of the row, determining which way the numbers increased, and following the pattern to the correct end. It didn't take a detective to figure that one out. There was a bathroom attached to the far side of the room with a pair of sinks, two toilets with privacy walls, two urinals, and a single shower stall. He assumed the women's accommodations were similarly arranged. Minus the urinals, of course.

From his pocket, he removed a slip of paper Dot had given him along with his badge and keys. Three numbers were printed on it. He unfolded the paper and read the numbers while dialing the combination lock attached to the front of his locker. It opened on the first try. Except for a trio of empty hangers on a cross bar, the interior of the locker was empty. Mitch used the bar to hang the two spare uniforms he had carried from the car, both still wrapped in plastic from the dry cleaners. In two of the cubby shelves on the left side of the locker's space, he deposited a pair of tennis shoes, jeans, and a flannel shirt he would change into in the morning after his shift. Finally, he pulled off the heavy coat he wore and hung it on one of the empty hangers. He was already dressed in his third, and last, uniform underneath the coat.

As it was his first time working a new job, he had changed at home to prevent any unanticipated snafus that might make him late. He imagined all kinds of things that could go wrong if he waited to dress at the police department. What if his locker didn't open? What if the keys he was issued didn't get him into the building? This way, in a worst-case scenario, even if he was stuck in the parking lot waiting for someone to let him inside, he was still ready to go to work.

"Hello, new guy," said a deep voice behind him.

Mitch turned to see a figure wearing a black t-shirt and uniform pants standing in the doorway. The man was about his own height though heavier, probably weighing over two hundred and thirty pounds. His skin was pale, with a light dusting of freckles on his nose under a pair of ice blue eyes. His bare arms were also covered with freckles where they had been exposed to the sun but had stubbornly refused to tan. The expression on his face was friendly, but Mitch still braced himself in anticipation of any 'new guy' hazing at his expense.

"You must be the transfer Sarge told us to expect. Mark, right?"

"Um, Mitch," he corrected.

"Yeah, yeah. Mitch. Sorry."

The man moved forward and stuck out his hand. "I'm Adam, but everybody here calls me Tink."

Mitch shook the offered hand. "Mitch," he repeated. "Should I call you Adam, or do you prefer … Tink, did you say? Where did that come from?"

"Tink is fine. People have been calling me that so long I sometimes forget what my real name is. They gave me that nickname when I was still a rookie working for Los Angeles P.D."

Tink pushed up his right shirt sleeve far enough to reveal a tattoo adorning his bicep. The image was a rendering of the iconic Disney fairy, Tinkerbell, complete with the jagged green hem on her miniskirt and little green slippers. Instead of a wand, however, she was waving a PR-24, side-handled police baton, and she sported a tiny, yellow, five-pointed star pinned to her chest. Beneath the fairy's dainty feet, inked in bold black letters was the word, "TINK."

"Wow," was all Mitch could think to say. "That's something."

Tink chuckled as he pushed his sleeve back down over the tattoo.

"There's got to be a story behind that. I mean people don't just start calling you Tink for no reason, do they?"

Tink shook his head. "Nope, there's a reason. It happened while I was still in training."

Tink stepped over to one of the lockers a few doors away from Mitch and dialed it open. Despite it being winter, he pulled out a short-sleeved uniform shirt. He picked up a nametag from one of the cubby spaces and pinned the tag above the right pocket of the shirt. The badge went on next over the left pocket. He continued chatting as he prepped for his first shift of the week.

"My training officer, a really good guy named Lennox Martin, he and I were on a call about some guy passed out in an alley. The caller thought he might be dead because he was banging his head on the brick wall for a couple minutes before he fell down and stopped moving. We found him pretty easily. He was homeless. His clothes were dirty and torn up and he looked like a pile of discarded rags when we got there. He smelled like hot garbage, too."

Tink removed a tactical vest and slipped it on over his head, pulling the Velcro tabs tight before patting them into place. The short-sleeved shirt went on over the vest.

"I pulled out my baton because, honestly, I didn't really want to get close enough to touch the guy. I figured if he got too close to me, I could push him back without having to put my hands on him. My F.T.O. leaned over him and kicked the bottom of his feet to try to wake him up. Before either of us could react, this guy jumps up and turns on Lenny. Dude was huge. Maybe only about six feet tall but built like a football linebacker. But that wasn't the worst part."

After tucking in his shirt, Tink fastened his duty belt around his waist and began snapping on the leather "keepers" that would hold it in place.

"When he stands up, he pulls this knife out. Blade is as long as my forearm. I have no idea where he was hiding it, but it was tucked away somewhere under all those rags he was wearing. He points it at my T.O. and he is way too close for him to get out of the way in time. The guy jabs his arm out and the blade sticks my training officer right in the stomach. Lucky bastard though, it caught the bottom of his vest so didn't go in too far. Lenny falls backward with the homeless guy following, and he's going to get stabbed again unless I can do something to help him, and quick. I'm left-handed, and I'm holding my baton in my left hand, so I would have to drop it or switch hands to draw my gun. I don't have time for that. By the time I could grab my gun, Lenny would already be dead. I did the first thing I could think of. I raised my baton in the air and brought it straight down on the homeless guy's head. I tagged him right on the top of his melon with the very end of my stick."

Tink, removed the magazine from his duty weapon and checked the rounds. Next, he press checked the slide to be sure the chamber was loaded. He jammed the pistol into his holster and fastened the snaps securely over the top. He didn't pause from his daily dress routine the entire time he was telling Mitch the story of his nickname.

"Soon as my stick made contact, this guy drops to the ground like a boxer that just took one too many punches. I don't know if I hit him in the perfect spot to put his lights out, or if his skull was already softened up from him banging against the wall over and over, but he was down for the count. We rolled him over, cuffed him and I called an ambulance for Lenny. While we were waiting, Lenny looks at me and starts to laugh. He told me, 'You looked just like Tinkerbell.' Then he laughs again. I asked what the hell he meant by that, and he says, 'you looked like Tinkerbell waving her wand and putting a sleep spell on that guy. Tap, and the fucker went out like magic.'"

Tink ran a hand over his equipment belt to make sure everything was accounted for, then swung his locker door closed.

"Well, when Lenny got back to work after healing up from his cut, he starts telling everybody the story of what happened, and pretty soon, everyone I know is calling me Tink. I tried to stop it at first, but that just made my partners think it was even funnier. After a while I gave up trying. Sometimes, you just gotta roll with things, you know? Now the only people that still call me Adam is my parents. My own sister calls me Tink."

"Wow," Mitch said again. "That is quite a story."

Tink glanced at his watch. "Come on, let's head up to the briefing room. I'll introduce you to the Sarge. He's probably already there since I think he fucking lives in this place. Brad won't show up until the last minute."

"Brad?"

"Brad Kodama. He's the other officer on our shift. Each night shift gets three officers and a sergeant. Day shifts get two officers, but they also have a bunch of cemetery staff and volunteers working, so the job is a lot easier."

The two men walked the flight of stairs up to the ground floor and, with Tink leading, located the briefing room. True to Tink's prediction, the sergeant was already inside seated at the head of a large, wooden conference table.

The sergeant was a pleasant looking man of average height and weight, with deeply tanned skin, black hair and dark eyes. His face could be called handsome, though unremarkably so. Mitch's eyes were drawn to the sergeant's long narrow nose. It bent slightly left and appeared to have been broken at some point in his life. The minor defect did nothing to diminish his good looks, and perhaps even accented what might have been an otherwise bland set of features.

"Hey, Sarge," said Tink, escorting Mitch into the room. "This is our new recruit: Mike."

"Mitch," corrected Mitch for the second time.

"Right, Mitch. Shit, I keep screwing that up. Do you mind if I call you Mike? It might be easier than trying to remember your name."

Mitch said nothing, unsure how to respond. The serious look on Tink's face melted into a grin, and he slapped Mitch on the shoulder good naturedly.

"I'm just fucking with you. Relax."

The Sergeant turned an exasperated look toward Tink. "Do you really think you're the one that should be making fun of people's names?"

Tink shrugged and dropped himself into one of the empty chairs around the table. The smile never left his face.

Mitch approached the sergeant and stuck out his hand. The two men shook.

"Jorge," said the sergeant. "Call me Jorge, George, Sergeant Smythe, or Sarge. Whatever you're most comfortable with. We're a tiny department and rank doesn't mean much around here except to determine who has to do most of the paperwork."

"He means us," clarified Tink. "We do the paperwork."

Sergeant Smythe nodded at the comment. "Yup. Pretty much."

After Mitch selected a chair next to Tink, Sergeant Smythe asked, "Do you have all your equipment?"

"I have keys, badge, I.D. card, and all my old patrol stuff. I still need a radio, though."

"Tink, do me a favor? After briefing, take him to the equipment room and get him a radio, a knife, and a handful of bullets."

"I have bullets," Mitch said. "And I always carry a knife on my belt."

"Are they silver?"

Mitch was again at a loss for words. He watched the sergeant closely, but the supervisor's face remained serious. When it became clear the sergeant wasn't joking, he stammered, "N-no."

Sergeant Smythe nodded as if he had expected the answer. "You're new here, so I understand that you're still figuring out what we do. I had hoped the chief or Dot might have filled you in a little bit, but I can see they left that for us. I know you've got a few years on and don't need to be put into a field training program, you're not new to patrol duties, but I think I'm going to partner up you and Tink for the next week or so until you get a feel for how things work around here."

"You got it, Sarge," agreed Tink.

"Maybe when you're finished with his gear, you could take Mitch out and introduce him to Harold," Sergeant Smythe suggested. "That might be a good place to start."

The door opened and another officer entered the room. He was a shorter man, somewhere in his early or mid-thirties. Straight black hair framed a set of high, sharp cheekbones and deep black eyes. His mouth was turned down in what appeared to be a permanent scowl, and upon noticing Mitch, his expression tightened further, his eyelids lowering as he gave the newcomer in the briefing room a suspicious glare.

The late arrival wore a standard sheriff's office department uniform, with the same patches and Dasan's Terrace badge as Mitch and Tink. He also wore a simple equipment belt with his duty pistol, handcuffs, radio and pepper spray. There was one detail, however that stood out as distinctly odd on the small man. Strapped across his back and hanging from right shoulder to left hip was a Japanese katana. The ornately wrapped handle of the sword protruded at an angle over his shoulder to a point only a few inches above the level of his head.

No one else in the room said a word about the very non-standard weapon, so Mitch kept his thoughts to himself.

"Brad, this is Mitch," said the sergeant casually. "Mitch, Brad Kodama. He's our senior officer on the shift. If you have a problem and I'm not around, you go to Brad."

"Nice to meet you, Brad," Mitch offered.

Brad said nothing. He only continued to glare as he pulled out a chair and settled in.

Mitch tried again to break the tension. "Do you study martial arts?" he asked lamely.

"Why? Because I'm Japanese? That's some stereotypical racist bullshit right there, pal."

Mitch's let his mouth fall open, shocked at the response. Before he could regain his composure and form some sort of response to the accusation, Tink bailed him out.

"Don't be a dick," said Tink to the stoic-looking officer, then he turned to Mitch. "Brad is a fourth-degree black belt in something I can't pronounce. He's also a third-degree in Kendo."

"Kendo?" asked Mitch.

"Yeah. You know," Tink pointed at the katana. "Swords."

Mitch blew out a small breath. "Okay. So, you see it, too. No one said anything and I was starting to wonder if it was my imagination."

"Oh, it's real," said Brad, putting on a thick Japanese accent for Mitch's benefit. "And it cuts real good, you round-eyed, white devil."

"Brad," said Sergeant Smyth. "This is Mitch's first day. Do me a favor and don't start messing with him until he's had a chance to get acclimated. Not all of us appreciate your sparkling personality."

In response, Brad gave Mitch a long slow wink. It reminded Mitch of a gunfighter in a saloon marking his next target. The gesture was scary in its malevolence. Then Brad did something completely unexpected: he smiled. The expression lit up his face and erased all suggestion of hostility.

"I can already tell you're going to be a lot of fun to have around," Brad said. "Welcome to Dead Town, Mitch. Where every shift is the graveyard shift."

Briefing only lasted a few minutes as it appeared that little of note had occurred during the past few days while B-Nights was off on their weekend. When Sergeant Smythe released them to go to work, Tink brought Mitch back downstairs to the equipment room. He pointed to a board with four rows of five small hooks. Eight of the hooks held gold-colored keys, and each key had a numbered metal tag attached.

"Those are the keys to the patrol fleet," said Tink, tapping one of the metal tags.

"Where do you keep the patrol cars? I didn't see any in the parking lot."

Tink chuckled. "Nope. Not cars. Golf carts. The chief has a car permanently assigned to him, and there is one other vehicle that can be checked out if one of us needs to get across town for any reason, but the rest of the keys are to golf carts. We used to use them all the time, but now they mostly sit in the lot behind the administrative buildings at the far end of the parking lot."

"Why don't you use them? Did they start breaking down?"

"Nah. Those things will run forever as long as you keep the batteries charged. We had to stop using them because the maintenance guys were complaining about the tire tracks all over the cemetery. They said we were messing up their landscaping." Tink shrugged. "I like walking better, anyway. It gives me some exercise."

Next, Tink showed Mitch a framed map of the cemetery hanging on the wall a few feet away from the key board. It had been blown up to the size of a movie poster. The cemetery property was roughly rectangular, with one corner of the grounds ballooning outward like a tumorous growth at the top left.

"This is the layout of the grounds that we're responsible for." Tink ran his finger over the picture as he explained how to read the map. On the bottom edge of the paper, from west to east along the property, he indicated a series of numbers from zero to nine. On the right edge, running from south to north were capital letters from A to Q.

"They broke the area up with a grid sequence so it would be easier to identify specific areas. If you ever need help in a hurry, memorize this map and use the grid to let people know where you are. Most of the time, you can call out landmarks and the rest of us will know what you're talking about, but for officers coming from outside, or for new hires," Tink gave Mitch a meaningful glance, "it helps to know the map."

Tink traced the tip of his forefinger along a bottom portion marked in green. "Right off the entrance and next to the parking lots is what we call the Front Lawn. It gets the most care and attention because it's what people see when they come onto the grounds. Management wants people to know we care about the place so they're comfortable burying their loved ones here. Further back from the Lawn is the rest of Front Half."

"Front Half?" asked Mitch.

"Yeah. Front Half and Back Half. The names are pretty self-explanatory. Front Half is still active. We have funerals and burials now and then, so the grounds are still tended. Back Half is older graves and mausoleums. There aren't any new plots being added, so it kind of gets ignored. There is some maintenance done out there, but for the most part, the only people that go that far back are us, the groundskeepers, and a few people every year trying to find the markers of older family members."

Tink pointed at the far corner of the map where the property bulged to the left. "This is Northwest."

"Because it's in the northwest corner of the cemetery?" asked Mitch.

"Nothing gets by you, does it? Yeah, it's in the northwest. It's fenced and gated so nobody can wander in by accident. This is where the oldest burial sites are. They go back over a thousand years, maybe more. You'll need a key to the gate if Dot didn't already issue you one. Put in a request through Jorge and he'll make sure you get one."

Mitch nodded. He had received keys to the main gate out front, the police department entrance doors, the locker room, and he had a general access key that would get him through every door on the first floor of the PD, as well as several more on the second. He also had two keys that belonged to the cemetery's administrative buildings. None of the keys on his ring were for the Northwest gate. "I'll ask for one. Should I ask Jorge for a key to the property room, too?"

"Nope. We don't get those. The chief has a key to that room and each of the shift sergeants has a key. That's it. Nobody else carries one."

"What if I need to get in there? What if I have to book property?"

"Give it to Jorge, and he'll book it in for you."

"What if I need to get something out for court or to follow up on a case investigation."

"Then you're out of luck," Tink said casually. "Look, Mitch. Once something goes in that room, it doesn't come out. You wouldn't believe the stuff we have locked away in there, and frankly, I think we're all better off not knowing exactly what this department has collected over the years."

"Shouldn't the officers have access…?"

"Forget it," interrupted Tink. "Property room is off limits. Deal with it. If you need something, talk to Jorge. C'mon. We need to get you outfitted before we start our first patrol."

Tink pulled open a drawer in one of the cabinets lining the back wall of the equipment room. Inside were yellow and green cardboard boxes of ammunition. He dug around the boxes until he found one he liked, then held it up where Mitch could see the cover. "Forty caliber, right?"

Mitch had been issued a Sig Sauer P226 when he was hired by the Sheriff's office. He had been allowed to keep it when he was notified of his transfer to Dasan's Terrace. His hand touched the butt of his gun unconsciously. "Yeah. Forty."

Tink set the box down before rummaging through another drawer. This time he pulled out two Sig Sauer, forty caliber magazines. "Extra magazines for your gun, and silver bullets," he said. He slid the magazines toward Mitch. "Load these up and find a place to carry them for now. You're eventually going to have to add extra magazine pouches on your belt.

Mitch opened the first box of ammunition and began loading one of the magazines. The rounds in the box were standard brass cartridges like the ones he already carried, but the slugs on top were not the jacketed, hollow-nosed bullets he was used to. Each round was topped with a solid ball of white metal.

Silver.

Mitch asked about the silver bullets as he clicked one gleaming round after another into the spring-loaded cartridge holder, but Tink shook his head in the negative. "Not now. Some things are easier to talk about after we walk around a little bit. You need to get to know this place first. Let's go see Harold. He can answer a lot of your questions. Well, maybe not answer them, but he can get you asking the right kinds of questions."

When Mitch finished loading the magazines, he slipped the extra ammunition holders into the side pocket of his uniform pants. Tink immediately handed him a Bowie style knife with a silver-composite blade and a boot sheath in which to carry it.

"What's the pig sticker for?"

Tink shook his head again. "Meet Harold first."

Mitch knew better than to push for information that was not forthcoming. He shrugged, accepted the knife, and affixed the scabbard into his right work boot. A few minutes later, Tink and Mitch exited the building and began their first patrol of the evening through the cemetery grounds.

At that time of year, it was already dark outside, but powerful vapor lamps placed throughout the cement-pathed, landscaped portions of the grounds provided plenty of light to see. Mitch had his Mag-lite flashlight with him, but with no immediate need for it, he left it in the carrier ring on his belt.

Walking through a cemetery at night, even a well-illuminated one, left Mitch feeling surprisingly apprehensive. He was not normally bothered by graves or death, and he had been on the grounds of this particular cemetery many times. More times than he cared to think about since the loss of his son. Still, he felt a definite sense of unease as he followed Tink past row after row of headstones. The silence around them began to feel oppressive, so in an effort to break the growing tension, Mitch tried to draw Tink into conversation.

"I know you don't want to talk about the bullets or the knife, so I'll wait to talk to Harold about that, but can you tell me what Brad meant when he said welcome to Dead Town?"

Tink chuckled softly to himself. "Don't let the chief hear you call it that." He spread out his hands to indicate the area around them. "*This* is Dead Town. The whole cemetery is Dead Town. You know how our initials are D.T.P.D.?"

"Dasan's Terrace. Right."

"Yeah. A long time ago, way before I got here, some of the officers started calling it the Dead Town Police Department. It's big enough to be its own town after all. We have over 300,000 citizens inside our borders if you count the native burial grounds and all the other unmarked or forgotten graves from before California was even a state. That's more people than most cities in this country. Dead Town was just a joke at the time, but it caught on. Kind of like my nickname. Most of the people that work here and a bunch of people that live around the area all call it Dead Town now. The chief hates the name. He thinks it makes us sound less professional. I think it's kind of cool, but I'm not the boss so I don't get a vote."

Tink stopped to glance around, getting his bearings. He stepped off the concrete path they had been following and led Mitch onto the manicured lawn through several rows of headstones. After a few minutes, he paused again. The location looked like every other spot Mitch had passed tonight, but Tink seemed to recognize some landmark or other. He nodded, then pointed to one of several stone benches that had been erected throughout the grounds.

"Let's take a seat for a bit," he suggested.

"What about Harold."

"Don't worry. Harold will find us."

Tink glanced at his watch then sat on the bench, releasing a grunting sigh as though he had been on his feet for hours instead of only a few minutes. Mitch sat next to him. Since he didn't have a watch himself, he pulled out his cellphone to check the time. His phone screen announced: 7:42 PM.

The two officers sat quietly for several minutes. Mitch twice attempted to initiate further conversation, but each time Tink quieted him with a wave of his hand and a quick "shush."

The larger man seemed to enjoy keeping the mystery going. Confused, and beginning to wonder if this was the hazing of the new guy he had been half expecting, he pulled out his phone again. It now indicated 8:06.

"Hello, Harold," whispered Tink, unexpectedly. "I was wondering when you were going to stop by."

Tink pointed north of their location, indicating a stooped figure that had appeared from behind several grave markers. The shadowy silhouette shuffled across the grass at an unhurried pace, oblivious to his two observers on the bench. The figure appeared to be a frail old man wrapped in a heavy wool coat. Wisps of stray gray hair could be seen moving in the wind over an otherwise bald head.

"Harold Petrovic. Husband of the late Amelia Petrovic. He comes by several times a night to visit her grave. He's very devoted that way. Do you see him?"

Tink's voice was still low, so Mitch spoke quietly to match it.

"Of course, I see him. I'm not blind. What's he doing here at night? How did he get through the gates? Did somebody feel sorry for him and give him a key?"

"Nope. No key. Doesn't matter though. We can't seem to keep him out."

"So, he's trespassing. Should we make him leave?"

"You're welcome to try. Why don't you go talk to him?"

Mitch stood, but a sudden thought occurred to him, causing him to turn back toward Tink.

"Is this a set up? Is he a friend of yours? I really don't want to shoot someone because you thought it would be funny to try to scare me."

"I've never met the guy personally. I see him out here all the time, but I usually leave him alone."

"Why?" Mitch was fully suspicious of Tink's motives for bringing him here, despite the fact it had been the sergeant's suggestion that he do it. "What aren't you telling me?"

"Go … talk … to … Harold." Tink jabbed his finger at the old man with each enunciated word.

Tink leaned back on the bench and folded his arms across his chest, clearly finished with answering questions. Mitch glanced toward Harold, who had by now stopped beside a stone marker and was gazing down at something in front of his feet. Mitch took a hard breath in and out, frustrated at being the only one that didn't know what was going on. Figuring this game was only going to end when he confronted the aged trespasser, he marched forward toward the stooped figure standing over the headstone.

"Hey, Harold!" he called out. The old man remained where he was, seemingly unaware that he had been hailed.

"Hey!" Mitch shouted again, then he froze.

Something was wrong with the picture in front of him. Harold remained beside what Mitch assumed was his wife's gravesite, unmoving. The old man's hunched form was between Mitch and two obelisk-shaped monuments, and he realized for the first time that he could see the narrow standing stones despite the fact the man was in the way. Harold was not quite as solid as he should be. Mitch could see *through* him.

All at once, Mitch understood what this was. It wasn't a hazing, per se, but it was a kind of test.

"Do you believe in ghosts?" Dot had asked him during his interview. The question had seemed out of place at the time, but it was starting to make more sense now.

Mitch approached the old man until he was directly behind him. Harold did not react to his presence. It was as if the officer behind him did not exist, and for Harold, perhaps that was true. This close, Mitch could see the man's body shimmered slightly, hazy and partially insubstantial.

"Hey, Harold," he said softly, reaching out, intending to touch the man's back. His hand passed through Harold's form. There was something there, but it was far from solid. It felt like he was pushing through multiple layers of thick, sticky cobwebs.

Harold startled and glanced back over his shoulder. The man's eyes searched helplessly as they tried to find the source of the disturbance to his nightly routine. It was obvious that although Mitch could see Harold, Harold was completely unable to see him.

The ghost, for that was what he was, flickered and dissipated. In an instant, he was gone.

"Well, that was new," said Tink. Mitch jumped. He had not noticed the other officer's approach. "You got Harold's attention for a second, there. Usually, he doesn't even notice when someone else is around."

"He's a ghost," said Mitch.

Tink scratched his head and looked pensive for a moment. "Not really," he said. "I mean, yeah he's a ghost, but he's not a real ghost."

Mitch shook his head slowly, confused. "Not a…?"

"Dot explains this kind of thing a lot better than I can, but basically Harold is what she calls an 'echo.' He isn't a full ghost, he's just an image of something that used to happen. Like a few seconds of movie footage that plays on repeat over and over. Dot says when something important happens to a person near their time of death, the emotion around that event can stick around for a while. Murder victims or accident victims sometimes leave echoes of the moments right before they die. For Harold it was a little different."

Tink pointed at the ground beside Mitch's feet. He glanced down to see a flat marker inscribed with the name, Amelia Petrovic. Tink pointed a few feet further away to another stone marked, Harold Petrovic.

"After Amelia died. Harold came by to visit her grave every day. There were probably a whole lot of emotions wrapped around those visits. Happy. Sad. Lonely. About two months ago, Harold had a heart attack and died during one of his trips out here. He died right about where you're standing. He left behind an echo. It still comes by to visit his wife's grave several times each night.

"Dot says echoes aren't real people so there's nothing we need to do about Harold. He's harmless, and he'll eventually fade away all by himself. That's what she told me, anyway. He's probably going to disappear pretty soon based on how faded he's already become. I can barely see him anymore."

Mitch held up his hand, wiggling his fingers in front of his face and remembering the feel of Harold's ephemeral form. It had been so fragile. Denny felt so much more solid…. Mitch pushed the thought away. This wasn't the time for personal introspection.

"Tink. Are you ready to start answering my questions now? I've seen Harold."

"Almost. Why don't we head back to the department first? I'll show you where Jorge's desk is, and we can sit down with him. He's been here longer than I have and can probably answer the questions that I can't."

"So, you met Harold," said Sergeant Smythe. Tink and Mitch had returned to the administrative building and the two officers currently sat in chairs arranged in front of Smythe's desk. He did not look surprised to see them back. "Now, you have questions you want to ask. Okay. Shoot."

"I already knew that ghosts were real," Mitch said to start the conversation. "I guess this helps though to know that you believe in them, too. I can ask questions without worrying that anybody thinks I've lost my mind."

Sergeant Smythe smiled briefly in understanding. "Ask whatever you like. I won't think you're crazy."

"I have a ghost in my house. How can I make it move on to … wherever ghosts are supposed to go?"

"There are people that can exorcise it," said Tink. "It can be forced out of the house."

"No. I don't want to hurt it. I want to help it… I want to help *him*. I want to help him to go where he needs to go."

"Sorry, Mitch," said Jorge. "That's beyond us. We aren't really experts in this area. I'm not a 'sensitive,' as Dot calls herself. I can only see spirits that animate strongly enough to be perceived by most people. I've never even seen Harold myself, although I believe everyone else when they tell me about him. Tink and Brad are more aware of spirits, but they don't have the ability for any major interaction with them. Talk to Dot about your ghost. Maybe she can help with your problem."

Mitch was disappointed by the answer. He had finally found people with whom he could discuss his son, but they knew nothing about how to help him. Was Denny permanently stuck here after all? If he couldn't find a way to help, what would happen to his son when Mitch died? Would the boy follow him into the afterlife? Would Mitch be stuck here too, in order to watch over him? Or would Mitch move on and leave Denny behind to haunt his old home on Christmas Eve for eternity?

He would talk to Dot about it, as Jorge had suggested. Hopefully, she would have more useful information. Shifting his thoughts away from his son, Mitch turned his attention back to Jorge and Tink. He still had other questions for the two men. Many other questions. His encounter with Harold had his mind spinning.

"Okay. If ghosts are real, then what else is out there that I've been pretending my whole life is only my imagination? What other boogeymen hide from us in the shadows?"

"You have to be more specific than that. There are many things people pretend aren't real because they feel safer not knowing the truth."

"Like ghouls," said Tink. He held up a finger, counting off items. "Witches, demons, fairies, elves, gremlins, zombies. I've run into all of those. Well, not a demon. That would suck to run into one of those, but I know they're real."

Mitch listened to the list Tink rattled off, trying to absorb the new information. He felt slightly untethered from reality as the world views he had held during the thirty-one years he had been on this planet began to unravel. Ghosts had been hard enough to swallow, but zombies? Demons?"

"Listen, Mitch," Jorge said. "I know this is a lot to take in all at once. That's why I wanted you to meet Harold first. Sort of break the ice, so to speak. The fact is, this job is going to be the easiest and the hardest thing you have ever done. Most of the time we sit around and babysit six hundred and fifty acres of uninhabited land. The trickiest part of that is figuring out ways to stay awake all night. Then, once in a while, something nasty is going to poke its head up out of the ground and it will be our responsibility to deal with it. Not only deal with it, but handle the whole matter quickly and quietly so the rest of the county has no idea that anything dangerous or supernatural has intruded into their lives. Can you imagine the panic if everybody suddenly knew that dragons were real, and the entire city of Sacramento could be wiped out overnight if we were unlucky enough to wake one up? Fortunately, most of the underworld agrees we're all better off not believing in them. They prefer it that way."

"They?" asked Mitch, unsure if he wanted to hear the answer, but too curious not to ask.

"Supernatural creatures. For example, elves are very powerful as individuals and as a species, but there aren't very many of them. The elves know if we ever organized against them, we could exterminate their entire race. A lot of people would die doing it, but then again, there are a lot of people on this planet. We have the numbers."

"Christ," uttered Mitch under his breath. "I should have let Hostler fire me."

Jorge pulled open his front desk drawer and removed a paper manual several inches thick from its recesses. He dropped the book on top of the desk in front of Mitch.

"Here. This is a catalog the chief, Dot and Sergeant Burke put together a few years back."

"Burke?" asked Mitch.

"He's one of the day shift guys," explained Tink.

"Anyway," Jorge continued, "It's a basic breakdown of the things we've run into and the best methods we've determined for dealing with them. Sorry, but the section on ghosts is pretty thin. There are a couple pages about exorcism of spirits that aren't safe to leave alone, but ghosts are mostly harmless, so we've been told not to mess with them. There are other important things addressed in the book, though, that you should be aware of. Like what creatures you are likely to encounter around here, and how to protect yourself from them. There's also a section on runes and common satanic symbols you may find useful. Most of those symbols are complete crap, but the book lists the ones you need to take seriously. You can consider this your field training manual. If nothing else, it will give you some interesting reading for the long nights of boredom ahead of you."

Tink clapped Mitch on the shoulder. "Like the sergeant said, most of the time this place is completely dead. Pun intended. Odds are you're gonna retire then die of old age before you ever have to face anything too bad. This stuff is real, but it's also really rare."

"What about vampires?" Mitch asked.

"What?" asked Tink.

"We work in a cemetery," Mitch elaborated. "Are they real? Am I going to have to worry about a vampire popping out of a grave some night and trying to eat me?"

Jorge laughed and shook his head. "No. That's a complete myth."

"Good," said Mitch, greatly relieved. For some reason, the idea of vampires frightened him more than any of the other supernatural creatures that went bump in the night. There was something viscerally disturbing to him about blood sucking monsters prowling for unwary victims in the shadows. It made him feel better to know they weren't real.

"I don't know where that rumor started," Jorge continued. "Vampires don't hang out in graveyards. There's nothing to hunt when everyone is already dead. They usually congregate in the middle of large cities where they can get blood more easily, and the occasional homicide is more likely to get overlooked as a robbery that got out of hand."

Mitch's painfully brief moment of quiet relief was suddenly dashed. Vampires *were* real. They lived in cities.

"Christ," Mitch muttered again.

CHAPTER 6

Despite Mitch's fears and expectations that at any minute the earth would break open and hordes of vampires, fairies, and the undead would come pouring out of the ground, the next three weeks with DTPD passed as Jorge and Tink had promised. Each day at work was like every other. The hours between seven o'clock at night and seven in the morning passed steadily and tediously, with almost nothing to do.

Jorge tried to keep the mood upbeat and help the time tick by a little more pleasantly. He cared about the team's morale, and he instigated several events during the long, quiet evenings to keep everyone awake, if not necessarily alert or active. Thursday night was movie night. On the second day of their work week, the sergeant brought a selection of three or four movies on DVD and, after the team had made their initial patrol rounds of the cemetery property, they would all gather in the upstairs breakroom. The command staff breakroom, where Mitch had interviewed with Dot and the chief, was the only room with a vending machine, television set and DVD player, so it was a natural congregating spot. As long as they cleaned up any garbage and cleared out before Simon or Dot came in for work in the morning, there was never any issue with the ritual.

On Fridays, before work, Jorge and his wife would cook a huge meal, and invite their entire family over for an early dinner. It was a ritual the sergeant and his extended clan had practiced for years. After dinner concluded, the sergeant packed up an assortment of the leftovers and brought them into work to feed his shift. Jorge's wife was an amazing chef, and the food was always better than restaurant quality in Mitch's opinion. It was certainly better than anything Mitch could fix on his own. On several occasions, he had attempted to give Jorge a small amount of cash to pay for the food he ate, but the sergeant always turned it down. He explained his wife would be very disappointed in him if he tried to make a profit off of all her hard work.

Despite the sergeant's valiant efforts to ease the tedium, it did not change the fact that working for DTPD seemed to consist of twelve hours each night sitting, walking, and sitting some more. Occasionally, when the boredom became too much, a member of the shift would be discovered tucked away in the locker room or in one of the meeting rooms upstairs catching a quick cat nap.

Absolutely nothing of note happened in Mitch's first few weeks assigned to Dead Town, unless he counted the night a driver on Jackson Highway got a flat tire outside the cemetery gates and Brad Kodama had helped the distressed man replace it with the spare out of the driver's trunk. Although Mitch had to admit the stares the driver kept giving the katana strapped to Brad's back were rather amusing, the whole event was hardly anything one might call interesting.

A few times, out of boredom, Mitch had gone looking for Harold. He thought observing the ghost again might remind him that as boring as Dasan's Terrace was, it still held potential to surprise. He was disappointed each time when he was unable to find the elusive old man. After several attempts, Mitch was forced to accept the fact that Tink had been right when he said the ghost was already fading when they met for the first time, and he would soon be gone. Harold did indeed seem to have vanished for good.

Mitch got more exercise these days, which was good. Walking the cemetery grounds had him moving most of the time. It certainly offered more of a workout than sitting behind a detective's desk all day. At least once each night, he would walk the entire perimeter of the property, checking for breaches in the wall or fence. The round trip was almost three and a half miles and took him most of an hour and a half at a leisurely pace. The remainder of his shift he would alternate routes back and forth through the center of the grounds depending on his mood.

While he enjoyed the nighttime strolls, and even somewhat looked forward to them, they still offered no excitement. They were peaceful and quiet, which to most people might seem ideal, but to a police officer that thrived on chasing bad guys and helping people when they needed it the most, it was soul-wrenchingly dull.

The only thing that kept Mitch on his toes was Brad.

After his initial introduction to the dark-eyed, dour looking officer, Mitch had assumed Brad was a loner and preferred the other members of the shift to simply leave him alone. He could not have been more wrong in his assessment. The angry cowboy persona he had displayed in the briefing room that first day had all been an act. Brad, it turned out, was a practical joker of epic proportions, with a wickedly keen sense of humor and no filter when it came to off-color jokes or bodily noises.

Only a few days earlier, Mitch had arrived for work and gone to his locker, only to discover he could not input the combination. A large amount of clear lubricant had been applied to the dial, leaving it a slick, shiny mess. Brad snuck up silently behind Mitch while his fingers slipped ineffectually over the small black numbered wheel.

"Vaginal lube, dude. It's supposed to make it easier to get into tight spaces, not harder. If you want her to open up, maybe you need to talk nicer to her."

Brad laughed and clapped Mitch on the shoulder. He then tossed Mitch a balled wad of toilet paper to assist in cleaning the mess he had created. Still chuckling to himself, Brad strolled out of the locker room as though nothing had occurred.

Mitch was not the sole target of Brad's attention, either. Tink, and even Sergeant Smythe found their way into his crosshairs on occasion. He was so personable and engaging, however, that his stunts never came across as malicious or ill-intended. Tink summed up the situation pretty well one night as he polished away dozens of white stripes of correction fluid Brad had painted onto his work boots, "It's just Brad fucking around. What are you gonna do?"

At the end of three weeks of painful boredom, movies, endless walking, good food, and dodging Brad's practical jokes, Mitch was finally settling into the routine. He felt he had a pretty good idea what the rest of his career was going to look like. He would be walking the grass-lined paths of Dead Town until he collected his gold watch and rode off into the sunset.

Tonight was Saturday, and it was the end of a long work week for the B team. Mitch sat in the briefing room at seven o'clock, daydreaming how to get back at Brad for his locker lubricant stunt while waiting for Jorge to start briefing.

The sergeant rifled through a small stack of papers and began the evening's activities as he had started almost every other night since Mitch was hired.

"Day shift has nothing in their log sheets to pass along. No reports of vandalism or trespassing. No notes on the admin board."

Jorge set the papers aside, clasped his hands together and set them on the table. Mitch expected him to offer up his nightly dismissal, "Go to work and try not to get eaten." The sergeant said it every briefing. It wasn't funny, primarily because it was not intended as a joke, but it was their cue for everyone to get up, leave the building, and begin their first round of patrols. The expression had started before Mitch arrived, most likely following an unpleasant event in the cemetery, and it had become the shift mantra.

Jorge did not say it tonight.

"It's a full moon," he said, instead. "We all know what that means."

Mitch looked around the table, then tentatively raised a hand to get Jorge's attention.

"In general? Like, it's a full moon and things might get crazy? Or is there something specific that the rest of you have neglected to warn me about?"

Jorge smiled. As Mitch searched the room, he discovered Brad and Tink were also grinning at him. He felt like the only kid on the playground not let in on a secret, and he didn't like the feeling.

"It's a full moon," said Jorge a second time, "and per our agreement with the local coven, they will be in the cemetery from ten o'clock until four tomorrow morning. I assume they will be in the northwest corner of the grounds since they prefer the older areas, and I expect you will all steer clear of them. They don't like spectators."

"Coven?" asked Mitch. "As in vampires?"

The other officers laughed. Tink banged a friendly fist on Mitch's arm.

"No, man. What is your fixation with vampires? You need to let that go. No, these are witches."

"Sacramento has a coven of witches?" Mitch asked, more to himself than anyone else. "I mean, of course it does. Why not? If there can be ghosts, why can't there be witches?"

"There are actually three covens in the area," said Jorge. "Alyssandra's is the only one allowed in the cemetery. She and the chief have an agreement that allows her to come in once a month on the night of the full moon. We leave her alone, and she gives us the same courtesy."

"Why is she the only one allowed in?"

"I'm not actually sure why she was allowed in. You would have to ask the chief that question. He's the one that approved her coven to enter the cemetery."

"I guess a better question then, is why were the others kept out? What's different about them?" Mitch asked.

"One of the covens is total bullshit," said Tink. "It's 13 women who have no idea what the hell they're doing. They chant spells that don't work, pretend they know more than they do, and dance around naked at midnight. I don't really mind that last part, to be honest, but the group is just a bunch of wannabes."

"And the other one?"

"Satanic," said Jorge. "Their leader has gained power by summoning minor demons. She calls herself, Chang'e." Jorge pronounced the name, Chung-uh. "She and her coven are dangerous. If you see any of them anywhere near the cemetery, you don't approach them alone. Come find the rest of us."

"That chick is crazy, of the batshit variety," added Tink.

"Alyssandra's coven worships Gaia," continued Jorge. "They draw their power from nature. She and her people are still dangerous, but as far as I can tell, they're honest and straight forward with us. You can trust them to keep their word. Even saying that, though, I don't know why Simon let them in."

"Do you want me take Mitch out and introduce him?" asked Tink.

"Yeah. That's probably a good idea. Take him to meet Alyssandra about ten o'clock. That way they haven't already started … whatever it is that they do out here. Let them know there's a new officer working for us, and let Mitch get to know them and what they look like. How can he know which witches to keep out if he doesn't know which ones we let in?"

A witch coven, thought Mitch with growing excitement. *So much for tonight being another boring shift.*

The next three hours were worse than most. With something to look forward to, the passing time insisted on crawling by even slower than usual. Mitch tried to make the minutes move faster by reading the section of his manual that dealt with witches, but he found himself unable to properly focus on the pages in front of him. His attention continually wandered to the time display on his cellphone.

A few minutes before ten o'clock, Tink at last announced they should go. He and Mitch hiked across the manicured lawns, through Back Half, and into the oldest parts of the cemetery grounds. The area they entered was off limits to normal visitors as it had long ago been designated by the state of California as historic lands. A separate fence had been built to separate it from the rest of the graveyard, and due to the lack of regular grounds maintenance, brush and mature trees had grown unmolested until achieving an almost forest-like appearance. The wooded space did not seem to inhabit the same world as Dasan's Terrace, much less the same cemetery.

Headstones and memorials in this region were much older as well, dating back hundreds of years. The surviving markers were weather-worn, faded, and overgrown with lichen and molds. There were older graves as well, going back to the first native tribes in California, but any decorations adorning individual gravesites from that far back were long since deteriorated to dust and rubble.

Tink unlocked the interior gate and let himself and Mitch into the northeast grounds.

"Does the coven have keys to this gate?" asked Mitch as he resecured the massive brass padlock that held the gate closed.

"No. I have no idea how they get in. I also have no idea exactly what we would have to do to keep them out if we wanted to. They sort of go wherever the hell they want."

"And how are we supposed to find them out here? Listen for chanting, or look for the bonfire?"

Finding the witches did not turn out to be a problem. Mitch and Tink's entrance into the secured area had not gone unnoticed. A tall woman dressed in a skin-tight black dress glided out of the shadows and directed the blinding beam of a flashlight into their faces.

"Officer Zapien, I know why you are here," she said to Tink in a defiant tone, "but I want you to know we had nothing to do with the vandalisms to those graves. They were all damaged when we arrived. You have no cause–"

"Damn it, Alyssandra, get that light out of my eyes! And what the hell are you talking about? Vandalism?"

The light dropped, now illuminating a patch of dirt at the woman's feet. As Mitch blinked the spots from his vision, he got his first good look at the leader of the witches' coven. Alyssandra was older, perhaps in her fifties or sixties, with dark skin and straightened gray hair long enough to touch her shoulders. The woman was thin almost to the point of being emaciated, and the lines of her jaw and cheekbones jutted out sharply from the narrow features of her face.

She peered at Tink, her eyes hooded and suspicious.

"You aren't here for the graves?"

"No. What graves?"

In response, Alyssandra played the beam of her flashlight across the ground, stopping at a row of worn headstones a few paces away. The burial plots she illuminated were in a line along the north side of the perimeter fence.

"Those graves. The ground has been disturbed and much of it removed."

Tink approached the graves, removing his own flashlight from his belt and turning it on. Mitch followed his example. The stone markers on the burial sites were still intact, although one was badly cracked with age and several pieces had fallen away from the etched face of it. The ground below each marker had clearly been tampered with.

"Sometimes the ground settles, causing the graves to sink. It leaves a shallow depression like this."

"Three graves in a row?" asked Alyssandra, skeptically. "And when a grave settles the grass and topsoil remain in place. These have had the dirt on top scraped away and removed."

"They look like someone dug a wide, shallow hole and carted away the extra dirt," Mitch agreed. "But why would anyone want dirt?"

"There are several uses for soil collected from a dead man's grave," Alyssandra stated, although Mitch had not expected a response to his question. "Most of them, however, we do not practice. They are darker arts. We had nothing to do with this."

"I believe you," Tink told her. "I didn't even know these holes were here until you pointed them out."

"Thank you, Officer Zapien," said Alyssandra, sounding slightly less hostile. "I did not want anyone thinking I had violated the terms of our agreement. I have done no harm to Dasan's Tears." The woman's eyes narrowed again. "If you aren't here for the vandalism, then why have you come to see me tonight?"

Tink waved a hand toward Mitch. "We came out so you could meet our newest officer. He got transferred to us a few weeks ago. Alyssandra, this is Mitch Loman. Mitch, this is Alyssandra Freid."

The two nodded toward each other politely.

"Officer Loman. Have you ever met a witch before?"

"I don't know," admitted Mitch. "If I have, I didn't know it. You don't look like a witch, so how would I be able to tell?"

"I don't look like a witch? What then does a witch look like? What were you expecting?" asked Alyssandra.

"I have no idea. You look like a normal person to me."

Alyssandra's brows pulled closer together and her lips tightened a fraction.

"Why wouldn't I look like a normal person? Are you trying to be insulting?"

"No. I-I'm not. I had no idea what you would look like. I didn't know what to expect."

She glided closer to Mitch. Though a few inches shorter than he was, as she approached, she seemed to loom over him. "Perhaps if my skin was green, you would have recognized me. Maybe if my nose was long and hooked? Or should I have a mole on my chin? Is that more witchlike for you?"

"He meant no harm, Alyssandra. His soul is clean."

A second figure strolled up behind Alyssandra, resolving out of the gloom and placing a calming hand on her coven leader's shoulder. Mitch had not heard her approach and startled a bit at her arrival. The new woman was shorter than Alyssandra and much younger, though she was also dressed in a form hugging black dress that covered her from the neck all the way to the ground. The dress looked much more flattering on the newcoming, even as it caused her body to blend into the surrounding shadows of the trees. Her face was a pale white oval in the moonlight, appearing to float unsupported in the darkness. Her tiny, pointed nose was almost lost between a mouth accented with heavy red lipstick and dark circles of kohl around her eyes. Long, straight black hair draped her head and trailed down her back to her waist. The overall image reminded Mitch of Morticia Addams from reruns he had watched as a child of the old black-and-white television show, The Addams Family.

"You're scaring him," she continued.

"I thought you'd look like that," said Mitch, pointing at the second woman.

Rather than be insulted by the bluntness of the comment, the younger woman laughed merrily. The sound of her amusement was light and infectious, and Mitch could see Alyssandra visibly relaxing.

"This is Violet," said Alyssandra with a wave toward the girl. "She is my second. I trust her, and in my absence, she may speak for the coven. If *she* makes you a promise, then *I* have made you a promise. Because she says you meant no offense, I shall take no offense."

Violet raised up on her tiptoes to be closer to Alyssandra's right ear. She spoke quietly. Mitch heard her whispering but could not make out her words.

"Is that right?" asked the coven leader.

Violet nodded, then spoke again, also too quiet for Mitch to hear.

"And you're sure of that?"

Violet nodded a second time and took a step back. Alyssandra raised a hand to the side of Mitch's face. She ran her fingers through his hair as though caressing a lover and Mitch flinched back involuntarily from the unwelcome touch. The witch merely smiled at his retreat.

"Violet seems to think very highly of you, Officer Loman. Do you know why?"

Mitch paused, thinking what he may have said or done in the past minute or two, but nothing out of the ordinary came to mind. "I have no idea," he admitted.

"Do you know what you are, officer? Do you know what you are capable of?"

"I'm a cop. Otherwise, I don't know what you're talking about."

Alyssandra turned to look at Violet. Mitch followed her gaze. The younger woman stared back at him intently and smiled, her teeth a bright white outlined by the red lipstick. A hazy orange light emerged, emanating from her head and shoulders and evolving into a slowly pulsing halo of flame. The spectral fire surrounded her face, bathing it in red, yellow and orange hues. It flickered and shimmered for a moment, then faded away as quickly as it had appeared.

Violet nodded once, and Alyssandra's attention returned to Mitch.

"Violet is willing to show you, Officer Loman. She can teach you to reach your full potential if you let her. Why don't you join us tonight, and in the morning, we can talk of how you may repay Violet's kindness."

Mitch didn't like the turn this conversation had taken. "Why don't you tell me right now what I'm capable of. And exactly what you mean by 'repay?'"

"Nothing comes for free. Violet does you this favor, and I feel it would only be correct for you to offer a favor in return. I am content to accept payment of this promised favor at a later date."

Mitch shook his head. "No. I'm not comfortable with the whole idea of owing someone an unspecified favor. Sounds like a good way to get fired or arrested. I've gotten this far without Violet's help. I think I'll make it a little longer on my own."

"Suit yourself," said Alyssandra with a casual shrug. "If you change your mind, you know how to find us. Of course, if you want answers in the meantime but don't want Violet's help, you can always go ask Harold Petrovic."

Mitch didn't know what she intended by that statement. It sounded vaguely ominous. Perhaps even threatening. Was she suggesting that Violet had answers to questions Mitch would otherwise have to die to find out? Was that what she meant by go ask Harold?

"I think it's time you gentlemen were on your way," said Alyssandra. "You've taken enough of our time this evening and it seems our business is concluded. You've introduced your friend to us, Officer Zapien, and you, Officer Loman, do not appear interested in our offered assistance. I think that leaves us nothing more to discuss."

Mitch glanced again toward Violet. When she noticed the direction of his gaze, she blew him a kiss, smiling and wrinkling her nose coquettishly as she wiggled her fingers at him in a brief wave goodbye.

"Thanks for your time," said Tink, pulling out his keys to unlock the gate.

The women disappeared, fading into the backdrop of the trees. They vanished completely. Mitch did not even see where they had gone. He shuddered. The whole interaction had been beyond creepy.

"How did Violet do that thing with the lights around her head?" he asked Tink.

"What thing?"

"Didn't you see the fire that glowed around her head back there?"

"The only light I saw was Alyssandra's flashlight in my face. Are you okay? Did you fall and hit your head when I wasn't looking?"

Mitch shook his head and laughed off the comment, trying to sound normal although he remained disturbed by his interaction with the witches. He had definitely seen something. Violet looked like she was making a point of letting him see … whatever it was. She was staring directly at him when it happened. If Tink hadn't noticed, then the display had been meant just for him.

What did that mean?

He sighed in frustration. Mitch felt like the butt of some joke he didn't understand. A dangerous joke that might explode in his face if he didn't figure out the punchline fast enough.

"I hope you don't have anything else planned tonight," said Tink, relocking the gate after they had exited the northwest grounds.

"What?" asked Mitch, jolted from his darkening thoughts.

"We had three graves vandalized and you're the junior officer on the shift. That means you've got a report to write."

CHAPTER 7

The diner was only about a third full at this hour, and the murmured conversations around the room remained low and unintrusive. Mitch sat by himself in a booth, scrolling through emails on his phone with a half-eaten cheeseburger on the plate in front of him. Living alone and having no culinary skills to speak of meant most of his meals were of the boxed, canned, or fast-food variety. Today, although he usually spent his days off on the couch in front of the television, he had opted to get some fresh air and treat himself to a meal out.

Cassie's Café was where he had landed today. The restaurant was close to home, reasonably priced, and the food was better than anything Mitch knew how to make for himself. Even if the service was not always stellar, the pros still outweighed the minuses.

It was early afternoon. The lunch rush had dissipated, and the dinner guests had not yet begun to filter in. The wait staff meandered leisurely from table to table, clearing away dishes and wiping down chairs and tabletops, while the cook stood in the service window chatting with one of the greeters between orders.

Someone approached Mitch's booth and paused beside the table. He caught the movement out of the corner of his eye but did not look up from his phone.

"I'm fine, thanks. I would take a refill on my soda, though, if you don't mind."

"Rude."

The voice was soft and cajoling. He glanced up and realized his mistake immediately. The young woman standing next to him was not his server. She did not work for the restaurant.

The woman had short blond bangs that stopped above eyebrows so pale they were almost nonexistent. The rest of her hair had been pulled back into a ponytail that jutted out behind her head, not quite touching the base of her neck. Striking blue eyes, the color of a motionless, deep, glacier lake, watched Mitch closely, and there was more than a hint of amusement in her stare. Her features had a healthy tanned glow, much darker than he would have expected for someone so fair skinned in the middle of February. She did not appear to be wearing any makeup, and Mitch found himself briefly wondering if she visited a tanning booth during the winter months.

His visitor wore a blousy, white T-shirt, cuffed at her shoulders and the tails tucked into a pair of faded blue jeans that showed off her slender curves admirably.

"I don't work here, she said," though there was no heat in the statement.

"I see that. I'm sorry for the confusion, I wasn't paying attention. Can I help you?"

The girl's mouth quirked into a disappointed scowl, giving her a mildly vexed appearance. Mitch found the expression ridiculously adorable, and he was unable to suppress a small grin in response.

"You aren't that observant, I guess," she huffed. "You must have made an absolutely terrible detective, Mr. Mitch Loman."

Mitch's grin disappeared and he peered at the woman's face more closely.

"I'm sorry, have we met? I don't remember."

The mystery girl stepped past the table and slid into the bench opposite Mitch's own. She set her elbows on the table and dropped her chin into her hands. Her lips pulled together in a pout causing the ridge of her nose to crinkle in an intriguing manner. Mitch found himself staring, desperately trying to remember where he might have seen her before, his eyes drawn again to her delicately pointed nose.

"So sad. I really had high hopes for you."

Then he remembered.

"You had black hair," he said. "That's cheating. It's not really a fair test if you change how you look. How are you, Violet?"

"Yay!" said Violet, tapping the fingers of her right hand into the palm of her left in a soft golf clap. "Maybe there's hope for you after all."

Mitch set his phone aside on the table and took a sip of his soda, trying to appear nonchalant, although in truth he was a bit unnerved by the witch's sudden appearance.

"Quite the coincidence running into you, today," he said.

"Oh, there is no such thing as coincidence, Officer Loman."

"Mitch," he corrected. "No need for any formalities here. So, if this isn't a coincidence, is this meeting intentional?"

"It very much is," Violet agreed. "Mitch."

"You followed me here?"

Violet's expression turned smug. She shook her head, causing her ponytail to wag back and forth. "No need to follow you. I can find you anytime I want. You should never let a witch take a strand of your hair. It can be very dangerous. Fortunately, we aren't your enemies and Alyssandra only used it to locate you."

Mitch remembered the coven leader's caress and the hand she ran through his hair. He shuddered as he realized what she had done.

Violet reached across the table and grabbed the edge of Mitch's lunch plate with a thumb and forefinger. She pulled the dish closer to herself, then plucked up a french fry. Mitch raised an eyebrow.

"Nothing comes for free, Mitch. The price of the lesson you just learned is a couple of fries. Consider yourself lucky it was so cheap. I have a great deal more that I can teach you if you want, but the price will be much higher than a couple bites of your lunch."

"I told you I'm not interested in that. The whole idea of a favor to be paid back later is not something I'm willing to go along with."

Violet reached for another fry, but Mitch snatched his plate back. She peered at him with her hand still in the air for several seconds before settling back into the bench on her half of the booth. There was a mischievous glint in her eyes.

"I know. I remember. How about this instead: we tell you what we want first, then you can decide whether or not the price is worth the information we're offering. Would that work better for you?"

"If I don't like the request, I can say no?"

Violet nodded.

"That sounds more reasonable. I think I can agree to at least hear you out in those circumstances."

"Great! First of all," Violet grabbed Mitch's plate again and jerked it to her side of the table, "I wasn't finished with these."

Mitch rolled his eyes but laughed softly. He held his hands up in surrender. "Okay. Okay. Help yourself."

Taking her time, Violet picked up a french fry, bit, chewed, and swallowed.

"Second," she said, removing a napkin from the table dispenser and dabbing demurely at the corner of her mouth, "we would like to have access to the cemetery more than once a month. On the nights we show up, we need you to make sure your partners don't know we're there. Keep them away with some excuse or other."

"No," said Mitch flatly. "That's never going to happen."

Violet shrugged and selected another french fry. She did not seem bothered by his response. "I didn't think so. Alyssandra wanted me to ask, though, so I asked. Plan B, then. Go to your chief and ask him to revise our agreement to allow us in twice each month. In exchange, I will agree to take you on as an apprentice and make sure you learn everything you need to know about your talents. Everything will be totally above board."

"What talents?"

Violet held up a finger and ticked it back and forth. "Nope. No more freebies. Go talk to Chief Jefferson and see what he says."

"I'll talk to him, but I can't guarantee he'll agree to anything."

"That's all I'm asking. Oh, and Mitch," Violet's tone turned serious. "Try to be persuasive. It's important. You have no idea who you are, what you are, or what you are capable of, but there are already some very dangerous people that are starting to take notice of you. I don't want to see you get hurt."

"If you don't want me to get hurt, then tell me what you mean. Who do you think I am?"

Violet shook her head with genuine regret in her expression. "If it were up to me, I would. This isn't my decision."

"Alyssandra," said Mitch.

Violet nodded. "Alyssandra."

Violet picked up Mitch's half-eaten burger. She raised it to her mouth and took a huge bite. Mitch's jaw dropped in surprise.

"What?" the blond, young witch asked around her mouthful of food. "A girl needs to eat."

Mitch pulled another napkin from the dispenser and held it out to her. "I guess so," he agreed. "Hey, out of curiosity. What was with all that black eye makeup and the wig the other night?"

"I have to look the part, don't I?" Violet asked, still chewing. She accepted the napkin. "Besides, I'm only twenty-nine."

"Twenty-nine? I don't understand the connection. What does your age have to do with it?"

"I'm the number two witch in that coven. I've earned my position there, but some of the others feel that I'm too young to hold that kind of power. They think my age makes me weak or vulnerable. The makeup makes me look older and a bit more dangerous. It keeps the challengers to a minimum."

"Makes sense, I guess," Mitch mused. "I like you better without it, though. You look much more normal."

Violet paused and gave him an odd look. "You used that word the last time I saw you. You said Alyssandra looked normal, and I'm starting to see why it pissed her off so much. It sounds like you're implying that I'm *not* normal."

"No, that isn't it at all. I'm only saying without the goth makeup and wig you look…"

"I look what?"

"Beautiful." Mitch flushed slightly when he realized what he had said. He had spoken without thinking. "I mean…"

"Stop!" Violet held up her hand. "Stop right there. I think that is the perfect place to quit talking."

Mitch shut his mouth. Violet wiped her chin with her napkin and dropped it onto Mitch's plate. She pushed herself out of the booth and left without another word. Mitch watched her as she headed for the doors. His eyes were drawn to the gentle sway of her hips as she went, and there was a little bounce in her step that he wondered if she had added for his benefit. He still had questions and wished she hadn't left so abruptly, but he reluctantly admitted to himself that she certainly knew how to make an impressive exit.

CHAPTER 8

True to his word, the following Wednesday night Mitch arrived at the police department three hours early for his shift hoping to catch Chief Jefferson before he went home. The chief's office was dark, and the door was closed, but he found the department's administrative assistant at her desk, typing manically on her desktop computer keyboard. The staccato click of the keys under her fingers was so rapid-fire quick, Mitch wondered if she was merely pretending to type at that speed for his benefit. Knowing Dot, however, probably not. She had many talents, making her a critical component of the Dasan's Terrace Police Department, she didn't need to pretend anything to impress anyone.

Dot's normally paper-cluttered workspace had been cleared and straightened, a rare condition for the busy woman. When she noticed Mitch entering the room, she paused her work and settled back in her chair, her hands folded in her lap as though she had all the time in the world and Mitch was the most important agenda item on her calendar. She smiled a warm greeting, and the expression on her face suggested she had been patiently awaiting his arrival. That was absurd. There was no way she could have anticipated Mitch coming in tonight, but he had a strange feeling that was exactly what she was doing.

"Hi, Dot," he greeted her. "Is the chief in his office?"

"No. I'm sorry. He has a Captains meeting at the Sheriff's Department this evening and he already went home to shower and change for it. Can I help you with something?"

Mitch nodded his understanding. Simon Jefferson had been appointed to Chief of Police at Dasan's Terrace by the Sacramento County Sheriff, but his official rank within the SCSO was still captain. As such, he was expected to attend the monthly, county-wide meetings with all of his peers.

"I don't know. I was hoping to speak to Chief Jefferson."

"Simon," Dot corrected.

"Simon. Right. I'm not sure I'm ever going to get used to that. Anyway, I was hoping to talk to Simon directly. Alyssandra's coven wants to negotiate two days every month in the cemetery in exchange for taking me on as an apprentice or something. I'm not sure I totally understand what's going on."

Dot smiled. "Simon already knows about that. Alyssandra came by to talk to him this morning about the same thing. They're working things out, I'm sure."

"Then why did Violet ask *me* to talk to the chief if Alyssandra was already coming in?" Mitch asked, more to himself than to Dot.

"I'm sure she figured you might have a better chance of convincing him than Alyssandra. The coven leader is … let's just say, less than subtle in her negotiation skills."

"Do I?" asked Mitch. "Have a better chance, I mean?"

"No. Simon will make up his own mind. You and I aren't going to sway him one way or the other on this. You're still welcome to talk to him about it, though. I'm sure he'd like to hear your opinion on the matter."

"Okay. I'll try to see him again tomorrow. Thanks, Dot." Mitch turned to leave.

"Wait, Mitchell. Do you have a minute?"

"I have three hours before my shift," Mitch admitted ruefully. "I think I can spare a minute."

Dot stood and stepped around her desk, gesturing for Mitch to follow her into the break room. She closed the door, then pulled out two chairs next to one another. She sat down, and Mitch followed her example, settling into the second chair. Dot looked at him seriously for a long moment, examining his eyes as though trying to peer through pupils and into the thoughts occurring behind them. The sensation of being studied left Mitch uncomfortable and fidgeting in his seat.

Finding what she was searching for, or perhaps not, Dot smiled and lowered her gaze.

"Tell me, Mitchell, if you don't mind my asking. What's your story?"

Confused by the question, Mitch wasn't sure how to answer. "I don't know that I have a story," he offered.

Dot patted him on the back of his hand; a comforting motherly gesture despite the fact she was five years Mitch's junior in age. "Almost everybody that comes to work for Dead Town has a story."

Mitch raised an eyebrow at Dot's use of the term Dead Town.

"I know," she continued. "Simon hates that name. I think it's cute, though. I've certainly heard people call this place worse. But let's stay focused on you. I know you see ghosts; you've demonstrated that already. There's more to it than simply seeing them, though. Isn't there? You're more sensitive to their presence than most people. When did that start?"

Mitch again shifted uncomfortably in his chair. This was not a topic of discussion he had expected, nor did he greatly desire to dwell on the details surrounding the death of his son with Dot. As nice as she seemed, and despite Jorge's earlier admonishment, she was still basically a stranger, and Denny's tragedy was not something he readily shared with others.

"I'm not sure I know what you're asking," he demurred. "What about you? What's your 'story.' How did you end up coming to DTPD?"

"That's fair," said Dot, accepting the shift in the conversation. "Here I am grilling you about a sensitive, and probably painful, event in your life. I should be willing to answer the same questions I'm asking. I'll share, and when I'm done, we'll see what you are willing to tell me about yourself in exchange. As you may already know, I am, like you, sensitive to spirits. But I can do more than that. I also see the auras of living people, and I periodically experience premonitions of future events. Particularly events tied to strong emotional responses. It's not like telling the future or anything that dramatic; I merely have feelings that something good or bad is going to happen, and I can feel a person's emotional state as a reaction to whatever they will go through. I have dreams sometimes about people that are going to experience desperate difficulty, but they're usually so vague I'm not sure what the visions are trying to tell me until after the event has already occurred. Not very helpful most of the time."

Dot rose from her chair and went to the refrigerator. She removed two bottles of water from an interior shelf, then returned to her seat. She handed Mitch one of the bottles without asking.

"I've been like this my whole life. At first, when I was younger, it would come and go, but about the time I turned eighteen, it became a more permanent part of me. I learned to control it. Well … mostly. When I was nineteen, I applied to Dead Town to be a receptionist at the Dasan's Terrace funeral home. Simon's predecessor, the old chief of police here, found me. He recognized my potential and brought me over to the police department. I've been the A.A. for the chief's office ever since."

Mitch held his water bottle in his hands and rolled it between his palms. He made no effort to open it. He wasn't thirsty. "That sounds pretty straightforward," he said. "I don't know that I would consider that much of a story."

"Patience, please. I'm not done," Dot admonished. "That is only the back story to how I got here. The important part is what happened before … and after … I got hired. I inherited these abilities from my mother who was the same way. Friends and family used to come to her to have their fortunes read in Tarot cards, although my mother admitted to me once that she had no idea how to read anything in the deck. The cards were props to give people something to focus on while she used her true abilities to read people's emotions. She mostly told visitors what they wanted to hear. She could look into someone's aura and tell when they were excited or sad, or when they were having a difficult time, and she would use the insight to draw out additional details."

Dot's gaze drifted to the top of the table, her eyes staring at nothing in particular as her memories pulled her attention away from her immediate surroundings.

"There was more to it, however, than simply knowing what a person was feeling. My mother could look into a person's aura and know immediately if they were sick. There was a darkness… a shade of wrongness that was unmistakable when someone was injured or ill. She saved my cousin many years ago when she warned him about a tumor growing on his kidney. She sent him to the doctor to get checked and they were able to remove it before it became life threatening. I have the same gift. And it truly is a gift. If I look closely, I can see if someone isn't feeling well, and I can often tell exactly where the sickness is growing. Unfortunately, my personal talent for reading auras did not fully manifest until I was an adult. If I could have used it sooner, I might have been able to save my mother."

Dot paused to take a drink of water. Mitch said nothing as he waited for her to continue. He had spent enough time interviewing people as a detective to know when someone needed to simply sit quietly and take a moment to organize their thoughts. Some stories needed to be told at their own pace, without any prodding or pushing. Mitch allowed her all the time she needed.

"When I was sixteen, my mother was diagnosed with breast cancer. It was advanced too far to successfully treat by the time the doctors found it; the cancer had already spread to other parts of her body. I couldn't see auras clearly at that age, so I never saw the sickness growing in her."

"Your mother didn't see the cancer in her own aura?" asked Mitch softly.

Dot smiled sadly. "I have met quite a few people that can see human auras. Some are stronger than others. My mother was one of the most powerful I've ever known, but out of all of them, I have never come across anyone that could see their own aura. I don't know why it's like that, but it is. No, my mother couldn't have seen the disease in herself. It would have to have been me. She died a few weeks before my seventeenth birthday."

Dot paused again, her blue eyes turning misty pale with unshed tears. She looked like a lost child at that moment and Mitch had to resist an urge to put his arms around her and hold her. Perhaps sensing his feelings, Dot sniffled and smiled at him, attempting to put him at ease.

"In the hospital, a little while before she died, I came to visit her. She was so wasted and frail, she was barely more than loose bones and skin in a hospital gown. The sight of her scared me. Regardless of her condition, when I came into her room, she seemed to light up at my presence. She forced one of the nurses to let her sit up so she could speak with me more easily. She told me she loved me, and she knew her time was short, but she wanted me to know that everything would be okay after she was gone. She had arranged for me to stay with family, and she had put aside enough money that I wouldn't need to worry about school or living expenses for several years.

"I couldn't believe what I was hearing. She was going to die. I was losing my mother and all she could talk about was how she was leaving me enough money to pay bills. I got angry at her for being so calm, so rational. There was no excuse for how I responded. I was a child, and my reaction was selfish, but that didn't change how I felt. I yelled at her. I yelled at a dying woman because I could only think of myself. I told her I wasn't ready for her to go, and she had no right to leave me. I needed her to be around to see me graduate high school, to go to college. To get married. I told her she absolutely could not leave this Earth until she had seen her first grandchild."

Dot swiped at her left cheek with a hand and sniffed again softly. She noticed Mitch had seen the tears, and she gave him a small laugh, letting him know she was alright. The true pain in the memory had long since been put to rest, leaving only a hollow sadness and longing behind.

"My words were silly and uncaring for my mother's feelings. She was still alive, but I was already feeling abandoned. In my heart, she had already left me behind. I put my face in her lap and cried, wanting to be comforted by the very woman I had been berating. That was when my mother stopped talking and went perfectly still. Her breathing slowed. I remember looking into her face and realizing that she didn't see me anymore. At least, not the me in that particular hospital room. Her eyes were focused on something far away, something beyond what I could see at the time. She put her arms out in front of her as if cradling something to her chest, and she started rocking gently back and forth. Back and forth.

"'I see him,' she said to me. 'Ah, he's so beautiful. Strong and healthy as a bear. And you look so proud, my fierce little girl. He is lucky to have you for a mother.'"

Dot looked toward Mitch. Her eyes were alight with childish delight and wonder. She shrugged at him, indicating the shock she recalled at her mother's behavior.

"Imagine that. I didn't know what to say to her. I couldn't tell if she was placating me or making fun of me. I even thought maybe the cancer had gotten into her brain, or the medications had addled her mind. Then she started to sing as she rocked. She was so quiet I could barely hear her, and it took me a second before I recognized the song. She was singing Time After Time, by Cyndi Lauper. I couldn't for the life of me figure out why that particular song was in her head. It went on for about twenty seconds, the singing and the rocking. Then her arms dropped to her sides and she fell asleep.

"That was the last time I spoke to her face to face. She didn't wake up again. She died a few days later."

"I'm sorry," said Mitch. "That must have been very hard for you."

Dot waved a hand toward Mitch and began to laugh. “Don’t be sorry. I didn’t know it until six years later, but it was a miracle that day. Like I said to you before: a gift.”

She shifted in her chair to face Mitch directly, her hands folded between her knees as she leaned toward him.

“When I was twenty-three, I gave birth to my son. On the day he was born, I remember I was lying in the hospital bed. My baby was in my arms, and I had just begun to nurse him. Before leaving the room to make some phone calls, my son’s father turned on a radio for me so I could listen to music. It was one of those 80’s pop stations. I love old 80’s and 90’s music.

“My son was suckling away contentedly, and I suddenly began to miss my mother. I thought about the last time I had talked to her and how I had desperately wanted her to meet her first grandchild. As I remembered the terrible day that we fought, I felt the pressure of two arms encircling me and my son. It wasn’t my imagination. I could feel and see the indentations where something pressed against my shoulders and chest. I started to cry. I was so happy at that moment when I realized what song had begun to play on that crappy hospital radio speaker.”

“Time After Time,” whispered Mitch.

“Time After Time,” Dot agreed, giving him another smile and a knowing nod. “She saw him. She saw her grandchild, and she held him in her arms. Even better, I got to say a proper goodbye. I got to tell her that I loved her.”

“That’s incredible,” said Mitch. As a realist and a cop, he wanted to remain skeptical of Dot’s story. The music could be pure coincidence, and the feel of her mother’s hug nothing more than delusion brought on by loneliness and the pain and hormones of recent childbirth. Dead parents did not reach across the years to hug their newborn grandchildren. He wanted to, but couldn't. The earnestness in her expression as she stared into his eyes convinced him. Besides, who was he to question other people's ghost stories? He thought about kettles and pots.

"I'm happy for you, and I'm glad your mother got to see your son." Then, to bring the conversation back to more world-bound topics, he said, "I didn't realize you had kids."

"Only the one. His father didn't want a family and skipped out on us pretty soon after our son was born. It's been the two of us on our own since then."

"What's his name?"

"Bear." Dot grinned fiercely at Mitch. "I named him that because…"

"Because that's what your mom called him when she saw him. 'Healthy as a bear.' I remember."

Mitch went silent. It was his turn to sink into the past, to lose himself in memory. Dot let him sit undisturbed for a minute or two.

"Do you want to tell me?" she finally asked. "Or shall we stop and do this another time?"

Mitch took a long, slow breath, then released it in a rush. "I had a little boy, too. His name was Dennis…"

Mitch told Dot the entire story, from Denny's accidental fall from his bedroom window to his surprise return the following Christmas Eve. He did not shy away from the painful details of wrapping his arms around his child every year since the initial tragedy and waiting out the clock as he felt the life draining out of the tiny body again and again. He even told her of his wife's inability to cope with the return of their son and her desire to sell the house and move out of the state. Mitch's refusal to move had led to her leaving to stay with her parents and subsequently sending him divorce papers in the mail a few months later.

Mitch omitted the weeks he spent blackout drunk following each of Denny's visits. He figured there was nothing to be gained in that revelation. Dot had most likely seen the Internal Affairs investigation paperwork, anyway. She could do the math on her own.

"It isn't the same happy ending as yours, I'm afraid," he said as he finished his tale. "I refuse to leave the house as long as he continues to come back. I can't let him go through that alone. I have to be there for him. I don't know how to help him, though, to show him how to move on to … to whatever should come next."

Dot placed a small hand on Mitch's arm. "I don't know if there is anything that can be done to help him move on," she said. "I don't think it's really Denny you're seeing every year."

Mitch pulled away from Dot's touch, suddenly furious. Was she calling him a liar? Did she think he was insane? "Of course, it's Denny!" Mitch shouted. "You don't think I know my own son?"

"No, no. That's not what I meant. Of course, you're right. It's Denny. What I meant to say was … how can I put this? Mitchell, first you have to understand a few things about spirits and how they occur. Has anyone ever explained this to you before?"

Mitch shook his head, no.

"There are five different types of spirits or ghosts that haunt our world. The first is what is called an echo. Echoes are formed when something very meaningful or tragic happens to a person right before they die. The actions they were engaged in before their death resonate and form an image. That image remains when the person is gone and simply repeats over and over until it eventually fades away all by itself. Echoes have no life of their own since the soul of the person who left it has already moved peacefully on to wherever they need to go."

"Like Harold?" asked Mitch. "Tink mentioned something about him being an echo."

"Yes!" Dot's face lit up. "Exactly like Harold. Harold's soul, or spirit or whatever you want to call it, has moved on to join his wife. What he left behind was a reflection of his love and devotion for her while he was alive."

Dot held up two fingers.

"The second group are poltergeists. These are similar to echoes in that they are caused by emotions at the time of a person's death. Poltergeists are more violent and dangerous, however. They are created when someone dies while experiencing rage, terror, or deep regret. The emotion itself is what is left behind rather than a picture of a specific moment in time. This emotion can grow, feeding on its own frustrated rage until it becomes strong enough to interact with the world around it. The more powerful ones seek out people to vent their anger upon, attacking their unfortunate targets like a child throwing a temper tantrum. While a poltergeist may act intelligent in its behavior, it is still not a real person. The soul of the deceased that created the poltergeist is gone and only the hate or fear remains."

Dot raised a third finger.

"The third type is the true spirit, or trapped soul. This is a person whose physical body has died but their soul has for some reason been unable to move on like it should. These are people that passed away before they could finish something they felt was too important to leave behind. These are also the ones that need help to be freed from the ties holding them here."

Dot placed her hand back on Mitch's arm. The sympathy in her eyes was almost too much for Mitch to take, so instead, he simply turned his attention to the water bottle in his hands.

"Mitch, I don't think Denny is trapped here. I think what you are seeing every year is an echo. I've never known an echo that repeated only once a year, but then there are lots of things I still have to learn about the supernatural. I believe you're reliving a repeat of Denny's death, a recording of an unpleasant event. Denny, himself, is at peace and has moved on."

"How do you know?"

"Never having seen Denny, I can't know for certain, but your story sounds like what I'm describing. You said he shows up at the same time every year? To the minute?"

"Nine forty in the evening, every time," Mitch agreed.

"And he stays downstairs with you the same amount of time before returning to his room. That makes me think echo. Have you tried preventing him from falling?"

"I closed the window and locked it the second year he showed up. The year after that, I nailed it shut and followed him up to the room. He still fell. He passed through the closed window like it wasn't there."

"He's replaying an event as it happened in real life," Dot explained. "Changing the physical surroundings does not alter what he experienced so he ignores anything different. It's as if he doesn't see the things as they are, but rather as they were."

"What about the fact he asks for his mother when he shows up? He's noticing that she isn't there."

"Did he ask for her on the night he died? Was she out of the room, maybe, and he didn't see her?"

"I…" Mitch paused as he thought about Dot's question. "I don't remember. I suppose she could have been in the kitchen, or out of the room for a moment. I'm not sure."

"I bet she was. In fact, if she was in the room with you this year, he probably wouldn't see her, and he'd ask about her again. He's on a loop. It's a recording of an event, a terrible, tragic event, but that's all it is."

Mitch sighed. "I hope you're right. If it is just an echo, how do I stop it?"

"You don't. It fades and disappears on its own. It usually takes weeks or months. A few last for years but those aren't common. I'm referring to echoes that repeat multiple times each night, though. For something that only occurs once a year, I have no idea how long it could take to fade away. But don't worry. Denny isn't in any pain. He's gone."

Mitch nodded, accepting the comfort Dot offered. She was the expert in this field so he figured she must know what she was talking about. Knowing his real son was safely away from this lousy world and didn't have to experience his own death once each Christmas was a relief. Mitch suddenly realized that Dot's explanation had left him feeling physically lighter, as though a pressure weighing him down across his neck and shoulders had been suddenly stripped away.

"So…," Mitch's voice choked off and he was forced to cough to clear the lump in his throat. "So, what are the other kinds?"

"Other kinds of what?" asked Dot.

"Ghosts. You said there were five, but you only mentioned three."

"Ah, right. Well, the fourth is demons, but honestly, those were never human and never had souls, so they only count as ghosts because of their tendency to haunt locations or objects.

The last one is revenants, which are creatures that have died and returned to life. They may or may not have their souls still attached when they come back. They usually get lumped in with things like zombies and vampires."

Mitch shuddered, and growled, "Vampires."

CHAPTER 9

Mitch strolled with Tink through the manicured front lawns of Dasan's Terrace, making a leisurely outing of their first patrol of the evening. Mitch's mind still circled around his conversation with Dot earlier that day, so he was only half listening as his partner prattled on about nothing of any real importance. Tink followed one of the paved pathways, his hands buried in the pockets of his uniform jacket as he speculated on Brad's current location, wondering if their teammate was out patrolling the grounds or, as seemed more likely, back at the police department dreaming up some new practical joke to spring on one of them unawares. Mitch did not respond to Tink's musings, paying little attention to the actual conversation occurring beside him. Internally, he could only hear Dot repeating her assurances that Denny was at peace.

He clung to that statement, hoping it was true, praying his son's soul wasn't trapped in the house to relive a Christmas Eve tragedy for the rest of eternity. The thought was too gruesome to contemplate.

"Dot knows what she's talking about, right?" he said, interrupting Tink's monologue in midsentence.

"What? What do you mean? When did you talk to Dot? What did she say?"

"She knows about ghosts. I mean, she knows as much as anyone can, right? So when she tells you something about spirits, you can trust that it's correct?"

"Dot knows more about ghosts than anyone I know. If there's something she doesn't know about souls and spirits then either she can find out the answer for you, or else it's not worth knowing."

Mitch nodded. He trusted Dot, but he had needed to hear the confirmation of her talents from someone else. This matter was too important not to double check.

"Why are you asking?"

"No real reason. I had a talk with her today about … something." Mitch stopped walking, distracted by an odd sight. He pointed across the lawn to direct Tink's attention. "What the hell happened there? Did the vandals start tearing up graves in the Front Lawn?"

Tink followed the line of Mitch's finger to a gravesite several yards to the left of the paved path. The lawn, normally smooth enough to mimic a golf course, with evenly mowed grass and flat marble markers spaced every few feet apart to indicate the individual graves, had a visible dip in its otherwise uniform appearance. One of the burial sites appeared to have collapsed, sinking downward to form a shallow bowl-shaped concavity in the grass.

The two officers strolled over to the irregularity to get a closer look. Tink played the beam of his flashlight over the damage, illuminating the shadowy hole.

"No," he said. "This isn't vandalism. Look, the grass is still there."

Mitch peered into the depression and saw, while cracked and uneven, the grass was indeed still present and intact. It had merely fallen into a sinkhole or unexpected gap beneath the lawn's roots.

"What causes this?" Mitch asked. "Water damage? Gophers?"

"Maybe water damage," agreed Tink. "It's possible when they filled this grave, there was too much air space in the dirt, and it settled when it got wet. I don't think so, though. The groundskeepers don't usually make that kind of mistake. I'm thinking it's more likely the burial vault broke or sank."

Mitch shuddered at the image that came into his mind. "Does that really happen?"

"Sure. The dirt on top of those caskets weighs a couple tons and sometimes, if the family got a cheaper quality liner, it can break apart. You know what a burial vault is?"

Mitch shook his head. "Um, not really, no. Is that like a crypt?"

"Nah. It's not a building. It's a concrete box the cemetery puts in the ground to hold the casket when they bury it. Even the best built caskets are going to fall apart over time, so to prevent … that," Tink pointed at the dip in the ground, "they put in a concrete casket holder called a burial vault. The concrete holds up better than just a casket and the cemetery lawn stays flat. Sometimes, though, if a family can't afford a regular vault, they get a liner instead. It's still concrete, but it only lines the walls of the grave and covers the casket. There isn't anything underneath except dirt. The walls are thinner and they can crack, or the whole liner can sink deeper into the ground. It doesn't happen very often, but this isn't the first time I've come across one."

Mitch played his light over the marble marker at the head of the damaged grave. It read, "Margaret Alido."

"Poor Margaret," he said. "What do we do about this?"

"Nothing," said Tink.

"Nothing?"

His partner pursed his lips and shook his head. "Nope. There isn't any crime here. It's a maintenance issue. I'll make a note of it in the patrol log so day shift sees it in the morning. They'll let the groundskeepers know, and someone will fill the hole and put new grass down. By tomorrow night, nobody will be able to tell anything ever happened here."

"Margaret will know," said Mitch, with a poor attempt at humor to lighten his own mood.

Tink laughed. "Yeah. But I don't guess Margaret cares much one way or the other."

"No, probably not."

Mitch grew pensive again. There were too many unpleasant thoughts swimming through his head calling out for his attention, his fears for his son's soul being paramount among them. The depressing clamor threatened to embrace him and drag him down into the darkness of his own subconscious. He found himself in desperate need of a distraction to keep his attention away from himself.

"Hey, Tink. What's your story?"

"My story?" Tink grabbed his equipment belt and hiked it to a more comfortable position around his belly. "I think I already told you. I clobbered some homeless dude who was trying to murder my partner."

"No, not about your name. Yeah, you did already tell me that one. When I was talking with Dot a while ago, she told me that everybody that comes to Dead Town has a story. They have a reason they ended up working here. I was just wondering why you're here. If that isn't getting too personal, of course."

Tink chuckled. "Oh that," he said. "There's no secret there. I don't mind talking about it. I guess it started with the fact that my parents were huge narcissists and didn't have much time to spend with a kid. They were more interested in making money, buying new cars, and going on expensive vacations. Without me most of the time. What? What's that look on your face?"

"Narcissists?" asked Mitch, grinning mischievously. "That's an awfully big word for you."

Tink huffed, feigning insult from Mitch's accusation. "I know big words. I'm not stupid. You want to hear another big word? You're-a-huge-asshole."

Mitch laughed. "Okay. Sorry, sorry. You're right. I'm a dick. Finish your story."

Tink pulled his jacket straight as though rearranging his damaged dignity before continuing.

"My parents were no-shows, so my grandfather basically raised me. He read to me, played with me, and kept me company when I was missing my mom and dad. He was always there when I needed him. I know that isn't an uncommon story. Lots of kids are ignored by their parents, and lots of them go to grandparents and aunts and cousins for attention. Where it gets interesting for me is that my grandfather died three years before I was born."

"Oh, man," breathed Mitch. "That's messed up."

"Tell me about it. When I was little, nobody knew he was there because I couldn't talk and tell people about it. As I got older, my parents thought I had an imaginary friend that I talked to. They didn't really care because it kept me occupied enough that they didn't have to spend any extra time with me. It started to become a problem when I was about five and I told my mom that I was talking to her father. I even described what he looked like. It scared her for a second, but then she convinced herself that I must have seen a picture of him somewhere and was repeating what I had seen in the photograph."

"I can understand that," said Mitch. "It's easier than believing your father's ghost is visiting your child."

"Sure. A normal mother would think that. I think in my mom's case, it was because it was easier than giving up a weekly tennis game and having to take her kid to the shrink, but your idea is good, too. Anyway, when I started going to school, I learned not to talk about my grandfather to my friends. It scared them away or got me labeled as the weird kid. I had to pretend I didn't see or hear him. He was always there, though.

"He got me in a lot of trouble, but he would also get me out of it, too. A bully would catch me talking to empty air and tell everyone I was crazy. My grandfather would follow the bully for a while, then tell me all the things he was doing that he didn't want anyone to know about. I would use the information to get him to leave me alone. Blackmail can be very useful at times. I think overall, I really liked having him with me. One of my favorite parts about having my grandfather around was that nobody could ever beat me at most games. He would always tell me what cards the other kids had, or what dice or tiles they had, or where their battleships were placed. I never lost a single hand of Old Maid as a kid."

"Is he still around?" asked Mitch. "Is he here, now?"

Tink shook his head. "If he was, I'm sure you'd see him, too. No, he disappeared a long time ago. I was about twelve years old when he told me his secret."

"Secret?"

"Yeah. Before he died, he buried a strongbox in his backyard. He didn't trust banks or lawyers and I guess he decided his stuff was safer in the ground. He left a note for his daughter, my mom, to find when he passed away to tell her where to dig to find it. Unfortunately for her, she couldn't be bothered to go through his things after his death. Instead of finding the note, she brought in a garbage hauler and threw out everything in the house that she couldn't sell or use. Including the directions to find the box.

"When I turned thirteen, I finally convinced my mom to go back to my grandfather's old house and dig it up. We had to pay the new owner $100 to let us dig in his yard, but we found it."

"What was in it?" asked Mitch.

"About two hundred grand worth of bearer bonds. Also, a bunch of old pictures and letters from my grandmother that she wrote to my grandfather before they were married. My mom was going to toss those in the trash, but I asked her to give them to me. I still have them."

"Wow. And your grandfather?"

"After we found the box, I never saw him again. I guess when we dug it up, we completed whatever business he had keeping him around. It's too bad. I miss him, and can you imagine the kind of damage I could do at a poker table with him helping me? Anyway, even though he's gone, I've been aware of ghosts and spirits ever since. When I got the opportunity to go to work in Dead Town, it seemed like a natural fit. I've been here almost three years, now."

"That's quite a story," said Mitch, "I have to say, you and Dot have happier endings than mine. My reason for being here is a bit of a nightmare."

"Sorry to hear that. Do you feel like talking about it?"

Mitch almost said no, but to his surprise, he realized he did want to talk about it. Sharing with Dot had made him feel immensely better, like a slowly tightening noose around his neck had finally loosened a fraction of an inch. It had let him breathe a tiny bit easier. The people he worked with were not only able to sympathize with his loss, but they, better than anyone else Mitch might find elsewhere, understood the aftermath as well.

"I think I do. Do you mind hearing it?"

Tink shifted his weight to his right, bumping his shoulder into Mitch's side companionably and knocking him off balance.

"Spill," he said. "I'm ready to listen to anything you need to say."

For the second time that day, Mitch told the tale he thought he would never share with another human being. He did not go into as much detail as he had with Dot, but he also did not shy away from the more painful moments of his time with Denny. With Tink, however, Mitch did mention his subsequent bouts of drinking and the disciplinary actions the department took afterward. He figured this man was his partner and deserved to know who he was working with night after night.

Tink did not react to the revelation. He took it in stride, offering no judgement or opinion on the matter. In fact, when Mitch finished talking, Tink suddenly grew excited as something new occurred to him.

"You said your son wanted a teddy bear?" he asked.

Mitch nodded.

"That reminds me of Teddy Boy."

"Who's Teddy Boy?" asked Mitch.

"I should have introduced you to him a long time ago. He's one of the ghosts here in the cemetery, but he's really shy. Nobody ever sees him."

"How do you know he's there if you never see him."

"Oh, he's there. I don't know how to explain it. It's better if I just show you. Come on." Tink waved a hand for Mitch to follow him. "We're not that far away. He's only a couple minutes of walking from the front parking lot."

Mitch fell into step behind Tink, and the two officers returned to the paved walkway. They followed the path to the east. When Tink stepped back onto the expanse of green, manicured lawn again, Mitch began to drag his feet. He was in a very familiar section of the cemetery, and he didn't like the direction they were heading.

"Tink, wait. Why do you call him Teddy Boy? Is there a teddy bear on his grave?"

"Yeah. How did you know? Oh, I guess you've seen it a couple times when you were patrolling."

"That's Dennis' grave," said Mitch, his tone flat and heavy.

"I think that's right. I think Dennis was the name on the stone. Dennis…"

Tink stopped. He turned toward Mitch and his face went pale. "Dennis Loman," he said. "Denny. Oh fuck, Mitch. I should have figured that out sooner. I'm so sorry, man."

"He's my son," Mitch confirmed. "You're taking me to Denny's grave. You don't have to show me the teddy bear. I know what it looks like. I'm the one that brings a new one to him every Christmas."

Tink's shoulders slumped. His eyes shifted left to right as though searching for an escape route. He looked like he would desperately like to be anywhere but standing in front of Mitch at that moment. He found his nerve, however, and met Mitch's gaze.

"We don't call him Teddy Boy just because there's a bear sitting on his grave," Tink said carefully. "It's more than that."

"What?" asked Mitch. "What else?"

"C'mon. I'll show you. More than ever, I think you need to see this."

Tink led Mitch the rest of the way to Denny's grave. Mitch reluctantly followed. When they arrived, he saw the familiar stuffed brown bear he had seen at this location for the past several years. Nothing had changed. There was nothing remarkable to find here. As he stared at the bear, Mitch realized for the first time that in the month since he had begun working in Dead Town, he had not once walked anywhere near his son's grave. He still visited frequently during his days off, but while working he had avoided the area. Was it his subconscious trying to separate his job from his personal life? Or maybe he simply hadn't wanted to deal with his emotional reaction to seeing Denny while at work. He didn't know for certain where the reluctance had come from.

He did know that the look Tink was giving him right now made him uncomfortable.

Tink looked at Mitch apologetically, then bent down to pick up the teddy bear. He held it awkwardly in his hands and took a noticeable breath as though stealing himself for something difficult.

"I don't think there's any way to do this except show you. I'm sorry," he said. Then Tink turned and hurled the teddy bear across the cemetery lawn as far as he could send it.

"Hey!" shouted Mitch, shocked and angered by the act of desecration. He had not known Tink very long, but the man already felt like a friend. Mitch could not understand why he would do such a terrible thing to a gift for a dead child. "What the fuck, Tink?"

"Easy. Trust me. This is the best way to show you what I was talking about."

Tink put a tentative hand on Mitch's shoulder. When Mitch did not immediately shrug off the touch, Tink slipped his arm around his back and guided him a few steps away from Denny's grave. He turned Mitch so they faced away from the boy's headstone.

"Wait a few seconds and don't look back."

"What are you doing, Tink?"

Tink shook his head solemnly but said nothing. After another moment, he turned around, indicating that Mitch should do the same. "Look at the grave," Tink said.

Mitch looked, and what he saw made his heart grow cold in his chest. The teddy bear Tink had tossed away was sitting in its previous location at the top of the gravesite, leaning against the headstone. The bear rested on the ground in the same place he had set it down two months ago on Christmas morning.

"What…? I don't…"

"There's more," said Tink. He went back and picked up the bear again. This time he did not throw it but instead tucked it under his arm and began to walk deeper into the cemetery grounds. "Come on, Mitch. Follow me."

Mitch trailed numbly after the other officer. When they had covered about fifty yards and Denny's marker was lost in the shadows behind them, Tink set the teddy bear on top of a nearby grave marker, then turned his back to it.

"Now you," Tink said. "Turn around so you're not looking at the bear or Denny's grave and count to ten.

Mitch did as Tink instructed. He counted quietly under his breath. When he reached the number ten, Tink said, "Okay. Turn around."

Mitch turned and found the bear gone from the headstone. "Is it…?" he asked, not able to finish the question.

Tink nodded. "Yeah. Let's go look."

The two men returned to Denny's grave and found the bear sitting its lonely vigil at the boy's headstone as if it had never been moved.

"It's always like that," Tink explained. "If someone takes it or moves it, as soon as they're not looking, it disappears and returns here. Nobody has ever seen who moves it. The spirit doesn't want to be seen. Not even Dot has been able to catch the bear moving, and she's the strongest sensitive I know, except for maybe Violet. We also used to wonder how a brand-new bear showed up every year, but after talking to you that's at least one mystery cleared up."

"It's a trick. This is some sort of prank. Brad!" Mitch shouted into the night. "Where are you. Stop this right now or I swear to God, I will beat you unconscious when I get my hands on you."

Tink placed a calming hand on Mitch's shoulder and spoke softly. "It's not a trick. Or, if it is, we aren't the ones doing it and it has the whole department fooled. Mitch, I think it's Denny protecting his teddy bear."

Mitch bent down and picked up the bear. "He always moves it back?" he asked.

"Always," agreed Tink.

Mitch began to walk. Tink fell into step right behind him, matching his speed and following silently. When they were again about fifty yards away, Mitch set the bear down on a random grave marker. The two men turned and stared off into the gloom of the dark cemetery. Mitch began to count.

"…Eight. Nine. Ten."

They turned, and Mitch saw the teddy bear still on the gravestone next to him. He looked at Tink quizzically. The other man shook his head, equally puzzled.

"I don't know," he said. "I guess Denny trusts you to put it back. You're his dad, after all."

Mitch didn't know the exact moment that he broke. The next memory he had was of Tink's arms around him, and the rough material of a uniform shirt against his cheek while he cried.

CHAPTER 10

The following Monday, during his days off, Mitch returned to Cassie's Café, where Violet had found him the week before. He chose the same time and again found the business sparsely occupied during the post lunchtime lull. Discovering his same booth empty, he asked the hostess at the register if he could seat himself. She agreed with a vague wave of her hand, showing as little interest in his request as possible without coming across as openly rude.

Mitch ignored the minor slight and moved past the disinterested woman. He slid into his selected booth and removed a menu from the metal holder at the end of the table. Scanning the laminated, tri-folded list from front to back, Mitch took his time. He already knew what he was going to order, but he also felt no particular urgency to place his meal request. He was in no hurry today. If anything, he was searching for ways to delay his eventual departure from the diner. He had nowhere else to be and nothing that needed his immediate attention. Having skipped breakfast, it was true that Mitch's stomach was now grumbling at the neglect, but a few more minutes of perusing the menu would not be an undue hardship.

It was rare that Mitch came to this restaurant two weeks in a row. The food at the diner was decent, but nothing stellar, and it was only one of a dozen places he could choose to eat near where he lived. It wasn't even the closest of his choices. In addition, he wasn't considered a regular. The staff didn't know him, and they weren't always the most engaged with their customers, the hostess at the front today being a perfect example of that tendency.

Still, here he was. Again. If he was being honest with himself, there was only one real reason he had come back.

Violet.

This was where she had found him last week, and there was a small part of Mitch that hoped she might come looking for him again. Although she didn't have any more of his hair to use to hunt him down, he figured she might think to look here. Even as the thought crossed his mind, Mitch knew it was a foolish hope. There was no further reason for her to talk to him. She had said all she needed to say last time before he … well, might as well face the reality head on … before he stuck his foot in his mouth, and she had skipped out of the restaurant laughing at him.

Twenty minutes passed. Mitch sent the waitress away twice with the lame excuse that he was still looking at the menu and deciding what he wanted. He had so far only ordered a soda, which had already arrived and been half consumed during that time. An older woman in a pink dress and white apron wandered over to his table for the third time.

"Ready to order, yet, or do you need a little more time. No hurry, dear." The sharp tone in her voice belied her words, as did the impatient twist to her mouth. She was probably beginning to wonder if he was going to sit in that booth all day, wasting her time asking for refills on his drink.

Mitch sighed and set the menu back in the rack. "No, I'm ready. Let's do the cheeseburger with a side of fries."

The woman scratched down his order on her pad and wandered away without another word. Mitch sipped from his soda, then pulled his phone out of his pocket. He brought the screen to life with the tap of a finger and began perusing his social media accounts to keep himself occupied while he waited for his food. With few other customers in the diner vying for the cook's attention, he didn't have long to wait.

His server returned with a heaping plate in one hand and a pitcher in the other. She set the burger in front of him, then reached over with the pitcher to top off his soda.

"Enjoy," she said. "If you need anything, feel free to wave me down and let me know. The name's Janice."

"Thank you."

Mitch grabbed a few napkins from the dispenser and reached for the ketchup bottle tucked away in the same rack with the menus. He felt a slight rush of air on the back of his neck, then heard a thump as his booth shook with the sudden arrival of another occupant.

"Hey, Mitch! Looks like I'm right on time."

He looked up to find Violet sitting in the booth across from him. She had her hair down this time, letting it fall until it barely brushed her shoulders. She also wore makeup today, though it was subtly applied, unlike the garish red lipstick and black eyeliner she sported when he first met her. A light shade of pink accented her lips, and she had done something to darken her eyebrows slightly, making them more visible. She wore a blue t-shirt under a red plaid, flannel shirt, giving her a casual, I-just-popped-out-of-the-house-for-a-quick-errand, sort of look.

"Hey, Violet. I… Hey!"

Violet snatched Mitch's plate and slid it over to her side of the table.

"Cheeseburger again? Is this all you eat? You know you'll give yourself a heart attack before you're forty if you keep eating like this."

Mitch reached to retrieve his food, but Violet playfully slapped his hand away.

"Mine, now," she said. "Get your own."

"If you keep stealing my food, I could argue that you owe me a favor," he suggested.

"Yes, you could. You wouldn't be wrong, either." Violet gave him an approving raise of her eyebrows, followed by a slow wink. "I guess you aren't as dumb as you look, Officer Loman. I'm glad to know I'm not wasting my time."

Violet brought a french fry to her mouth and bit it in half with an exaggerated click of her teeth.

When she noticed the new customer in the booth with Mitch, his server returned to check on him.

"Do you need anything else?" she asked, indicating the empty space in front of Mitch where his burger had once been.

"Yeah. I'd like another cheeseburger and fries, I guess. And…"

He looked at Violet who was helping herself to the ketchup.

"Hot tea, please," she said, her attention focused on the upturned container. The condiment bottle was either empty or incredibly stubborn. Giving up, she looked at the waitress. "And another ketchup. This one's done."

When the server disappeared to put in Mitch's second order, Violet picked up her burger and took a small bite.

"This is delicious," she said. "I definitely owe you one."

She said the last five words slowly and with deliberate emphasis. Mitch understood immediately what she was telling him. Violet had been ordered by her coven leader not give Mitch any information without extracting favors in return. By taking his food, she was allowing herself to be in his debt if only in a limited sense. She was, in her own way, giving him an opening to ask a few questions that would not otherwise deserve any response.

Violet was still technically following Alyssandra's directions, but she was also playing a little bit fast and loose with the rules. Mitch understood the line she was walking. He also wondered if this second meeting was Alyssandra's idea, or Violet's.

Regardless of the reasons, Mitch took the opportunity Violet was offering.

"Last week, you told me that there are people taking notice of me. What did you mean by that?"

Violet set the burger down and wiped her hands together, brushing crumbs onto her plate. "Is that really the question you want answered? Not very inspired."

"What is it about me that's worth noticing? Why am I drawing attention?"

"Better," she said. "Okay, let's start there. You interact with spirits. That's why you're drawing attention to yourself. People want to use that gift to their advantage. Or, if they can't use you directly, they want to make sure you can't use your ability to interfere with their plans."

"What plans?"

"Nope." Violet wagged a finger at him. "That's another question. You only get the one."

"This doesn't make any sense. Lots of people interact with ghosts. Why is that a big deal?"

"Lots of people *see* ghosts. That's different. Very few have the ability to speak with them and physically touch them. That is extremely rare."

Violet paused for a moment, frowning, then shrugged. "Oh, well. I'm going to count that as an extension of your first question. But that's all you get for today. I have a question for you, though."

"Sure. Go ahead."

Violet laid her right hand on the table and tapped her forefinger on the glossy plastic several times.

"Do you see this?" she asked.

"See what?"

She tapped her finger again.

"Right there. Stay focused and keep looking. Tell me if you see it."

She tapped her finger a third time.

"See what? I don't know what you're asking me to…"

Mitch stopped talking. He did see something. Where Violet tapped her finger, a circle of soft blue light appeared, slowly expanding across the surface of the table. She tapped once more, and the light grew incrementally brighter.

"You see it, don't you? What color is it?"

"Blue," said Mitch. "What am I looking at?"

Violet removed her hand from the table and the light immediately began to fade. A few seconds later, it completely disappeared from Mitch's sight. He reached out a tentative hand and touched the spot where he had seen the blue glow, tapping it as he had seen Violet do. The light did not return.

"What was that? Where did it go?"

"You just gave me some very important information, so in return, I will share something with you," Violet told him. "I don't want you claiming I'm still in your debt. What you saw was a tiny display of magic. I released a bare trace of power into the table to see if you could see me do it. You did. This means that you're not only sensitive to spirits, but you can also see magic."

"What does that mean? Are people that see magic rare?"

"Some people can manipulate magic by learning spells and using enhanced objects, but there aren't many practitioners who can see magic as a visual emanation. The fact you saw a blue light tells me you are one of these people. Coupled with your talent for working with spirits makes you quite the unicorn, Officer Loman."

"Mitch," said Mitch.

"Sure. Mitch. As all debts are paid, I think our business is concluded for today."

She took another bite from her burger.

"You're going to stay and eat with me? You're not leaving?"

"I answered your question, and I shared my observations about you. That makes us even. I earned this burger, so I plan on sitting here and enjoying my lunch. Why? Do you want me to leave? Were you hoping to stare at my ass again when I walked out?"

"I-I didn't..."

"Oh, please. Of course, you did. You were staring so hard I could feel the warmth on my butt from twenty feet away. I'm surprised I don't have a sunburn down there."

Mitch stammered out another denial. Violet only laughed at his discomfort.

"You know, you're kind of cute when you're embarrassed," she told him, easing the sting of her teasing.

The waitress arrived at that moment with Mitch's second burger, saving him from any further pointless attempts at saving his dignity.

The rest of their lunch together was pleasant, if not terribly informative. They chatted about various topics including where they had been born, their families, and what schools they attended. Every time the talk drifted toward Dead Town, Alyssandra, or the coven, however, Violet would shake her head in warning and change the subject. She had meant it when she said their business was concluded for the day.

When the check arrived, Violet stood up, revealing she was wearing the same faded jeans she had worn the week before, or perhaps an identical pair to the first. She thanked Mitch for the meal and headed for the door. Before exiting, she glanced over her shoulder and found Mitch still watching her.

With her left hand she hiked up the tail of her flannel shirt, while with her right index finger, she pointed at her butt. Mitch grinned and nodded enthusiastically, giving Violet a double thumbs up in appreciation. The door closed behind her, and she was gone.

On the drive home Mitch replayed their conversation repeatedly in his head. He could interact with spirits, and he could see magic. That's what Violet told him, but what did it mean? And why was it drawing attention from others when he didn't even know if he could do anything with the abilities? The information Violet gave him was less helpful than he had hoped. Rather than providing real answers, it created a hundred new questions; questions he would not get to ask unless he could reach some sort of agreement with Alyssandra and the coven. He hoped his chief was in the mood to negotiate with Alyssandra, because he would really like to know what the hell was happening to him.

Mitch turned into his driveway and all thoughts of Violet and magic evaporated. A young-looking girl sat on the concrete step of his front porch, her head bowed and her white-blond hair covering her face. At the sound of Mitch's car pulling in, the girl looked up.

It was Dot.

At first, Mitch was merely puzzled as to why she would turn up at his house, but as he got closer, he noticed the splotchy red marks on her cheeks and the wet shine of her eyes. She was crying.

Heart racing and pounding painfully in his chest, Mitch threw the car in park, turned the engine off and bolted out of the vehicle to check on her.

"Dot! What's wrong?"

She stood as he approached, wiping ineffectually at her face with a sodden tissue in her hand.

"I'm so sorry, Mitchell. I completely misunderstood the situation. I didn't realize your son was the teddy bear boy."

Dot stepped into Mitch and wrapped her arms around his waist in a fierce hug, which only frightened him more.

"What do you mean, you misunderstood?"

"Tink called me about an hour ago and explained what happened last week. He told me what you talked about. He said the boy with the teddy bear is your son, that the child buried there is Denny."

"He is." Mitch felt ice forming around his heart as he saw the look of pure distress in Dot's face. "The boy with the teddy bear, that's my son."

Dot stepped away, sniffed and coughed. She wiped at her nose with the useless tissue.

"When we talked, I thought what you told me was everything. I didn't know there was anything more than the visit at your house once a year."

"I didn't either," agreed Mitch. "I didn't know about the bear until Tink told me. What does it mean? Why are you so upset?"

"He isn't an echo, Mitchell. Denny guards that bear all year long. If it ever goes missing, he always finds it and brings it back. That shows intelligence guiding his actions. It isn't the work of an echo or a poltergeist."

"My son is…" Mitch couldn't finish the thought.

"He's trapped here. His soul is bound to his body, not your house. It stays with his gravesite most of the year. He isn't only appearing once a year, he's always here. He's visiting the house on Christmas Eve for a reason. He's looking for something, something he needs to find or fix in order to move on. I'm so sorry, Mitch. I should have figured this out sooner, asked more questions, or … something."

"You couldn't have figured it out any sooner. None of us had all the pieces before now. Don't blame yourself. But, if he really is trapped here, that means when he dies every year, he feels…" Mitch trailed off, unable to say the words.

Dot hugged him once more. This time, Mitch wrapped his arms around the diminutive woman and held her as well. She sniffled then began to cry once more.

"That poor little boy. Mitchell, I promise I'm going to try to figure out how to free him. When you come in for work on

Wednesday, I'll stay after my shift and we'll go to his grave, together. I'll try to have a talk with him and find out what he's waiting for. Okay? I'll fix this. I won't quit until we help him."

CHAPTER 11

The next two days crawled by interminably slow for Mitch. He ate little and was unable to sleep more than a few restless hours. His mind refused to be quiet as he waited for Wednesday to arrive, taking all his attention away from the normal processes of going through day-to-day life. He could think of nothing but his son now that he knew the boy's spirit was trapped. Even when he tried to focus on Violet and the brief flash of magic she had shown him at the restaurant, that minor miracle could only keep him distracted for a brief time.

At last, the start of his first shift of the week arrived, and true to her word, Dot met him in the briefing room when he walked in a few minutes before seven o'clock. When they heard what the chief's secretary was planning, the entire B-Nights shift offered to join Mitch and Dot at Denny's grave. They all wanted to help in any way they could to put the boy at last to rest.

At first, with the entire shift volunteering to participate, Dot was hesitant.

"Was Denny a shy child, or did he enjoy being around people," she asked Mitch.

"He loved people," Mitch responded. He absolutely adored being the center of attention, and the more spectators around the little ham, the better. He's been like that since he learned to talk."

Dot pressed her lips together into a tight line as she considered Mitch's answer. "Okay. I don't want a crowd of people scaring him away from us, but if you're sure Denny wouldn't mind, we can all go."

The proclamation was met with triumphant smiles from the patrol team, and Jorge announced briefing was cancelled to allow them to begin the séance immediately.

A few minutes later, when they had all gathered at Denny's burial plot, Dot directed them to sit in a circle. Tink and Dot claimed one side of the gravesite, while Jorge and Brad sat on the other. She directed Mitch to sit at the foot of the grave so that Denny's headstone closed the circle.

It was already dark in the cemetery as the sun had set almost an hour earlier. A sliver of moon hung in the sky, and the path lights several yards in the distance provided only partial relief from the evening gloom. No one seemed to mind, least of all Mitch. His eyes had already mostly adapted to the surrounding dark.

Mitch half expected candles, drawn symbols in the dirt, and odd chanting to be included in the ritual. His only experience with seances or drawing out the supernatural came from movies and books, and he was unsure how much depicted in popular culture was based in reality and how much was pure fiction. To his surprise, and partial disappointment, there were no candles or props of any kind used. Dot did not even have them join hands. Instead, she simply began talking to Denny as if addressing a child in a room full of adults.

"Hi, Denny. We're all here because we're worried about you. Your daddy especially. He's right over there. Do you see him?"

She paused but there was no response.

"Mitchell, say something to him."

"What do I say?"

"It doesn't matter. Talk to him about anything," Dot responded.

"Hey, buddy. Can you hear me? If you can, I'd love to see you. Can you come out and talk to us? I have some friends here. I think you'd like them. Daddy works with them, and they are really nice people. They want to meet you."

"Hi, Denny," said Tink. Jorge and Brad also chimed in.

"See? We'd all like to see you. If you're here, please come out and talk to me."

Another pause as they waited to see if Mitch's pleas had generated a response. They were rewarded with more silence.

"Denny," said Dot. "We want to help you if we can. I know you're stuck here, and I'd like to figure out why. I can't do that if you won't talk to me."

They listened again but Denny seemed unwilling to respond to Dot's and his father's entreaties. The wind picked up at that moment and the gust of air moaned and whistled through the empty branches of nearby trees. There was nothing supernatural about the sound however, as Denny continued to ignore the group of people around his grave.

Dot reached out and gathered up the teddy bear resting against Denny's headstone. She hugged it lovingly to her chest.

"This is a really nice bear. We all know how much you like it and how well you take care of it. Do you want to tell me why it's so important to you?"

"Come on, buddy. I really need you to come out. Talk to me, please," Mitch begged. "I want to know why you haven't moved on from here. Why are you staying? What's keeping you here? Is it me? Did I … do something wrong?"

Dot placed the teddy bear back on the ground, but instead of sitting it upright as it had been before, she left it lying face down in the dirt. "I think I'll leave it like this," she said. "I like it better on its face."

With a quick wave of her hands, she indicated the others should remain quiet. They all sat motionless, waiting silently for any reaction to her announcement. Mitch did not see or hear anything. After several long seconds had passed, he felt his legs beginning to cramp and he shifted to relieve the pressure. He stretched out one booted foot and rotated his ankle to work out the kink, then froze.

The bear moved.

It shifted slowly at first, almost imperceptibly. It rocked to one side, then the middle of the bear's stuffed body flattened as though under the weight of a hand. The bear sat suddenly upright, sliding back to its former resting place against the tombstone.

No one moved.

"Mitchell," Dot whispered. "Did you see Denny?"

"No," he responded, equally softly. "I only saw the bear move."

"He's trying very hard not to be seen. I don't understand why he won't show himself. He's obviously here and he can hear us."

Dot removed the bear and placed it on its face once again. This time several minutes passed before there was any reaction, but the bear eventually righted itself and moved to its previous location. Denny still did not make a full appearance.

"Why won't he come out?" Dot asked, talking to herself more than to any of the others gathered nearby.

"Is he afraid of you, Mitch?" asked Brad. When Mitch glared back at the accusation, Brad waved his hands in a calming gesture. "No, I know he's not afraid of his dad. What I mean is, on the night he died, did he do something wrong? Something that made you mad at him, or that he was embarrassed about?"

"He didn't do anything wrong," Mitch said, defensively. "He's a great kid. He could never do anything to make me angry. The only thing he did that night was be a normal, regular little boy. He was so excited about Christmas, he kept crawling out of bed to check for Santa. He got out of bed and came downstairs so many times, his mom and I both warned him he needed to go to sleep. We told him if he wasn't asleep when Santa showed up, he would fly right past our house. Of course, that still didn't stop him, but that's just what kids do."

"I know you believe he shouldn't be upset," Brad continued, "but would Denny be embarrassed by his behavior? Is he afraid to face you because he didn't do what he was told?"

Mitch didn't answer. He didn't know.

"Should I leave?" he asked Dot.

She shook her head. "No. You need to be here. You're the only person that Denny would have any reason to talk to. If you go, we might as well all leave with you."

Mitch decided to try again. "Denny, I'm not mad at you and you aren't in any trouble. I'm worried about you. I want to help; we all want to help. Can't you come out and talk with us? Just for a little bit?"

"Is there something we should know about the bear, sweetheart?" asked Dot. "Are you afraid to leave the bear? Will he be lonely if you go away without him?"

"The bear will be fine," assured Tink. "In fact, that isn't even the same bear. Your dad told us that he buys you a new one every year."

The temperature dropped several degrees, and a new wind picked up. This time there was nothing natural about the chill breeze. It swirled in a small eddy around the five seated people, and Mitch felt his ears pop from the sudden change in pressure.

"Denny," he said. "What are you doing?"

The teddy bear exploded. Stuffing and strips of fuzzy rag flew out in all directions, pelting everyone gathered around the gravesite. Fortunately, the debris was only cloth and cotton, so no one was harmed. Several pieces of the fragmented bear were caught up in the narrow funnel of wind and carried away into the night.

Everyone flinched back from the unexpected violence. Brad had even somersaulted backwards and came to rest on his feet, ready to fight or run as the situation demanded.

"What the holy fuck was that!" shouted Tink.

Only Dot, of the five people around the small grave, appeared more thoughtful than startled.

"I don't think he liked what Tink said," she mused. "Mitchell, did Denny know that you were the one buying him the teddy bears?"

"Of course, he did. I bring him one every…" he paused. Did Denny know? The bears were Christmas gifts, and to a four-year-old boy, Christmas gifts came from Santa. Did he believe the teddy bear came directly from Santa Claus? He might have, at least until ten seconds ago when Tink had revealed the truth.

"Maybe not," he admitted, reluctantly. "It's possible he believed they came from somebody else."

"Santa," said Dot.

"Santa," agreed Mitch.

"I think I'm starting to get a clearer picture of why Denny is here. I'm not certain yet, so I don't want to give you any false hope. I need to do some research and talk to a few friends to see if they have any suggestions."

"Can you tell me anything right now?" asked Mitch. He was beginning to resent all the people keeping secrets from him. Dot was trying to help him, he knew that, but she was holding something back from him as well.

"I don't want to be wrong again. I gave you bad information last time because I jumped to a conclusion. I don't want to do that again. Give me some time. Right now, I can only tell you that I think I can help Denny. I can give him what he needs to move on if I can only figure out a few more little details. In the meantime, do me a favor and get your son a new bear. Put it back on his grave and see how he reacts to it."

"Okay, I'll do that. But, when? When can you help him?"

"I can start reaching out to my friends first thing tomorrow morning. But if I'm right about what I suspect, I can't help Denny until he's ready to show himself."

"And when would that be?"

"I think that part is obvious. The same time he always shows himself. Christmas Eve."

Mitch groaned. Christmas was ten months away. An eternity when your child's soul hung in the balance.

"It can't be sooner?" he asked, though he held little hope of a positive reply.

"Maybe," agreed Dot, "but honestly, I think probably not. I don't want to promise anything I can't deliver."

Mitch nodded. If there was nothing more to be done, he had to accept Dot's answer at face value. She was the expert in these matters, and he needed to trust she knew what she was doing. "Okay. For now, we wait."

A stray thought occurred to Mitch, a question he had meant to ask many times before, but the opportunity had never arisen. "Can I ask you one more question?"

"Of course. Ask me anything."

"Why do you call me Mitchell? Everyone else calls me Mitch."

Dot frowned, considering his question. "Because you look like a Mitchell to me. No, that's not quite right. You *feel* like a Mitchell to me. Do you mind?"

"I suppose not. I have to admit it sounds a little strange to me at times, but I guess it's not a big deal. I haven't been Mitchell since my mother died. She was the only other person that ever called me that."

Dot smiled, although her eyes turned distant and sad as they gazed into his face. "I know," she said, cryptically. "That's probably why you need me to say it."

"Why I need…?" began Mitch, but Dot had already climbed to her feet and begun walking away.

Mitch debated rushing after her, asking what she had meant by that odd reply. Instead, he remained sitting beside Denny's grave, staring at the tattered remains of the teddy bear. Maybe there were some things, he decided, he didn't want an answer to.

CHAPTER 12

Professor Solomon Schick sat in the breakfast nook of his kitchen with his coffee mug cupped between his hands and the morning paper spread out on the circular dining table in front of him. The plated remains of a homemade cheese omelet had been pushed to one side to make more room for the paper. He turned to the crimes and police blotter portion of the Local Pages section and meticulously read through the stack of two and three-line activity reports for the County of Sacramento. It was the same morning routine he had been following for the two months following the burglary of his home.

Three times previously in the past eight weeks, he found disturbing information during his breakfast ritual. A burglar in the Rancho Cordova area was breaking into private homes, stealing money, jewelry, and small electronics that could be easily carried away. Three residences had fallen victim to this thief, and the method of the break-ins was the same each time. The back door leading into the house was broken open using brute force, then a systematic search was conducted of all rooms in the house. When the entire building had been thoroughly ransacked, the burglar exited using the same door through which he or she had entered.

The forced entry and thoroughness of the search inside the home was not unique to the crime, nor were the items typically targeted by the thief, but Solomon knew without doubt these three break-ins were the work of the same criminal. He wished he could convince himself otherwise, but to do so would only be burying his own guilt in these events. He had to face the obvious truth: someone had figured out his secret.

The piece of evidence that linked these three crimes in Solomon's mind and made them unique from so many others occurring every day, was the trail of dirt left behind by the culprit in each house. Significant amounts of soil, rock and debris were cast off, either intentionally or accidentally, leaving a clear path for police to follow, and identifying exactly where the burglar had walked while searching each room throughout the homes. Solomon could not ignore the obvious clue.

The journalists documenting the crimes in the paper had even noticed the odd distinction and had labeled the thief with the nickname, Dirty Bandit.

Police currently had no leads on the suspect, and there were no known witnesses to the crimes.

Solomon was not similarly stumped. He knew exactly who the thief was, or rather, *what* it was. He had remained silent this long only because he knew if he spoke up, he would not be believed. The police would decide he was merely an attention seeker, or perhaps crazy. Or both. There was nothing to be gained by providing law enforcement with information that would only be ignored. Besides, Solomon told himself, nothing had been lost besides property and money. That could all be replaced.

This morning things changed.

Solomon reread the article he discovered, hoping he had made a mistake. Perhaps he had misunderstood the reporter's intention and made assumptions without actual facts. But no, the damning information remained exactly as he recalled. Two nights ago, another home had been invaded by the Dirty Bandit. This time, the house had not been unoccupied; somebody had been in the residence when the burglar entered. The homeowner must have heard the noise of his door being broken open, confronted the thief, and then been killed during his efforts to defend his property. The details of the murder were as bloody and brutal as they were brief. The article stated the victim was bludgeoned with a heavy, blunt object that had broken his skull in multiple places. The homeowner was long dead when a neighbor noticed the open back door the next morning and went to investigate.

Solomon had to admit these were no longer solely property crimes. The thief had moved way beyond simple larceny. A man was dead, and others might follow soon. He could no longer remain silent and pretend his inaction was the correct path. Even if the police laughed at him and rejected his information, he needed to at least try. Common human decency demanded that much.

He scanned to the end of the article and found the paragraph he wanted. Police had no useable leads and were searching for witnesses or anyone who might have information leading to the identification and capture of the murderer. A tip-line had been created at the Sacramento Sheriff's Office and a phone number was provided. The article stated callers could remain anonymous if they so wished.

Solomon exhaled slowly. He did wish to make this call anonymously, but he knew that would be a waste of time. They would absolutely ignore the information if there was no name attached to it. Who could possibly take it seriously in those circumstances? He had to tell them who he was and explain how he had gained the information if he had any hope of being believed.

There would be repercussions. If word of this reached the university, his name would become nothing more than a joke to the rest of the staff. It could even get him fired if he embarrassed the wrong people. That was, of course, if no one believed him. If they did believe, things could get a whole lot worse.

He sighed again, then picked up his phone.

CHAPTER 13

A week passed after the failed attempt to speak with Denny. It was the longest week of Mitch's life, and given his experiences over the past few years, that was quite an accomplishment. As Dot had suggested, he immediately purchased a new bear for his son. He overnighted the order so it would arrive as soon as possible, and by Friday it had arrived on his front porch in a neat cardboard box. Mitch brought the bear to work with him that same day and placed it on Denny's grave.

Within seconds of being placed beside the boy's headstone, the hapless stuffed toy was rendered into its component parts exactly like its predecessor. Denny was still upset, and there was nothing Mitch could do for him. He wasn't even sure why his son was so angry. Was it Tink's admission that the bear had not come from Santa Claus? Was it Dot's attempt to get Denny to talk to them against his wishes?

Or was it something Mitch himself had done?

There were too many questions, and too few answers. Mitch trusted Dot, but after he shared the details of the second bear's demise, even she could not offer him any explanation. All she seemed to know for sure was Denny was stuck in this plane of existence, and it centered around something that occurred the night he died. That meant that there was nothing useful or practical that could be done to help him in the foreseeable future. She again asked him to wait while she continued to study the problem, suggesting the only window of opportunity they might have to help would be when Denny returned next Christmas Eve. After the agonizing slowness of the last week, Mitch did not think his sanity would survive another ten days, much less ten months.

Sitting in the briefing room on the following Wednesday, Mitch, Tink, and Brad sat around the table as Jorge perused the evening activity log. They waited for his usual announcement that there was nothing going on and they all should go to work, but to everyone's surprise, the sergeant discovered a manilla envelope pinned on the activity log clipboard addressed to their shift. He opened the envelope and removed two sheets of white paper.

"We have a follow-up request from dayshift, gentlemen. Apparently, homicide detectives for the county are investigating a new murder. They have been observing a series of burglaries over the past six weeks by a guy the media has been calling the Dirty Bandit. He leaves mud and debris all through the homes he breaks into. A month ago, during his second burglary, he left behind a fist-sized piece of rock with two numbers etched into it. The detective assigned to the case thought it could be a piece of a tombstone or perhaps a commemorative marker of some kind. It was bagged and placed into evidence, then forgotten.

"Last weekend, the Dirty Bandit killed someone, and the case got bumped up to Homicide. The new dick on the case did a little digging and found a report of vandalisms at our cemetery.

He thought it might be worth a check to see if the piece of rock matches any of our damaged gravesites."

"How come they didn't follow up a month ago when they first found the rock?" asked Tink.

"We hadn't found the vandalized graves, yet," Mitch reminded him. "Besides, it was still just a property crime then. The Property Crimes detectives don't have the resources to investigate more than ten percent of their caseload. Each detective in the bureau gets fifteen new crime reports every day and they only have time to follow up on the cases they can close quickly. Reports that don't have any good suspect leads to chase down get filed as unsolved and are left for the insurance companies to take care of."

"That's right," said Jorge. "I had forgotten you worked property crimes before you came here. So, yes, the rock got zero attention until the Dirty Bandit suddenly became a murderer. Now they want to chase the leads that they didn't have time for earlier."

Tink nodded. "Okay. That explains the time delay, but why didn't dayshift do the follow-up when they got the request?"

"Mitch wrote the vandalism report. I guess they figured it was his case."

"Or Dot figured I could use something to do, even if it only killed an hour or two," muttered Mitch.

"Maybe that, too," admitted Jorge. He separated the two pages in his hands and slid one of them across the table to Mitch.

The paper was a blown-up copy of an evidence photograph. Despite the enlargement, the photo was remarkably clear and detailed, showing a roughly triangular piece of stone with the numbers "08" etched into it. The stone was worn and mottled with lichen and mold stains, suggesting a great deal of aging, but the numbers remained easily legible. An "L"-shaped ruler lay beside the broken rock to demonstrate to anyone viewing the photograph the perspective and size of the object depicted.

"I'll go take a look and let you know what I find," Mitch told the sergeant.

"Okay," Jorge announced, placing the second page back in the manilla envelope and setting the document aside. "That's everything for now. Go to work and try not to get eaten."

Mitch left the briefing room and exited the building, heading off in a brisk walk directly for the northwest section of the cemetery grounds. It was the oldest part of Dead Town, and it was where Alyssandra had initially pointed out the vandalism to the graves. It was a fair hike, but Mitch's nightly treks throughout the property during foot patrols were getting easier as his body adapted to the exercise, and he arrived at the fenced perimeter several minutes later only slightly out of breath. He let himself into the gated area with his department-issued key and turned on his flashlight to more closely examine the damaged burial sites.

When he wrote his report, there were only three disturbed graves. Tonight, as he played his light over the area, he found a fourth grave had been tampered with, the topsoil disturbed, and the dirt removed. The fourth site was beside the other three earlier ravaged locations creating a row of four desecrated graves, one next to the another. This did not come as a complete surprise to Mitch. The detective requesting this follow-up had noted the Dirty Bandit had committed his murder this past weekend during a fourth burglary, and the fourth damaged grave only confirmed Mitch's suspicions that the murderer and the Dead Town vandalisms were somehow connected.

The piece of stone was found after the second burglary, so Mitch started his search by checking the second of the four gravesites. The marker on the selected site was a granite plinth about two feet tall, supporting a rough-cut circular column peaked with a Celtic-style cross. The entire piece appeared to be cut from a single stone.

As he expected, the marker at the head of the plot was cracked and fragmented. Pieces had fallen away from the main carving, and the entire structure appeared fragile enough that a good earthquake would send it tumbling to the ground for good. In the square base, a simple inscription had been etched into the face. It read:

MARIA PLUMA DE NOCHE
1775 – 18

After the eighteen, a jagged triangular hole marred the rockface, leaving the specific year of death uncertain. Mitch was certain that date was going to be 1808. He removed the picture from his pocket, unfolded the paper and held it beside the grave marker. The shape of the broken rock matched the hole in the headstone, and the numbers "08" aligned perfectly with the missing portion of the date.

"Thank you, Maria. You just provided us with a lead in a murder investigation."

Mitch locked the gate on his way back out and returned to the police department to let the sergeant know of his findings. He checked the briefing room and Jorge's desk, but the sergeant was in neither location. That was not unusual. Next, he went upstairs to the second floor to see if Jorge was hanging out in the break room. With a television set and easy access to snacks, this was generally where Mitch's boss could be found when he wasn't in either of the first two locations.

On the second floor, he passed by Dot's desk in the reception area intending to go directly to the hallway leading to the break room. Instead, he paused when he heard a voice from somewhere close by talking in a low tone. Glancing around, he noticed that the door to the assistant chief's office was open a crack, and light was emanating from somewhere inside.

Not wanting to eavesdrop or overhear something he wasn't intended to hear, Mitch tromped heavily across the room to the open door and announced himself loudly enough to warn anyone inside that he was coming.

"Hey, I heard voices and thought I'd come see who…"

He trailed off as he saw the hunched figure in the office. It wasn't Jorge. It was the assistant chief himself, Tim Delaney. The man was seated at his desk looking through a spread of papers fanned out over the entire usable surface of this workspace. He was talking to himself, muttering as he traced a forefinger along a paragraph of writing on one of the papers. The assistant chief wore his Sheriff's Department uniform tonight rather than a suit. The uniform was an old-style, green wool, class-A outfit, complete with the archaic gold and green patches adorning his sleeves. The department had moved on to black uniforms and patches over twenty years ago. Apparently, Chief Delaney was either nostalgic for the good old days, or else extremely cheap.

"Um, sorry to bother you, Chief," Mitch apologized. "I didn't realize you were here so late tonight."

The assistant chief glanced up, distracted. He took a moment to focus on Mitch standing in his doorway. "What do you want?" he snapped.

"Nothing, sir. I saw the light on and came in to investigate." Mitch pointed at the chief's attire. "I love the old uniform. I've only seen those patches in pictures before. I didn't know we could still wear green."

Chief Delaney peered down at his shirt, then back at Mitch. His lips tightened and his eyebrows pulled closer together. "Of course, we can wear green. Son, I wore these patches when I was sworn in on my first day on the job, and you can bet your last dollar if you ever see me lying in a pine box, these will be the patches I'll be wearing on that day, too. You hear me?"

"Yes, sir. I'm sorry. I wasn't…"

"Now, did you need something important? Or did you come in here to make fun of my fashion sense?"

"No, sir. I'll…" Mitch paused as a new thought occurred to him. "Chief, I was coming back from doing a follow-up on the new murder investigation in the county."

The chief perked up at the news, the cross expression on his face smoothing noticeably.

"You're investigating a murder?" he asked.

"Yes, sir. Well, no. You see, I think the vandalisms that have been occurring in the old part of Dead Town are connected to the Dirty Bandit."

"Dirty Bandit?" The chief's interest began to wane as suddenly as it had occurred.

"I would like permission to investigate the vandalisms on our end. Who knows? If I get lucky, I might be able to solve a murder. If not, no harm done, right?"

Chief Delaney turned back to the papers on his desk. He waved a dismissive hand toward Mitch. “Go ahead. Investigate the vandalism.”

“Thank you, sir. Will you tell Chief Jefferson what I’m doing the next time you see him?”

The assistant chief nodded. “I’ll tell him.”

Mitch started to back out of the office.

“Wait!” Chief Delaney barked, his attention once more on Mitch. “You are doing this on your own time. I’m not paying overtime, and you still need to work your regularly assigned shift. Understand?”

“Yes, sir.”

The assistant chief flapped his hand at Mitch again, indicating a final dismissal. Mitch left without another word, walking quickly through the entrance lobby and heading for the stairs before Delaney could change his mind.

The following morning, after his shift had ended, Mitch wandered into the officers’ report writing room on the first floor and dropped himself into a chair behind one of the desks. He had already completed his supplemental vandalism report on the fourth grave during his regular shift, so while he had time to kill at the moment, he had nothing to do with it. Bored, yet still excited to have a case to investigate after all this time, he watched the second hand of the clock ticking out a patient circle on its face, minute after minute. He had learned long ago that police work was more about patience than it was car chases and gun battles. Paperwork, research, and timing were the true keys to catching criminals. Knowing how important it was, however, didn't mean he necessarily enjoyed having nothing to do.

Tapping his fingers impatiently on the desk, he waited for eight thirty to roll around so he could call the Sheriff's Department Homicide detectives office. Most of the deputies in that unit got to work around seven, but he wanted to give everyone time to chat, drink coffee, and get settled into their desks before he called. The detectives were more likely to answer their phones if they weren't still up and wandering around through their early morning routines.

He gave up his lonely vigil a few minutes early, deciding the last of the stragglers had probably found their desks by now. He dialed the direct line into the homicide office and listened to the recorded greeting. The calm, professional voice on the phone invited him to dial his party directly if he knew their extension, otherwise please wait until someone was free and available to answer his call. The message repeated three times before a living person picked up the phone.

"Homicide. This is Detective Garza."

Mitch had been hoping the person answering would be a detective he knew, but he did not recognize the name Garza.

"Hi, detective. My name is Mitchell Loman. I'm an officer over at Dasan's Terrace PD. I got a request last night for a follow-up on one of your recent cases. I'm trying to reach Detective Ali Minhas. Is he at his desk?"

"Just a second, Officer … Loman, you said? Just a second and I'll see if he's in."

Mitch waited on hold, listening to a recorded piece of classical music he did not even try to identify. Even as a kid, he had never been much into music, especially anything older than the 1990's. After about two minutes, the line clicked and Officer Garza's voice returned.

"Ali asked me to put you through to his desk phone. Hold on and I'll route you through. Just in case I mess this up and lose you, his extension is 4482."

"Thanks…" but he was already listening to the hold music again.

The music paused and he listened to a series of clicks before a new voice answered.

"Hello. This is Ali. Can I help you?"

"Hey, Ali. This is Mitch Loman. I don't know if you remember me, but we met a couple times while I was assigned to a desk over in Property Crimes."

"Yeah. I do remember you. Hi, Mitch. I thought I recognized the name on that vandalism report. When did you leave the Sheriff's Office?"

"Actually, I didn't. Dasan's Terrace is still part of the Sheriff's Office. It's one of their contracts. I transferred over a little while ago."

"It is? No shit? I've never heard of it before."

"You and a lot of people," Mitch muttered. "Listen, I was able to do that check for you last night in the cemetery. That rock from your earlier burglary is definitely from one of our markers."

"Weird. I wonder what our guy was doing in the cemetery."

"I don't know, but it looks like it's part of a routine. We have four graves vandalized in the same area and from what I've heard, your Dirty Bandit has hit four houses. I don't think that's a coincidence."

"No. It doesn't sound like it. Can you do me a favor and take some photographs of the graves and send them to me?"

"Sure," Mitch agreed. "And maybe you can help me out as well. I've got the green light from my chief to investigate this at our end. Can you send me copies of all your notes and evidence on the crimes so far? I can pull up the basic reports on my end, but they don't tell me much except what the patrol officers documented when they first came out. Maybe there's something in your case notes that will help me know what I'm looking for. Of course, in return I'll share anything I find out in the cemetery with you."

"I don't see a problem with that. Do you still have department email?"

Mitch sighed, but then quickly tamped down his impatience. "I still work for Sac County, so yes, I do. Email would be fine."

"Right. Sorry. Sorry. We have a cemetery department? How come I never knew that?"

The question was rhetorical, so Mitch did not bother to answer.

"I'll make copies of my notes and get them out to you today."

"Great. Thanks," said Mitch. "I'll take photographs tonight when I get back in for my next shift and send those to you."

Mitch exchanged cell phone numbers with Ali before hanging up in case they needed to talk again. Finding a detective at his desk was always an iffy event and it would help to have a way to contact each other directly should any new information turn up.

Yawning and stretching the kinks out of his back, Mitch headed downstairs to the locker room to change into his street clothes. It felt good to have a case to investigate again. He hadn't realized until his conversation with Ali truly how much he missed being in the detective bureau, and this homicide was a perfect opportunity to keep himself busy during the long empty hours of his shift. It would also help him keep his mind off Denny, at least a little bit. He looked forward to reading through Ali's case notes.

But that could all wait until tonight. He was exhausted, and the only thing he wanted currently was to head home, crawl into bed, and get some much-needed sleep.

CHAPTER 14

Mitch slept through the day and returned that night refreshed and ready to get to work. As soon as briefing concluded, he walked out to the northwest section of the cemetery and took photographs of the damaged gravesites for Ali. Since the sun was already down for the evening, instead of using his phone to take the pictures, he borrowed a digital camera from the department equipment room that had a decent flash attachment. The images came out clear, but they were still a bit dark due to the surrounding gloom. Mitch decided he would send them anyway, and Ali could always request additional photos to be taken in the daylight hours if these did not meet his needs.

After the photos were done, Mitch returned to the police department, downloaded the relevant files to a thumb drive, and checked the camera back into the proper equipment room storage cabinet. Next, he plugged the thumb drive into one of the officers' work computers and emailed Detective Minhas the photographs. While logged into his email, Mitch saw he had received a message from Ali with several files attached. He downloaded each of the files and saved them to a folder on the same thumb drive he had used to download his pictures earlier.

Tonight was Thursday, so it was movie night. Jorge brought in a selection from his classic horror movies of the 1970's and 1980's and announced the titles to the team during briefing. The films he picked for this evening were Season of the Witch, The House that Dripped Blood, and The Howling. Mitch hated to miss movie night, especially when the sergeant brought in videos with supernatural themes. When the shift watched horror movies, they frequently discussed the events portrayed as if they were training films. Mitch had learned a great deal over the past weeks listening to Tink and Brad talk about which creature traits seemed accurate and which were complete nonsense made up by writers and directors looking for a cheap scare. Assuming of course, that those two had any idea what they were talking about, and they weren't intentionally trying to confuse Mitch more than he already was.

Regardless of his reluctance to miss, Mitch had gotten Jorge's permission to skip the movies tonight and focus on the homicide files he had received from Detective Minhas. Mitch knew he could go through Ali's files tomorrow night and hang out with the shift tonight like a normal Thursday, but it had been so long since he felt like a useful contributing member of the police force, he was eager to dig into this homicide case.

The first four files in the email were the initial reports written by the responding officers to each of the related burglaries. Ali knew Mitch had access to these files already through the department report writing system but had included them anyway for convenience. Mitch appreciated the detective's thoroughness, but he had already reviewed these reports the night before, printed out hard copies, and placed them into a folder he had created to organize and store all collected case documents. The incident reports were little more than notes on dates, times, and items of property removed from the homes. As Mitch already knew, no witnesses had been identified and no significant evidence had been left behind. Despite the amount of dirt and debris left in each residence, there were no useable footprints, fingerprints, or suspect-related evidence discovered during the initial forensic sweeps of the homes.

Even in the case of the homicide, the only blood, hair, or DNA collected had been from the victim. The murder weapon was also missing, presumed to have been carried away by the suspect or hidden somewhere around the house in an as yet undiscovered location. Mitch skimmed these reports, checking for anything he may have missed on the first readthrough. He did not find anything new.

The property taken in each theft was unremarkable. Cash and jewelry seemed to be the primary targets. Small items throughout the house that could be easily sold for additional pocket money were also missing. These were not rare or special items. There also did not seem to be anything about the homes or property that made them stand out as targets of the burglar. The residents all lived within the Rancho Cordova area, but they did not know each other or have any obvious connections to one another. Based on everything Mitch could see, the victims seemed totally random.

The only information that seemed noteworthy were the dates of the crimes. They each occurred on a Friday night, two weeks apart. The homicide had occurred exactly six weeks after the first known burglary attributed to the Dirty Bandit. The reasoning for this consistency was unclear. It could be an unplanned coincidence, the crimes could be tied to some other cyclical event, or it could be their suspect was intentionally baiting the police by being predictable. It could be anything.

Hell, the murderer might be a patient in a psych ward and only got a hall pass every other Friday. Without more information, it was impossible to tell why the pattern existed or if it would continue. If it did follow its previous sequence, the Dirty Bandit would not strike again until next week. Of course, the fact that the burglar was now a murderer and had drawn more attention to him or herself, might cause them to alter their prior behaviors, and any attempt to forecast future crimes would be pointless.

Just in case, Mitch made a mental note to stay close to the northwest corner of Dasan's Terrace next week.

The next files he opened were compressed data files of all the photographs taken by deputies and CSI officers of the burglarized residences. Although the images gave Mitch a better mental picture of the muddy trails left behind by the suspect, they did little to help determine who the suspect may have been. He did note that the soil and earth left on the floor of the houses comprised only a fraction of the dirt missing from each of the vandalized burial sites. The majority of the missing grave dirt remained unaccounted for.

Mitch made a note to himself to pass this bit of information along to Ali. It may not be significant, but it also could be a pivotal piece of evidence. It was hard to tell this early in the investigation. Regardless, he had promised to share anything he found with the homicide detective, and he intended to keep his word.

After the scene photographs, he sorted through a collection of images of the homicide victim. He flipped through them carefully, but again, other than appeasing his own morbid curiosity, they offered no further insights.

The final files Mitch opened were eight pages of phone call records. With no other leads to follow, the Sheriff's Office had opened a tip line to the public, asking for anyone with potential information about the murder to call in. The first page was titled, "Unrelated calls," and listed dozens of numbers and brief two or three-word synopses of the reason for the citizen's contact. Mitch skimmed the page with a finger, reading notes such as, "lost cat," "loud helicopter overhead," and "package delivery on roof."

He laughed. It was the typical venting from those fringe elements in every population that thought they had a direct connection to a police officer's phone. It was why every deputy selected to man one of these tip lines was required to attend a four-hour training class on how to remain polite while telling someone to go to hell and not call again.

Each of the remaining seven pages was topped with a single phone number and a name, although four of the seven pages were simply listed as "anonymous." Under the title was a typed outline from the deputy answering the call explaining the nature of the initial message. Below this were the notes regarding the follow-up and any return calls to the initial informant. Mitch assumed this second write up was done by Ali or someone else in the homicide bureau.

Five of the seven pages concluded with, "No useable information." Page six listed a possible suspect vehicle seen at the scene of the third burglary. Ali's conclusion on the bottom of the page advised that the car had been located a few days later and turned out to be a teenaged boy driving through the neighborhood with his headlights out because he was dropping off his girlfriend past her curfew. Another dead end.

The last page was a college professor who claimed he didn't know who had committed the murder, but he did know how they had done it. Ali's typed remarks following his conversation with the man said simply, "Monster breaking into houses. No suspect information." Below that summary, handwritten by the homicide detective was a county report number and the opinion, "Nutjob!"

That was all there was. Mitch clicked through the files again to be sure he hadn't missed anything, but there was nothing of use in any of it. The case looked dead in the water at the moment. Barring any new activity or a sudden break in the case on the tip line – which clearly seemed unlikely – there was little left to be done. No wonder Ali had handed over his personal files so easily. He had nothing further to go on and was probably hoping Mitch would be the break he needed to crack this investigation.

With nothing else to do, Mitch made physical copies of everything he had and added them to his growing folder. He found it easier to skim through paper documents by hand than to open and close a series of electronic files. Maybe he was being a Luddite, but the feel of a solid binder in his hands always made him feel closer to a case. When the folder was complete, he pocketed the thumb drive and began flipping through his collected documents. He decided to focus on the pages from the tip line files. Maybe something in there would give him a hint as to how to proceed. He came to the last page, the one concluded by Ali's dismissive opinion of the caller, and he saw the handwritten report number at the bottom again. He thumbed through the folder once more, looking for anything with the referenced report number, but found it did not match anything he already had.

Curious, he typed the case number into the report writing program on his computer. It came up as another burglary report. The victim in this report was documented as the same person who had called in to the department's tip line. At first Mitch was intrigued, thinking that this might be a fifth crime from the Dirty Bandit, but the report soon discouraged his excitement. The incident date was long before the first appearance of the Dirty Bandit. The Deputy's accounting of the crime documented a standard break-in like a million others that happened every year. No dirt trail was left behind. The entrance was through an unlocked window rather than forced through a back door. Finally, the items stolen were some ancient artifacts from Northern Africa, specifically selected from a display case.

None of the details matched the Dirty Bandit's modus operandi.

Mitch printed a copy of the file for his folder. It did not seem related, but Ali had included it for some reason, so he figured he should keep it for the time being. He closed the program on his screen and powered down his computer. Ninety minutes of research had provided him with very little information he did not already have, and nothing that would help him to further the investigation. He had his first case in two months and in one night he had already crashed headlong into a dead end.

"Shit."

Closing the folder and scooping it up from the work desk, Mitch rose to his feet. Maybe he could still join the team in the breakroom in time to see the end of the first movie.

The following morning, Mitch decided to call Ali before going home. There wasn't any reason for the phone call other than to let the detective know about the amount of missing grave dirt, and that could have been handled in an email, but Mitch also wanted to satisfy his curiosity on one particular issue. He was still wondering why the college professor thought his burglary might be related to the homicide. He might truly be a nutjob, as Ali's notes suggested, but maybe there was something else going on as well. Whatever the case, Mitch had an annoying prickling in the back of his mind that he knew would not go away until he asked about it.

He'd had that prickling on more than one occasion both as a detective and a street officer. Occasionally, it led him nowhere, but more often than not, it had occurred for a good reason. He had learned to trust it, even if he didn't fully understand it.

At seven-thirty, Mitch pulled out his cell phone and dialed Ali's number. The homicide detective picked up on the second ring. From the background noise and the echo to his voice, it sounded like the man was in his car driving somewhere.

"This is Ali," he said.

"Hi, Ali. This is Mitch, from the cemetery PD. We talked yesterday."

"Oh, yeah. Hey, Mitch. Did you get the files I sent you?"

"I did, thanks. Did you get my pictures? If they're too dark, I can take more."

"They're probably fine, but I haven't gotten into the office yet to check. I'm running a little late today. My kid is sick, and I couldn't get out of the house until my wife's mother got there."

"Sorry your kid isn't feeling well. Hope it's nothing serious."

"I think it's a serious case of him not wanting to go to school today, but otherwise he's fine. So, what's up? What can I do for you?"

Mitch paused, almost deciding to say goodbye and end the call. This was probably nothing but a waste of both their time, but before he could back out, the itching at the base of his skull returned.

"Look, it's not a big deal, but I have a question about one of your calls on the tip line. Something caught my attention and got me curious."

"The tip line was pretty much a bust, so I don't know what I can tell you other than what's on the note sheets. What do you want to know?"

"The college professor. What's his deal? Is he actually a professor, and what did he tell you about the murder?"

Ali laughed out loud "Oh, that guy. Yeah, I remember him. He said he's a professor at Sacramento State University. Teaches religious myths and mythology. I think he's been doing it a little too long and it made him soft in the head. He's starting to smoke his own product if you get my drift."

"He told you a monster was breaking into houses?" Mitch asked. "What kind of monster?"

Another laugh. "Yeah. He told me my killer was that little dude from Lord of the Rings. You know, that funny looking, trollish thing? What's the name … Gollum? That's it. He told me Gollum was the burglar and he was the one that killed my victim."

Mitch paused, taken aback. He wasn't sure what he had expected to hear, but he was pretty certain this wasn't it.

"How does he know? Did he say how he found out? And did he tell you why he thought his burglary was connected to the Dirty Bandit?"

"The whole thing was weird. I think he watches too many fantasy movies. That or teaching a bunch of college kids has finally made his mind slip. He said whoever broke into his house took some rocks or something that were given to him by an old friend. The professor said the rocks would summon the little monster dude."

"None of that makes any sense."

"Tell me about it," said Ali. "That's why I finally stopped talking to the guy. I can't exactly ask for an A.P.B. on a two-foot tall, bald, gray dude with bad teeth. I'd be in a rubber room by tomorrow. Was that it, or did you need anything else?"

"No," said Mitch. "That was it. Oh, and I wanted to let you know that I looked at the pictures of the crime scenes. The amount of dirt at your burglaries is barely a fraction of what was taken out of the cemetery. I don't know if that helps, but if you find four huge piles of grave dirt in someone's backyard it might be a clue."

"Alright. Thanks for that. Call me if you have anything else or have any more questions."

"Thanks, Ali. Take care. Hope your son's okay."

"Bye."

Mitch hung up and slipped his phone into his pocket.

Another dead end.

CHAPTER
15

The following Monday, Mitch settled into his usual booth at Cassie's Cafe for a late lunch. Since meeting Violet here three weeks ago, it had become part of his weekly routine. Mitch wasn't sure about his feelings for the witch, she could be mysterious and, at times, a tad infuriating with her secrets, but he found he enjoyed her company, nonetheless. She had a quick wit, a devastating sense of humor, and no one could deny her physical charms. She also seemed to enjoy being around him as well, although she was careful to keep the conversations light, never straying from simple, inconsequential topics. She definitely had some personal walls up whenever she was with him.

She also frightened him a tiny bit.

Mitch had not yet fully adjusted to his new reality of ghosts, witches, magic, and creatures that went bump in the night. He wondered if he ever would. He could not imagine a time when these things might feel normal to him, but then, when he was first hired as a police officer, wearing a ballistic vest and carrying a gun on his hip had felt strange and unnatural, too. Things changed, and people had to adjust with those changes.

After ordering, Mitch glanced around the restaurant, hoping to spy Violet coming in. The place was quiet, with only the few afternoon regulars he was beginning to recognize by sight. There was no sign of the bouncy, blond coven member yet. She hadn't turned up last week, either, which had left Mitch strangely disappointed. His feelings made little logical sense. She didn't owe him an RSVP, or an apology for standing him up; it wasn't as if they had a standing date or anything. They met here twice, and that was the extent of their interaction.

Still, here he was, despite feeling more than a little self-conscious. He didn't have anywhere else he was supposed to be today, so the diner was as good a place as any for him to end up.

His food arrived a few minutes later. For a change of pace, he had ordered a bacon, lettuce, and tomato sandwich along with a bowl of split pea soup. He enjoyed his cheeseburgers, but Violet had been right when she said he'd never see forty if that was all he ever ate. He thanked his server, then reached for a handful of napkins. While his head was turned, he felt a slight rush of air and felt the familiar vibration of someone crash landing on the bench on the other side of his booth.

Mitch smiled to himself and pulled a few more napkins without looking toward his visitor.

"Hello, Vi," he said. "I missed you last week."

"Nope. Don't," she said. "Not Vi. Never Vi. I can't stand the name. Say it again and I'm out of here."

Mitch turned toward her and noticed that despite her correction, she was grinning devilishly at him. "Sorry. I'll keep that in mind, Violet. Where were you last week? I even ordered an extra burger for you. It sat and got cold. The waitress probably felt sorry for me for getting stood up."

"I know," Violet said, then puffed her cheeks and blew a loose strand of hair from her face. "I saw you, and I saw the burger on the table. It looked good."

"You were here?" asked Mitch, surprised by the revelation.

"Yup, but when I saw you had ordered for me, I left. A girl does not like to be too predictable. I have to keep you on your toes."

"I must admit, you are anything but predictable. I never know what to expect when you're around. I know almost nothing about you."

"I can't say that I mind keeping you guessing," she admitted. "You're much more fun when you're confused. Besides, what do you think you need to know about me that would change anything? You know I'm a witch, and you know I belong to a coven that uses your cemetery once a month. You don't need anything else."

"What about your name?" asked Mitch. "I don't even know your last name. You know mine. You probably read it on my name tag the moment we met. I figure it's only fair that I know yours. Don't you think?"

"Guess," she said. "See if you can figure it out."

"Figure it out? What do you…? Um, okay. Jones? Smith?"

"Boring," Violet huffed. "Think about it carefully. What is my name?"

"Violet," Mitch said, then repeated it. "Violet. Vi-o-let. I don't know. Roses are red and violets are blue. Blue?" he guessed.

Violet perked up, a wide grin spreading across her face.

"Yes!" she exclaimed. "Or rather, Blue is my middle name. My parents wanted me to have a unique name, something that would make me stand out. I would say they were successful in that regard. I've been teased for my name my entire life. My last name is Rose."

"Violet Blue Rose," said Mitch.

"Go ahead. Say it," dared Violet.

"Say what?"

"It's a stupid name."

Mitch nodded. "It is a little bit stupid," he agreed. "It's also really amazing, and endearing and lovely. It's intriguing and mysterious, like the name of a French spy in a World War II fantasy story. It's a unique name that could only belong to the right person. It fits you."

Violet glowered. "You're making fun of me."

"I absolutely am not. I mean it. It fits you. It's the perfect name."

Her features softened, and a small smile pulled at her lips. It was perhaps the first time that Mitch had seen Violet smile where it looked absolutely genuine, rather than merely part of a mask she used to hide her true feelings. When the silence stretched to the point it became uncomfortable, Mitch tapped the side of his soup bowl lightly with his spoon and attempted to steer the conversation away from the unexpected moment of intimacy.

"So, should I start eating, or wave down the waitress and order myself another meal while you eat this one?"

Violet glanced at the offering and wrinkled her nose at the soup. "I'm not a fan of split pea, so you keep it. I'll take half the sandwich, though. I'm glad to see you've moved on from burgers."

Mitch slid his plate forward so Violet could take half of his lunch. "Does this mean you owe me a favor?" he asked.

She bit into the corner of the sandwich, then shook her head. "Nope. Half a favor for half a sandwich."

Violet, with the sandwich in her left hand, raised the index finger of her right and twirled it in a small circle. A small bead of yellow light appeared at her fingertip. When the light coalesced into a solid-looking sphere, she placed it on the table and rolled it toward Mitch. The ball reached the end of the table and continued off the edge where Mitch put out a palm to catch it. As soon as the sphere touched his skin, it popped like a bubble, dissipating into nothingness.

Violet shook her head, looking disappointed in the effort. She repeated the twirling motion with her finger and created a new orb of sparkling light. As she placed the second ball on the table, she raised an eyebrow at Mitch. "Catch it this time," she told him, then sent the glowing ball rolling.

Again, Mitch put out a hand to catch the sphere as it fell off the edge of the table. Again, it popped out of existence. Violet grimaced her displeasure.

"Okay," she said. "Here's your half favor. You could catch that ball if you really wanted to."

"How would I do that?" Mitch asked.

"Sorry. We're even again. Better luck next time."

"Well, isn't this a cozy little gathering," a new voice interrupted.

Mitch jumped. He was getting tired of people sneaking up on him. He used to think he was an observant person, but lately he was learning that he was oblivious to a lot of things to which he needed to be paying closer attention.

They both turned to find Alyssandra standing next to their table. The older woman's glare of displeasure moved back and forth between the two of them. Violet replaced the partially eaten sandwich on Mitch's plate and wiped at her mouth with the back of one hand. She couldn't quite meet Alyssandra's eyes, and her posture made her look like a child who had been caught playing dress up in her mother's room. A room that was apparently supposed to be off limits.

"What did I tell you about teaching him before we had an agreement with the Lost Child?"

Violet did not respond. She simply deflated a bit more. Alyssandra slipped into the booth beside her coven member and Violet shrank further into the corner.

Alyssandra stared at Mitch with a cold, calculating expression. She did not smile, and Mitch was grateful for that. The way her skin pulled tight along her sharp jawline and cheekbones made him think of a living skull already, if she smiled it would only complete the image. He realized his shoulders were tensed and hunched forward, and he had to consciously force himself to relax.

"You have no idea what game you're playing here," Alyssandra said, the words raspy and harsh, like fingernails across a chalkboard. Mitch shivered. "Do you know what she is? My dear little Violet? What she is capable of?"

Mitch did not respond. He didn't think there was anything he could say that Alyssandra wanted to hear. She nodded, content with his silence.

"She isn't your pretty little plaything, Officer Loman. You wouldn't know by looking at her, but my girl is one of the most dangerous creatures you will ever meet."

Mitch's eyes flickered toward Violet, at her slumped and defeated posture. She stared at the corner of the table in front of her, her expression frightened and embarrassed as Alyssandra talked about her.

Dangerous? Mitch wondered. Her attitude around Alyssandra argued against it. She had power, he knew, he had seen glimpses of that, but dangerous? That was a little harder to swallow.

"Ah, I can see you don't believe me," continued Alyssandra. "Well, perhaps a small demonstration is in order. Violet, touch the officer. Show him what you can do."

Violet remained slumped in her corner of the booth. She shook her head meekly. "Please, Alyssandra. I-I don't want to."

"Are you refusing an order?" Alyssandra's voice hardened further. "Are you challenging me for leadership of the coven?"

Violet's eyes grew wide. "No! Of course not. I would never challenge you."

"Then do as I say. Officer Loman, would you be so kind as to hold out your hand?"

Unsure of Alyssandra's intentions, but confident that Violet would never harm him, Mitch held out his hand. Violet blinked, and a tear rolled down her cheek. She mouthed the words, "I'm sorry," then lunged forward, grasping his hand. Violet pulled.

The world went black around him. There was no light, no sound, no sensation of touch. There was only pain. It filled his body and his mind so completely there was no room for anything else. A wrenching sensation climbed his arm, like muscle pulling free from bone, but it went much deeper than mere bone. Mitch was being twisted from the inside out.

He screamed. At least, he thought he screamed. He could not be sure since he heard nothing in that moment. His mind felt completely disconnected from his body. The only sensation throughout his physical form was the pain. The only thought he could focus on was the pain. The only reality he could experience was the pain.

It was his new universe, blackness and agony, and it held him in its grasp for only a moment, but also for an eternity.

Then the light came back. The restaurant, the sounds, the smells, all flooded back to the forefront of his awareness. The world returned and the overwhelming agony that had held him at last receded. Though the pain faded, a sick feeling of internal damage, of wrongness, remained. He didn't think he was injured in any way, but at the same time, he felt broken.

Mitch realized he was shaking. His shirt and pants were wet, and a waft of putrid air in his nostrils alerted him that he had vomited on himself.

Violet was back in her corner of the booth. She was crying, her shoulders hitching as she attempted to muffle her sobs.

"Officer Loman, do you understand a little better, now?" Alyssandra leaned toward him, demanding his attention. "Violet is an exorcist. Spirits act at her direction. She has the ability to cast souls from this world on a whim, and those souls, as you yourself have just experienced, do not need to already be separated from their bodies before she does it."

Mitch tried to speak, but the effort almost caused him to throw up again. The room was spinning, and he felt as though he had been run over by a truck.

"Don't worry, officer. She did not do you permanent harm. You will recover soon enough. I expect you will not soon forget this little lesson, however. Come, Violet. We are leaving."

Violet followed Alyssandra as she exited the booth. She did not look toward Mitch. She could not face him. The shame in her face was clear for him to see, even in his weakened condition.

Customers stared toward the commotion, making Mitch wonder if he had actually managed to scream during the ordeal. Or perhaps they had simply heard him emptying his stomach and were trying to figure out the nature of his distress. Their waitress rushed toward the table, and Alyssandra detained her with a hand on her arm.

"The food here is abysmal," the coven leader hissed. "You should be ashamed of yourself. My friend has grown quite ill, and I expect you to take care of him."

She released the server's arm, then with Violet in tow, she marched out of the diner.

Violet followed Alyssandra out into the parking lot. She glanced back over her shoulder at the diner, but the door had closed behind her, and she could no longer see Officer Loman inside. He would not be coming after them any time soon, she knew, not after what she had done to him. The officer would be incapacitated for some time yet.

"I don't think that was necessary," she said softly, more to herself than to Alyssandra. The coven priestess heard her comment, nonetheless.

"If you followed my orders and stayed away from that man, then perhaps it would not have been. Since you did not listen, I needed to make a statement, both to him and to you, apparently."

"I'm sorry about that, but I think this may have been a mistake."

Alyssandra halted, whirling around to face Violet.

"I decide what is or is not a mistake. The officer needs to understand our strengths, and he needs to know we are not to be trifled with."

Violet wanted to argue the point further but held her tongue. Alyssandra had been good to her, protected her when she needed protecting, and the coven leader deserved her respect and obedience because of that. Still, Violet worried about repercussions from her attack on the Dasan's Terrace officer.

Instead of debating Alyssandra's orders, Violet simply said, "I looked into him. He isn't the type to be frightened away. He will be stubborn. Dig his heels in. I'm afraid if we are not careful, we may make an enemy of that man. I don't think that would be good for us or the coven."

Alyssandra's face softened in contemplation. She appeared to consider Violet's words.

"Are you sure about him?" the older witch asked. "That he is … like you?"

"The echo in the cemetery is gone. It was still too strong to fade away on its own, and I did not remove it. That isn't proof, but I don't think I'm wrong about him. Everything I've seen suggests it."

Alyssandra paused to consider the situation again.

"Maybe I was hasty after all. It would be better to have him on our side rather than opposing us."

Violet looked toward the restaurant doors. Officer Loman still had not emerged. She hoped she had not hurt him worse than she thought.

"Okay," said Alyssandra, bringing Violet's attention back to the conversation. "You may continue to see him."

"I'm not sure he wants to see me after … well, after that." Violet gestured toward the diner.

"Hmm. True. Then tell him you only did it because I made you. It's the truth. Make me the bad guy and see if maybe he'll feel sorry for you. Tell him you like him and didn't want to do it. Offer to make it up to him in whatever way he might like. Men are idiots when you appeal to their baser needs."

"Sure," Violet agreed, though she knew Officer Loman was not the type of person to take advantage of that kind of offer.

Violet regretted hurting him, and she did want to make it up to him somehow, but she knew it would take more than the simple offer of sex to gain back his trust. Alyssandra had given her permission to continue talking with Officer Loman, so she would start there. If she was careful and let him see how genuinely sorry she was about what had happened, maybe he would open back up to her.

Maybe.

"In the meantime," continued Alyssandra, "we need to move things along. If you can't get him to be more friendly towards us, we should at least have some leverage over him."

Violet felt a cold lump form in the pit of her stomach. *Now what?* she wondered but kept her thoughts to herself.

"Free up your evening on Wednesday." Alyssandra said. "I will make us an appointment with Chief Jefferson. We need to make the Lost Child recognize our value to him, and we need to do it right away. This is not an opportunity we want to squander."

CHAPTER 16

As Alyssandra had promised him, Mitch did recover after a few hours. Physically, at least. Mentally, he could not forget the feeling of pain that enveloped him and the sense of being disconnected from his body. When he tried to sleep over the next couple of days, he woke frequently, disturbed by formless nightmares that he could not properly remember upon waking.

Once, he was jolted awake by his own shouting. His body was covered in sweat and his pajama pants clung to his legs as though he had recently climbed out of a swimming pool. He tried to hold on to the remnants of the dream that had terrified him so badly, but it was already breaking apart and drifting from his conscious mind. He only had vague, fragmented images of a roiling darkness and something amorphous reaching out to ensnare him.

He arrived for work on Wednesday night, already fatigued and in poor humor. He sat at the table during briefing and in the thirty seconds it took for Jorge to tell everyone that nothing had happened during their days off, he almost fell asleep.

"Hey, sleeping beauty," said Tink, giving Mitch a push on the shoulder. "Did you hear Jorge?"

"Yeah. Nothing happened," said Mitch.

"No," chipped Brad. "The part where he said you need to go upstairs to the Chief's office."

"What?"

Jorge sighed. "Simon wants to see you in his office. He said send you the second briefing is over. That means now. So, go."

"What does he want?" asked Mitch, too muzzy from lack of sleep to be properly concerned that the chief had stayed behind after work to talk to him. He could only generate a general curiosity in the haze that constituted his waking thoughts.

"Go and ask the chief. When he tells you, come back and tell me, then we'll both know what the hell is going on."

"Fine," mumbled Mitch, crossly.

He pushed his chair back from the table, dragging the feet over the laminated floor and creating a loud screeching noise. Tink covered his ears in mock annoyance. The look on Jorge's face indicated there was nothing feigned about his own impatience at Mitch's antics. Apparently, Mitch's bad mood was becoming infectious. That would not do if he was about to talk to the boss, so he tried to wake himself up with a couple deep breaths as he headed upstairs.

Walking through the reception area of the second floor, Mitch noticed Dot was not at her desk. Her shift ended at five, and he figured she must have already left for home. The chief's office door was ajar, and Mitch heard a woman's voice speaking from inside. He recognized the sound almost immediately and his feet froze in place. It was Alyssandra.

What the hell was she doing here?

Mitch forced himself to keep moving, stepping up to the partially open door. He paused, then rapped a knuckle on the wooden frame.

"Chief? I was told you wanted to talk to me. I hope I'm not interrupting anything."

"Come in," responded Simon. The chief's voice was carefully neutral, he noted.

Mitch stepped into the office. It was a large space, fitting for the chief of police of a much more populated department than the DTPD. At the far end of the room, Simon was seated behind his desk. In front of the desk, Alyssandra sat in one of the leather guest chairs with Violet standing over her left shoulder, hands clasped behind her back. Violet wore the black wig and goth makeup she had been sporting the first night they met, though she was dressed in a pale blue, long-sleeved blouse and a jean skirt that stopped at her knees.

"Come in," repeated the chief. "You know Miss Freid and Miss Rose. They came by my office tonight to make one last appeal. They believe you could benefit from their assistance, and in exchange they want additional access to the cemetery. I previously told Miss Freid, here," he indicated Alyssandra, "that I was not interested in such a concession. She is insisting that this would be beneficial to all of us, including yourself and Dasan's Terrace. I am reconsidering my stance, but I thought I should hear from you first, since this is primarily about you."

Violet turned. She smiled when she saw Mitch and raised a hand in greeting.

Mitch flinched and took an involuntary step back. The smile sputtered and died on Violet's face, and she let the lifted hand fall back to her side.

"I want nothing to do with any of them, sir," said Mitch bluntly.

Alyssandra rose to her feet and spread her arms as though welcoming Mitch into an embrace. "Dear boy. Don't be like this. Perhaps I was a bit harsh during our last talk, but don't let your enmity toward me push you into making a rash decision. You have a gift that needs training. A gift that, if left unaddressed, could eventually cause you and those around you great distress."

"I'm familiar with distress," Mitch shot back, flicking a glance toward Violet. "I think I'm better off staying as far away from you and your coven as possible."

Violet wiped a hand across her cheek, smearing the kohl makeup under her left eye.

Simon rose from his chair. "I think that is your answer, Miss Freid. Thank you for coming by."

Alyssandra whirled toward the chief of police. Listen to me, Lost Child. In the interests of complete transparency, I will speak clearly. Your officer is an exorcist, and probably will be a very powerful one. He is only now coming into his powers, and without training, he will become a threat to us all. If you send me away from your office tonight, you will be bringing me back in six months or a year to request my assistance in hunting him down. I do not wish to see it come to that. Violet is the only person I know in five hundred miles with the ability and experience to train him how to use his power without breaking his mind.

"I am also not a philanthropist. I will not offer Violet's services for nothing. I have asked for only one extra night of access to the cemetery each month in repayment. I think that is more than fair."

Violet straightened and met Mitch's stare directly. He could see the regret and concern in her look. He wanted to believe the emotions were genuine. "Please, Mitch," she said. "Let me help you. Afterwards, if you want, you'll never see me again."

He wanted to say no. The "lesson" he had experienced in Cassie's Cafe was still too fresh in his mind; too raw. He did not trust Violet. No, that wasn't completely true. He *did* trust Violet, damn it, despite what had happened. She hadn't wanted to hurt him. It was Alyssandra that he truly did not trust. As long as Alyssandra was leader of the coven, he was not safe. But maybe, if he learned enough from Violet, one day he might be strong enough to fight back. Or, if not fight back, at least be strong enough to defend himself.

Mitch gave a small, reluctant nod toward Chief Jefferson.

"I accept your offer to help," said Simon. "But not for twenty-four days each year. I'll allow the coven eighteen days. Each full moon and six additional nights of your choosing. As Coven Priestess, you may select the dates you wish, but you will notify me at least one week in advance before entering the cemetery. In exchange, you will teach Officer Loman how to harness and use his abilities safely. You will teach him everything he needs and wishes to know. You will provide information clearly, without riddles or confusing language, and you will hide nothing from him."

Alyssandra raised an eyebrow disapprovingly. Before she could speak, the chief continued.

"You, of course, may deny him any information that compromises the integrity, safety, or privacy of your coven."

The eyebrow dropped and was replaced by a predatory smile. "Acceptable," Alyssandra agreed.

The coven leader held out her hand, palm facing upward. A spiral of blue light coiled from her outstretched hand traveling in an arc toward the chief. Simon extended his own hand, allowing the end of the light bridge to touch his palm.

"My word is my oath," said Simon.

"My word is my oath," repeated Alyssandra.

The spiral light flared red at the spoken words, then disappeared.

"I would have accepted fourteen days," Alyssandra cackled at the chief. "Thank you for eighteen."

"I would have given twenty-four if you pushed a little harder," said Simon. Alyssandra's laugh choked off and she glared at the chief.

"When am I supposed to start?" Mitch asked.

"The sooner the better, I would think. If nothing comes up during your shift, why don't you start tonight? Miss Rose, are you free?"

"She is," stated Alyssandra. Violet remained respectfully mute, not interrupting the coven leader.

Violet and Mitch walked side by side through the cemetery grounds, moving away from the police department building and deeper into the shadowed areas of Dasan's Terrace. Alyssandra had disappeared as soon as the deal was struck, leaving Violet behind to honor the terms of her agreement. The two walked several minutes in awkward silence. Finally, unable to take the quiet any longer, Mitch said the first thing that came to his mind.

"I like you better without the wig."

Violet reached up and jerked the wig from her head, running the fingers of one hand through her shorter blond hair to straighten any tangles. "Better?" she asked, a tentative smile pulling at her lips.

"Much."

The silence descended once again. This time it was Violet that tried to fill the void between them.

"I'm sorry I hurt you. I shouldn't have done it. I should have told Alyssandra no."

"It didn't sound like you had much choice. What would have happened if you had refused."

Violet shrugged. "Maybe nothing."

"But?" prodded Mitch.

"But she could have cast me out of the coven. The other witches could then either chase me from the city or kill me. Maybe both."

"Then I'd say you did what you had to do."

Violet turned suddenly to confront Mitch. She placed a hand on his chest, stopping his forward progress and leaving the two of them only a few inches apart. She had to tilt her head back to meet his eyes.

"And I say that I will never harm you like that again."

The earnestness in her face and the wet sheen in her eyes melted the last of his resolve not to trust her. Mitch knew he was probably being careless to forgive her so quickly, but he could not help believing … or maybe simply wanting to believe … in her sincerity

"Please don't make a promise you don't know you can keep," he said, not unkindly.

"Why wouldn't I keep it?"

"Alyssandra said something about my abilities breaking my mind. I don't really understand what that means, but if it happens, I don't want to hurt anyone, and I hope that you would do everything in your power to stop me."

"You have absolutely nothing to worry about," she assured him. "Your soul is the source of your ability to manipulate ghosts. Spirits, and sometimes a stubborn poltergeist, can fight back during exorcisms so that, as you banish them, they can latch on and tear away tiny pieces of your soul when they go. Over time, an untrained exorcist's own spirit breaks down beyond repair from all the repetitive damage, that's what makes them go mad. There are ways to avoid that if you know what you're doing. I'm here to make sure it doesn't happen to you. I won't let it."

Violet bounced up on her tiptoes and surprised Mitch with a kiss, a quick peck on the side of the face. With a flush rising up across her chest and neck, she spun on her heel and started walking again. Surprised, Mitch touched a hand to where her lips had brushed his cheek. He smiled, deciding he had enjoyed the brief contact. In fact, he found himself wishing she would turn around and do it again.

She didn't.

Violet kept walking, leading him deeper toward the north end of the cemetery grounds, away from the manicured lawns and perfect rows of headstones, into the roughly wooded areas. Minutes later, when she found a place she liked, she turned to face Mitch and held up an index finger. She twirled it slowly until a ball of yellow light appeared. Mitch recalled the diner and the odd game she had played with him there.

Violet flicked the tiny ball toward him. "Catch," she called out.

Mitch snatched at the yellow light but, as he had anticipated, it blinked out of existence the moment it touched his hand.

"Lesson number one," Violet said.

She held her hands a foot apart and moved them like she was packing a snowball between them. A larger yellow ball formed between her palms. When the ball was the size of a grapefruit, she hurled it directly at Mitch. He yelped and jumped but was unable to dodge out of the way before it struck him in the chest. The ball passed harmlessly through him and fizzled to nothing a few feet away.

"Magic must be shaped and controlled. Otherwise, it is simply … magic. Nothing more than a ball of light to those that can see it, and literally nothing at all to those who can't. When I toss it to you, focus on catching it. You have to want it in your hand so badly that it obeys your will."

She formed another ball. "Catch."

Mitch focused on the yellow light. He pictured it staying intact in his hand as he caught it, but it passed through him again.

"Better," congratulated Violet. "I saw you deflect it a tiny bit that time."

"Alyssandra called me an exorcist," Mitch said, changing the subject. The statement had been weighing on his mind since he heard it in the chief's office. "She said you're one, too."

Violet nodded.

"And earlier tonight you mentioned using my soul to exorcise spirits. What does that mean? What is an exorcist? I mean, I've seen the movie, so I kind of get that part, but there's more to it, isn't there?"

Violet's gaze wandered into the sky as she tried to figure out a way to say what needed to be said. There was only a sliver of moon overhead, and they had left most of the cemetery's electric path lights behind. Stars shone overhead by the thousands in the late evening heavens. "I told you a while ago that you had the rare gift of interacting with spirits. Remember?"

Mitch agreed. He did remember that conversation.

"That's basically what an exorcist is. It's someone who can manipulate ghosts and spirits to their will. You don't just see ghosts, but you can touch them and force them to do your bidding."

"You can do this, too?"

Violet nodded. "You and I are exceedingly rare, Mitch. We're also considered really dangerous. Our abilities aren't restricted to the dead." Violet's eyes lowered, suddenly unable to meet Mitch's own. She was obviously remembering her demonstration of that power in the diner. "If I didn't have Alyssandra and the coven protecting me, there are people out there that would try to use me or … to get rid of me."

"They would do the same to me?"

"They would. Fortunately, you have Simon and the police department protecting you. And now you have me."

Mitch felt a warmth growing in his chest. It was comforting to know someone cared about him and was looking out for him. He hadn't felt this way since he began dating Linda all those years ago. It felt nice to have these feelings again, even if he knew he needed to be cautious about expressing them. He had no idea if Violet felt the same way or was merely feeling guilty about hurting him earlier.

"How does it work? The exorcisms?"

"You use your natural gift, and you focus it the way I will train you to focus it. Why do you think we're out here tossing stupid light balls around? I'm trying to teach you the tricks you're going to need for everything else you have to learn. It can take a lot of willpower and desire to use your gift intentionally. Sometimes it's easy and you do it without realizing you're doing it, like you did with Harold. But it's those times you act without thinking that are so dangerous."

"What?!" barked Mitch. "What did I do to Harold?"

"Harold was a fragile old echo. He was harmless and no threat to anyone, so he wasn't about to fight back when you banished him. The moment you touched him, your pity for his condition triggered your gift. You tore him apart and scattered his essence."

Mitch's mouth dropped open, aghast. "I killed him?"

Violet laughed. "No, silly. There was nothing to kill. He wasn't real. He was only an echo. Do you kill movie actors when you turn off the film? Do you kill characters in a book when you close it and put it away? Of course not. they never really existed."

So, he was the reason that Harold never came back. Mitch touched him and ended the echo. That explained a few things, the feeling of cobwebs parting under his touch, and the startled look on Harold's face when he disappeared. It also created a few questions. Mitch peered suspiciously at Violet.

"How do you know I was the one who banished him?"

"I didn't actually know for certain until just this minute," Violet admitted. "I suspected it, though. I noticed Harold was gone and it was much too early for him to simply have faded away. I realized there had to be a new exorcist in the cemetery, or at the very least, someone with a magical item that could banish echoes. A few days later, I met you and I got my first good look at your soul. I could tell immediately that you were like me. Your soul was … well, it was obvious to me what you were, and exorcists are so rare, I figured it had to be you that erased Harold."

"Violet. You said you met me a few days after you noticed Harold was gone? When did you notice he was gone, and what were you doing in the cemetery a few days before the full moon?"

"Oops," she said. "You're right. I wasn't in the cemetery before I met you. That wasn't our night to be in Dead Town, so of course I wasn't there."

"Your coven already comes in whenever they like, don't they?"

Violet patted him on the chest, dragging her nails across his shirt as she paced a small circle around him. "As per our agreement with your chief of police, I am not required to provide information that may compromise the security of the coven."

"You sneaky little…"

"Officer Loman! Be very careful how you finish that sentence."

"Witch," he finished. "How many of you are there, by the way? In your coven?"

"Three, seven, and thirteen are standard numbers. Sometimes there can be many more, depending on the power of the leader to maintain order. We have thirteen in ours."

"And all of you can do magic?"

Violet paused again, seeming to debate with herself whether or not she should answer the question. "Anyone can do magic, Mitch. There are many practitioners that utilize magical forces using spells and enchanted objects designed for that purpose. The ability to see magic and manipulate it directly is a huge advantage for witches, sorcerers, and others, but it is also not terribly common. Most people, including many of those in my coven, only know that magic is working because of the effects it causes when it is being used."

Violet rolled her hands as if physically trying to find the proper words to explain the image she had in her mind. "Try to imagine roasting a marshmallow over a campfire when you can't see the fire. Someone else has already lit it, and you can use it, but you are never sure exactly how high or low the flames are. You observe that the fire is there because the logs are turning black and breaking down so you trust that you can cook your marshmallow, but if you hold it too high over the fire, it never turns brown. Also, more importantly, if you hold your marshmallow too low…"

"It burns up."

"Exactly."

"But *we* can see the fire, so the chances of roasting our marshmallow properly are much better."

Violet laughed. "More than that. We can actually light the fire for everyone else, and if we feel like it, we can reach our hands in and pull out hot coals. Which brings me back to our original lesson."

Violet held her hands together, bringing another yellow ball of light to life. She rotated it against her left palm like a major league pitcher preparing to hurl a fastball to home plate.

"Catch!" she announced, flinging it toward Mitch.

CHAPTER 17

Mitch and Brad wandered the Front Lawn of Dasan's Terrace on the last night of their long work week. Working twelve-hour shifts was not physically demanding in Dead Town, but when all you did was work, go home, sleep, then go back to work, for four straight days, it left a person mentally drained and ready for a day off. It didn't help that they worked nights, either. Trying to stay up all night four nights in a row and then trying to live on a normal schedule on your weekends often left a person permanently sleep deprived and lethargic.

With eight hours still remaining in their shift, Brad already looked like he was ready to pack it in and go home. Mitch was sure his own giddy behavior wasn't helping the man's mood any, but he didn't really care. He had learned quite a lot about magic and what it could do from Violet during their first night of lessons, and he was looking forward to next Monday when they were scheduled to meet again.

They weren't meeting at Cassie's Cafe this time. Mitch was pretty certain he would never be allowed back there again after the fiasco during his last visit. The staff had acted understanding and polite as they helped clean him up and get him to his car, but the angry glower on the manager's face as Mitch drove away made it clear he was not on their favorite customer list.

During the four hours that Violet worked with Mitch on Wednesday, he had finally reached a point where he could perceive and draw magic from the air around him and even, with concentration, hold it in his hands. The first time he successfully held the insubstantial yellow ball without popping it left him with an incredible sense of accomplishment he hadn't felt since getting hired by the Sheriff's Office. He still could not manipulate magic into anything useful, but merely holding it was a huge step forward from where he had been only days ago. He also began to understand why the coven was so attracted to Dead Town. Magic was sparse and mostly unavailable throughout Sacramento County, although there were a few pockets of power here and there where it was thick enough to be visible to Mitch's careful inspection. Here, in Dasan's Terrace, power permeated the ground and the air like dense fog, especially in the older parts of the cemetery.

All he needed to do was concentrate and focus his awareness on the magic and he could see the wispy tendrils of power drifting along beside him and flowing under his feet. It was a simple matter at that point to reach out and grasp it; to collect it in his hands. In childlike delight, he waved cupped fingers like a scoop in front of his face and gathered energy from the air, compacting it as he collected it until the mass glowed a soft yellow, exactly like the balls of pure magic Violet had demonstrated for him. He held it in his upturned palm.

"You can't see this?" he asked Brad, holding the ball in his hand between them. It glowed clear as a lightbulb to Mitch's perceptions.

"For the hundredth time, no. I don't see anything."

The annoyed edge to Brad's voice made Mitch chuckle. He felt like a kid with a secret, taunting all his friends with the knowledge of something he would not share with them. Mitch flicked the ball of power into Brad's face. It puffed away to nothing when it made contact. His partner did not so much as blink as it made contact and Mitch wondered at Brad's complete lack of awareness of what was happening. But then, only days ago, Mitch himself had been similarly clueless. The major difference between the two of them was that regardless of how much training or coaching Brad received, he would never be consciously aware of the magic that surrounded him.

It was a strange feeling to be so singularly aware. Mitch began to understand how lonely it could be for someone who saw ghosts and magic but didn't have anyone around to explain to them what they were experiencing. The isolation would be enough to make a person believe they were losing their mind. For the first time since getting kicked out of the Detective Bureau, Mitch was glad he had landed in Dead Town. It had saved more than his job; it was responsible for returning his sanity.

This was where he was supposed to be.

He formed another ball of light.

"Can you see this one?"

Brad sighed and ran a hand lightly over the handle of his katana, perhaps unconsciously reassuring himself it was there in case he decided to cut Mitch into several pieces. After all of Brad's practical jokes targeted against him in the past weeks, Mitch felt no guilt as he irritated his partner to distraction.

A skeletal figure dressed in black resolved from the deeper darkness in the distance to appear in front of the two officers. The intruder had a hood pulled over its head, leaving the face shrouded in shadow and giving Mitch an uneasy impression that he was facing the Grim Reaper. Mitch let the ball in his hand blink away as he grasped the butt of his service pistol. He noticed that Brad beside him had also reached for his gun.

"What are you doing so far away, Officer Loman?" The figure asked. "You have duties in the northwest you should be attending to."

Mitch recognized the voice. He relaxed marginally but did not remove his hand from his pistol. "Alyssandra. What the hell are you doing here?"

"This isn't your night," warned Brad. He had gone so far as to draw his weapon now and he was holding it beside his thigh, barrel pointed toward the ground. "Should I be reporting a violation of our agreement to the Chief?"

"No time for pleasantries," the tall woman mocked. She pointed a gnarled, bony finger at Mitch. "The vandal is back. He is desecrating a new grave in the northwest as we waste time here. I thought you wanted to catch him."

Mitch silently kicked himself. He knew, based on the vandal's past behavior, that he might be showing up in the cemetery this week. When nothing happened on Friday, the suspect's usual day, he had let his guard down. Coupled with his preoccupation with Violet's lessons, he hadn't seriously considered their quarry might make an appearance tonight.

"What's she talking about?" asked Brad.

"The homicide case I'm working for County," he said. "Our suspect is in the cemetery right now."

Mitch took off at a slow jog, conserving his energy. He was in a hurry, but he didn't want to arrive completely winded and incapable of defending himself in a physical confrontation with his suspect if necessary. Brad ran right along behind him.

Mitch heard him speaking into his portable radio as he relayed their grid location and intentions to the rest of the team. He overheard Brad advising the shift they were responding to a 901, which left him momentarily confused. A 901 was a traffic accident according to standard radio codes. Had Brad forgotten and made a mistake? If he had, it was an odd mistake to make. How often did people crash their cars in the middle of a cemetery? He decided the code must have a different meaning in Dasan's Terrace than in the rest of Sacramento County. Mitch made a mental note to review the training manual he had been given – and so far completely ignored – at the next opportune moment. He had assumed he knew everything in it already, but what other idiosyncrasies of his current assignment was he missing out on?

Mitch tucked the thought away for later. Right now, he needed to focus on not tripping and falling in the mud.

Brad Kodama was in better shape than Mitch, and as soon as he finished his radio broadcast, he put on a small burst of speed to catch up. Mitch noted that as soon as Brad pulled even with him, the other officer slowed to match his pace. It was the smart move. Brad might have been able to get to the vandal's location faster without Mitch, but the officer that planned to live to see tomorrow did not make a habit of leaving his partners behind.

It took a little over ten minutes of jogging interspersed with fast walking to reach the northwest corner of the property. Rain had pelted the entire county in brief but torrential bursts the night before, and the still wet ground dragged at their boots as they ran, slowing them and causing them to work harder in their efforts at haste. When they arrived at the gate leading into the older section of the grounds, Mitch could see a newly violated grave site torn up beside the other already vandalized locations.

A trail of newly disturbed earth marred the ground from the recently excavated grave, leaving an easy-to-follow path that led through the bars of the security fence and away in an easterly direction. Mitch didn't waste time trying to unlock the gate to inspect the damage, he simply veered to follow the dirt tracks.

The lighting in this portion of the cemetery was poor, and both men had their flashlights out as they ran to avoid tripping over or stepping into unexpected obstacles. Mitch played the beam of his light ahead of him, illuminating the direction of the path they followed. He worried it might turn suddenly or, worse yet, stop completely, leaving them with no way to continue pursuing their quarry.

He needn't have worried. As the light of his flashlight peeled away the shadows in their way, he spotted two figures in the distance. They were walking away from the running officers, moving at a leisurely pace through the night-shrouded graveyard. The silhouettes of the two people looked like they belonged to an adult and a child, the shorter figure barely reaching the level of the taller subject's chest. Neither appeared to have a flashlight or any other source of illumination other than the limited city glow from nearby Rancho Cordova and the twinkling stars overhead. As the beam of Mitch's flashlight touched them, the smaller figure turned to search for the source of the unexpected light.

"Stop! Police!" Mitch shouted.

Despite his best efforts to conserve his energy earlier, he was breathing hard from his run across the cemetery, and the command was uttered with less force than he had hoped. He slowed to a walk but continued to move forward, drawing his duty pistol as he attempted to close the distance between himself and the two subjects. Following Mitch's lead, Brad also slowed and removed his weapon from its holster.

The shorter figure stopped, waiting for the officers to move closer. The larger subject took a few more shuffling paces forward before noticing his partner was no longer at his side. The taller figure paused, turned around, then moved to stand directly behind his smaller companion.

Mitch played his light over the pair of trespassers, trying to keep them in his sight. He did not see any weapons, but he knew that situation could change in a heartbeat. The shorter one raised a hand to shield his eyes from the glare, while the larger figure did not move. Shuffling closer, Mitch got his first good look at the pair, and he did not like what he found.

Not at all.

The shorter figure was male, but he was not a child. Mitch saw red hair and a pale white face belonging to a young man in his late teens or early twenties. Towering over the first man was someone – something? – standing over eight feet tall and staring back at Mitch with hollowed out sockets where its eyes should have been. In fact, all of its facial features were twisted, excavated versions of what should have been there, with no nose to speak of and only a rough gap where a mouth would have been on a normal human being. The hulking form wasn't human, that much was clear immediately.

The creature behind the red-haired man appeared to be covered in dirt from head to toe, with small cascades of rock and soil falling from its body with each movement. Mitch and Brad paced slowly and carefully toward the odd pair, weapons pointed in front of them.

"Don't try to run," Mitch ordered. "Both of you drop down on your knees and place your hands on top of your heads."

The young man laughed. "I'm not running anywhere," he said. "It's probably you guys that should be running."

Mitch dropped his finger from the ready position along the side of his pistol and rested it on the trigger. The words had definitely been a threat, but he was unsure what they meant. He still did not see any weapons, although the dirt-covered creature was large enough it probably did not need one. Mitch's mouth went dry, and the hair prickled on the back of his neck.

"I'm not going to tell you again. Get on your knees."

"Number Five, stop the police officers," said the redhead, glancing over his shoulder at the behemoth behind him. "Make sure they don't follow me. When you're done, come join me again." He turned his back on Mitch and Brad and began to walk away, moving through the cemetery grounds with the casual stroll of a daytime tourist.

Mitch pointed his weapon at the man's back. This was a murder suspect trying to get away and he briefly considered shooting him to stop him from escaping. The man was not an immediate threat however, and despite the need to apprehend him, Mitch couldn't bring himself to shoot an unarmed subject in the back.

"Stop!" he shouted, taking another step forward.

The creature reacted to his movement and stumbled into motion, trying to intercept Mitch. The thing moved slowly, awkwardly, but it was so large, Mitch knew it could do a lot of damage if he let it get its hands on him. As it lumbered in his direction, Mitch made another unpleasant observation. The thing wasn't covered in dirt as he had first thought. The entire creature *was* dirt. The missing earth from the desecrated grave site had somehow been shaped and brought to life by the young man disappearing in the distance, and the hulking, animated result was right now bearing down on him like a sentient avalanche of debris.

"Stop!" Mitch shouted again, this time at the creature. It continued to rush forward, picking up speed.

Mitch and Brad fired. Multiple rounds struck the monster, punching holes in the packed earth of its body and causing small puffs of dirt to erupt where the bullets made contact. The metal projectiles had no noticeable effect on the creature's behavior.

The thing charged directly at Mitch, swinging a massive arm in an effort to bludgeon its target into submission. The attack was clumsy, giving Mitch barely enough time to dodge to the side and roll out of the way. The creature staggered forward several more steps, its massive bulk dragging it twenty more feet through the cemetery before it could halt its charge and turn back around. It oriented again on Mitch. It appeared to be ignoring Brad for the moment and focusing its energies on one opponent at a time.

Mitch jumped to his feet, raised his gun, and fired another volley of shots at the creature. He expended round after round until the slide of his pistol locked back, announcing he had run out of bullets. He ejected the spent magazine and searched his belt for a moment, locating the magazine he kept loaded with silver ammunition. He launched another flurry of gunfire, but the specialized bullets had as little effect on the animated dirt creature as the lead ones had.

Seeing Mitch's futile assault, Brad holstered his weapon and reached over his shoulder to draw his katana. The towering behemoth leaned forward in preparation for a second charge against Mitch when Brad slipped silently behind it. He swung his blade in a vicious downward arc that slashed the monster across the side of its neck. There was a high-pitched ringing noise, and a spark flashed as the edge of Brad's sword struck something too hard to cut through, then rebounded away. The blade caused no more damage than the guns. The creature seemed invulnerable to the only tools the two officers had to work with.

The thing opened its mouth and roared at Mitch in obvious rage, though no actual sounds came from the creature. It lurched toward him, still uttering its silent scream. Bullets were ineffective and Brad's sword had been less than useless, so Mitch decided to try something more direct. He stepped into the charge and kicked, driving the heel of his boot into the creature's chest.

The monster never slowed. Mitch's foot made contact with the mass of rushing rock and earth, and it felt like he had kicked a brick wall. An oncoming brick wall. The impact threw him onto his back, forcing him to roll aside at the last instant to avoid being trampled by the rampaging creature.

It again rushed past him, unable to adjust quickly enough to follow Mitch's roll. The creature halted and turned. From his hands and knees, Mitch let his vision blur slightly, using the trick Violet had taught him to see magic more clearly. He wanted a better idea of what he was fighting. Was it alive? Maybe even sentient? If he could only see what drove the creature, he might have an idea how to stop it.

He peered into the massive form, seeking a glimpse of the thing's source of power. He found nothing. Well, no, not exactly nothing. Mitch did see something flickering, barely visible along the rough surface of the earthen monster. A black, shimmering aura surrounded the creature, holding it together and directing its movements. The monster was not alive, it was nothing more than it appeared: a walking pile of grave dirt. It was the oily magic surrounding it that kept it on its feet, kept it moving. Kept it attacking.

Mitch pushed to his feet and prepared to meet yet another charge. As the creature turned its head, tracking him with those hollow eye sockets, Mitch wondered if he could disrupt the magic that animated the thing. He knew he could touch the ambient magic in the air around him. He could even gather it and disperse it if he concentrated hard enough. Maybe he could physically draw away the magic animating the dirt giant, reducing it back to its component elements.

Nothing else was working, he told himself, so he might as well give this a try.

Before the lumbering horror could start its next attack, Mitch took the initiative. He bolted forward. He ran directly at the towering horror and slapped his open hands against its enormous chest. Curling his fingers like claws, he scraped along the dirt surface of the creature's torso, trying to gather the black magic flickering at the edges. His fingers slipped through the dark aura like he was trying to grab at wisps of fog. He couldn't find any purchase against the animating magic, and he came away with nothing more than grave dirt under his fingernails.

The attempt took only a moment, but in that moment, Mitch was stationary in front of the creature for too long. The monster took that opportunity to strike. An arm the size of a small tree trunk swept through the air. Mitch did not see the attack coming, only felt the impact across the left side of his skull. The world swam crazily, and darkness swooped in from the corners of his vision.

He did not think he passed out, but his next memory was of lying on his back, staring up at the stars as they spun sickeningly counterclockwise in the sky. The world bucked and heaved beneath him and he felt a sudden urge to throw up.

The creature stepped into Mitch's view, eclipsing the stars as it gazed down at him with its vacant eye holes. Mitch could not see it clearly, his vision remained fuzzy, but he recognized that he was moments away from his own death if he could not force himself to move. He managed to roll onto his stomach but that was as far as he got before the dizziness drove him back into immobility.

"Hey! Number Five!"

Mitch heard the voice. It was Brad, trying to distract the monster from its chosen prey. He turned his head to look in the direction from which the shout had come. The effort made his stomach leap into his mouth. Brad was waving his arms in an attempt to gain the giant's attention.

"Number Five. You're done here. You stopped us from going after your master. Now follow his orders and go find him."

Mitch waited for the creature's foot to cave in the back of his head. Seconds ticked by but the killing blow did not land. Mitch pushed himself to his hands and knees, still feeling as weak as a newborn kitten but not wanting to die without putting up as much of a fight as he could manage.

"Hey, look. We're done. No one is going to follow you if you leave. We are both staying right here. I promise."

Brad dropped the katana in his hand, letting it fall to the ground. Then he sat down beside the fallen blade, tucking his knees to his chest and wrapping his arms around his legs as if he were a tourist settling onto a blanket to enjoy a picnic. His posture demonstrated he intended to stay exactly where he was for as long as it took for the monster to realize he was telling the truth.

Mitch collapsed back onto his chest. It was not an attempt to emulate Brad's surrender, he simply had no strength left in his body. The brutal dizziness had also returned, ending any hopes of remaining off the ground, much less managing to lever himself upright.

"Not following," he gasped.

To his relief, Mitch heard the creature moving away, its massive blunt feet dragging along the grass and soil as it shuffled off in the direction the red-haired man had gone.

A thought flashed through his brain as he listened to the footsteps retreating into the distance: *should I go after it?* That thought was followed immediately with: *Oh God, I think I'm going to puke.*

Brad clambered to his hands and knees and crawled to Mitch to check on him.

"Are you alright?" he asked, helping Mitch roll onto his back so he could examine his face.

"No. Head hurts. A lot."

"I'll bet it does," agreed Brad. "You took a pretty good shot to the melon, partner. I would not be surprised to find out you are sporting a nasty concussion right now."

Mitch stared up at the stars swirling in mad circles overhead, then closed his eyes to shut the image out.

"Yup. Probably right," he agreed. "What the hell was that thing? Ever seen one before?"

"No," Brad admitted. "Nothing exactly like that. It looked like maybe an earth elemental, or a golem of some sort."

Mitch opened his eyes wide in surprise, then immediately regretted it. He raised a hand to his aching head as a memory, previously lodged far back in his brain, was teased forward by Brad's comment.

"A what?" he asked Brad.

"Earth elemental," Brad repeated.

"No, the other thing."

"Golem. I've read a little about them. Most of the time they're clay, but they can be dirt, wood, or pretty much anything that will hold together in a solid form."

Mitch began to laugh. He stopped when he tasted bile at the back of his throat. He coughed and spat to clear his mouth.

"Golem," Mitch muttered. "Not Gollum."

"What are you talking about?" asked Brad. "Are you hallucinating? Do you know where you are?"

Mitch nodded. The motion hurt his head, so he stopped. "The professor isn't crazy. He knows exactly what's going on. I need to talk to him."

"Who? What professor?"

Brad quickly gave up trying to make sense of Mitch's mumbling and keyed his radio mic, asking for back up and medical assistance.

The world swam around Mitch, and his vision narrowed to a shrinking tunnel of light.

"Need to talk to him," he whispered, his words slurring. "But first, I think I'm going to pass out."

CHAPTER 18

Mitch woke in bed. It wasn't his bed. In fact, it wasn't any bed with which he was familiar. He shifted under the thin, scratchy sheets and decided it wasn't a terribly comfortable bed either. He opened his eyes and tried to sit up. The room pitched around him, and his stomach twisted in reaction to the unsteady image. He let his head fall back into the pillow, too dizzy to do anything else. Above him, white acoustic ceiling tiles layered the ceiling and emergency sprinkler heads poked through into the room every eight feet or so.

In front of Mitch, a television hung on the wall. The screen was currently off, showing only a black reflective surface mirroring a blurry image of Mitch surrounded by white sheets. The room was silent, although the muffled echo of voices reached him from somewhere on the other side of a closed door.

A metal rail ran the length of Mitch's bed along the left side. The railing and the polished white, laminate floor beneath him were the final clues he needed to decide that he was in a hospital. He attempted again to sit up, and although the physical reaction wasn't as bad as the first attempt, the walls and ceiling still swam in sickening waves and whorls. He paused, letting the world settle. Moving his head slowly so as not to set the room spinning once more, he took in his surroundings. Opposite the door, three chairs lined the wall in a tight row, armrest touching armrest. In the center chair, sat Brad, his elbow propped on the arm of the chair and his head resting in his hand. Mitch heard a soft snoring coming from the officer as Brad's chest slowly rose and fell in the breathing rhythm of deep sleep.

Brad still wore his uniform, Mitch noted. Mitch himself was now adorned in a thin cotton gown that wrapped around his torso and tied together at his right hip and under his armpit. The hem of the gown stretched past his hips to a few inches below his knees. Shifting to get a better look at Brad, Mitch felt something pull at the back of his right hand. He glanced down to find a plastic tube taped to the skin of his hand where, he assumed, a needle had been placed into a vein. The tube trailed away from his hand, across the bed, and up to a bag of clear liquid hanging from a metal hook erected on a four-wheeled post.

If there had been any doubt in his mind before, he was now absolutely certain he was in the hospital.

"Brad," Mitch croaked. His throat closed and he was forced to swallow several times to clear the thick, dry lump that had formed there. This led to a brief coughing fit. "Brad," he said again when the fit passed.

Brad's head slipped from his hand and he jerked awake. His eyes shifted left and right as he tried to orient himself and recall where he was. His gaze landed on Mitch, and Mitch could see memory of the situation come rushing back as the groggy officer pushed to his feet and hurried over to Mitch's bedside.

"You're awake. Good."

Brad grabbed what looked like a video game joystick hanging from a cord beside Mitch's pillow. He pushed the button on the end of the handle several times before letting go.

"When the ambulance brought you in, they couldn't wake you up. The doctors didn't know if you would eventually wake on your own or if you were going to slip into a coma. That thing in the graveyard clobbered you good. Nothing broken in that hard skull of yours, but you've got a nasty concussion and some swelling."

There was no further time for Brad to talk or for Mitch to ask questions. A slender woman in hospital scrubs entered the room. She looked to be of Indian descent, with black hair tied back into a severe bun, and alert dark eyes that crinkled around the corners when she smiled at the sight of Mitch sitting up.

"Officer Loman, I'm Doctor Pandey. I'm the attending physician on this floor. I must say that I'm very happy and relieved to see you awake. The bruising on your brain was serious and if you didn't wake up on your own by tonight, we were contemplating opening you up and relieving the pressure. I think we are safely past that option now. How are you feeling?"

"Like the aftermath of a car crash," he said. "And I don't mean I was in a car crash, I mean I *am* the car crash. Can I get some water? My mouth is really dry."

"Of course."

Doctor Pandey retrieved a gray, plastic pitcher and a paper cup from somewhere behind Mitch's head. She filled the cup with water from the pitcher and handed it to him. He drank slowly, making sure his stomach wasn't going to reject the offering before swallowing a little more. The liquid stayed down, but only barely.

"What's the last thing you remember from last night?"

"Last night?" Mitch echoed. "What time is it?"

"It's almost noon, Mr. Loman. On Sunday."

"Mitch. Call me Mitch, please," he said as he attempted to digest the information he had received.

Sunday, he marveled. He had lost over twelve hours lying in this bed unconscious.

"Can you answer my question?" the doctor said. "What do you remember?"

"I remember getting sucker punched by a right hook I was too slow to avoid." Mitch didn't elaborate. He didn't think telling the doctor he had gotten knocked out by a dirt golem in the middle of a cemetery would do much for her opinion of his mental health. "I don't remember anything after that until I woke up here."

"Good. You recall up to the moment of the injury, so there doesn't seem to be any memory loss. That's a good sign. Does your head hurt? Dizziness? Nausea?"

"Yes, ma'am. All of the above."

"Okay. I'm going to recommend that you stay with us at least until tomorrow so we can keep a close eye on you. I think you're probably going to be fine, but you're not completely out of the woods yet. If there are any complications from the concussion, I want you where we can get to you quickly. Does that sound all right?"

"I'd rather go home," said Mitch. "I'm not a fan of hospitals, and I think I'll feel better sleeping in my own bed."

"I can't force you to stay, Mitch," the doctor told him. "But I highly recommend against leaving."

"Well, if you can't force me…"

"I can," interrupted Brad. "The chief told me if I let you try to leave here against the recommendations of the doctor, he's going to fire your ass and write me up for insubordination. I don't think he was kidding. At least, I'm not going to take that chance. If you try to get out of that bed, I'm handcuffing you to the railing."

Doctor Pandey gave Mitch another little smile. "So, you're staying with us. Wonderful. I will let the nurses know to check in on you every half hour. If you decide to leave before tomorrow morning, I will instruct one of the staff to call Chief…" The doctor glanced toward Brad.

"Jefferson," he supplied.

"To call Chief Jefferson and inform him of your decision to go home against my recommendations. Does that sound acceptable to you?"

Mitch glared at Brad, but the expression made his head start to pound. He flopped back onto his pillow. "Sounds great, doc. Tomorrow morning it is."

"In the meantime, try to stay awake for the next few hours while we keep an eye on that bruising. I know it's not very exciting around here, but I'd rather you didn't fall back asleep until I'm comfortable the swelling under your skull is subsiding. Are you hungry?"

Mitch thought about the question for a moment. His stomach felt more settled since drinking a little water and he realized that he hadn't eaten anything since five o'clock the previous evening.

"Yeah. I could eat."

"I'll let someone know to bring you a lunch. They have chicken breast today and corn on the side. It's not bad." The doctor chuckled. She had a pleasant laugh, the kind that put people immediately at ease, Mitch thought. "It's not good, either, but it's not bad."

A little over an hour later, Mitch lay with his eyes closed, the head of the bed raised to an almost seated position. He wasn't asleep, he was simply resting as he listened to a station on the radio in his room playing nineties pop selections. His lunch had gone down easily and seemed content to remain in his stomach. A petite, energetic girl who didn't seem old enough to be out of high school, much less working with patients in a hospital, had brought his food and cleaned up his dishes when he announced he was finished. The bubbly nurse had white-blond hair as pale as the chief's administrative assistant's. Unlike Dot's, however, the nurse's hair color was not natural; the pale shade belied by her full dark eyebrows and deep, chocolate brown eyes. She introduced herself as Amanda and flirted casually with Mitch as she helped him out of the bed to use the bathroom after his meal. She told him how handsome she thought he was and that she wished for the good old days when the hospital dressing gowns were always flying open in the back.

Before leaving, she dimmed the lights in the room after Mitch complained of a slight sensitivity to the bright overhead bulbs. His headache subsided considerably in the lowered lighting.

Out of boredom, Mitch tried watching television, but the flickering images on the screen hurt his eyes and made him dizzy. He experienced the same result flipping through the pages of a magazine a few minutes later.

The radio proved the perfect compromise. It offered a little distraction to keep his mind busy and awake, while not causing him any further discomfort.

Brad Kodama remained in the room despite Mitch's insistence that he should go home and go to bed. Brad wasn't much company at the moment, however. After assuring Mitch that he would stay and help him stay awake as long as necessary, Brad had curled back up in his prior position in the chair and promptly fallen asleep. Mitch let him doze, content to sit and listen to the music.

While he listened to Kiss Me, by Six Pence None The Richer, on the radio, the door to his room swung open. Mitch heard the slight creak of the hinges and the sound of footsteps entering. Opening his eyes a bare crack, he expected to find the tiny blond nurse returning for her thirty-minute check-in. Instead, he spied Chief Jefferson strolling into the room.

Mitch shifted forward and sat straighter when he saw the chief. The motion made his head throb, and his vision blurred for a moment. He blinked, eyes watering with pain, and tried to bring the room back into focus. As he peered toward the chief, the man's face and form began to shimmer. A veil seemed to part in front of Chief Jefferson and in his place, Mitch saw a skinny black youth who appeared to be barely into his mid-teens. The boy had the same broad features and pale smokey eyes as the chief but appeared at least twenty years his junior.

The dizziness intensified and for a moment, Mitch feared he was about to lose his lunch. He closed his eyes to let his head and stomach calm down, and when he opened them again, the boy was gone. Only Chief Jefferson remained in the room.

"Hello, Mitch. Glad to see you're feeling better. Brad called me and let me know you were awake, so I thought I'd come by and see you for myself."

"Hi, Chief… Um, Simon. Thanks for coming."

"What did the doctors say?"

"Doctor Pandey thinks I'm going to be fine but wants to keep me here under observation for another day. I'd rather go home, but it sounds like you would rather I followed her directions. You weren't really going to fire me, were you?"

The chief's face screwed up into a puzzled expression.

"How hard did you get hit?" he asked. "What are you talking about?"

"Brad told me what you said to him, that if he let me go against the doctor's recommendation you would fire me, and then write him up for not keeping me here."

Brad began to laugh softly in his chair. His eyes remained closed, but it was obvious he was now awake and listening in on the conversation.

"I didn't tell him anything of the sort," said Simon. "But now that you mention it, I agree that you should stay until the doctor says it's safe to leave. In fact, I'm giving you a direct order to stay put. Enjoy the down time and the private room. It's one of the perks of working for Dasan's Terrace."

"What about the golem, and the Dirty Bandit?" asked Mitch.

"What about them? Whatever the Bandit was going to do, he's already done it. Another home was burglarized at one o'clock this morning. Fortunately, nobody was injured." Simon paused, then gestured at Mitch with a hand. "Sorry son. I should have said, no one *else* was injured. Anyway, there's nothing more to be done about it right now. The County detectives will have to deal with the aftermath. Brad filled me in on the information he had, and I agree that it sounds like a golem."

"I think I may have a lead."

"You know who the Dirty Bandit is?"

"No, not the bandit. But I may have information about the golem. A professor, a guy named Solomon something, I don't remember his last name. He called the tip line and reported he knew something about the golem. I ignored it because I thought he was a crank, but now I think he might actually have information we need."

"Okay. Give me his contact information and I'll pass it along to the detectives. This is their case after all, not yours."

Mitch felt his heart sink. After only a week, he had already been kicked off the case.

"You're pulling me off this investigation? What did I do wrong?"

Simon shook his head, looking confused again. "Pulling you off what investigation? Since when were you working it?"

It was Mitch's turn to look baffled. "The Dirty Bandit," he explained. "I was able to link our grave vandalisms to the homicide that the County was working. I asked Chief Delaney if I could work the case from our end and he said yes. He also said he was going to tell you what I was doing. I guess he forgot to mention it to you."

"Delaney?" asked Brad, suddenly fully alert in his chair.

The chief's face hardened, but he didn't appear upset. Mitch thought it looked more like he had come to an uncomfortable realization or conclusion. Simon turned to face Brad.

"Brad, why don't you head out. Your shift is over and it's time for you to get home. I appreciate you looking out for Mitch while we waited for him to regain consciousness. Go get some sleep."

"You sure, chief? I don't mind staying a little longer."

Simon nodded. "Go home. Get some sleep."

"And thank you," added Mitch. "Thank you for saving my life."

"I wouldn't go that far," said Brad with a shrug. "I called an ambulance and sat with you for a while."

"No, I mean before that. You stopped the golem from finishing me off. He was about to stomp me into a bloody puddle before you convinced him to leave."

"Oh, that. That was no big deal. You would have done the same for me."

Mitch shook his head. "Maybe. Maybe if I had been smart enough to think of it, which I'm not sure I would have. Anyway, thank you. I owe you one."

"I'm going to hold you to that," said Brad. Then he waved at the chief. "Alright, I'm going. Good night, or rather, afternoon."

The chief walked with Brad to the door and ushered him into the hallway. When the officer was gone, he closed the door behind him and turned to face Mitch. He paused for a long moment, clasping his hands together in front of his chest as he considered what he wanted to say.

"I didn't think that I would be the one to have to tell you this," he began. "In fact, I thought you already knew, but it has suddenly become clear to me that you don't."

"Sir?" asked Mitch.

"Assistant Chief Delaney is dead, son."

"Oh my god." Mitch was stunned by the news. He had spoken with the man only last week. "What happened?"

"He interrupted a robbery at a convenience store. He was shot and killed at the scene."

"I didn't hear anything about that. Nobody said anything in briefing. When did it happen?"

"1992."

"I … I … What?!"

Simon stared at Mitch for a long moment, disbelief warring with the urge to laugh. “You really didn’t know?” he asked.

Mitch didn’t respond. He couldn’t seem to make his mouth work properly, so he settled for shaking his head.

“How is that possible? I thought the first day you met him, during our interview, that you figured it out. You even shook his hand. Well, tell it to Sweeney! When Dot and I saw you physically touch him, that was the moment that I decided I was going to hire you. We see him all the time, but none of us has ever actually touched him. And you truly did not realize he was a ghost when you shook his hand?”

Mitch gave another mute shake of his head.

“What was your first reaction when you met Tim? Chief Delaney?”

“I didn’t like him,” said Mitch, honestly. “He had a cold hand, and I immediately didn’t like him. Which is strange now that I think about it because I don’t usually feel that negatively about someone I just met.”

Simon sidled over to the bed and peered down at Mitch. “That was a little voice in the back of your mind telling you something was wrong with the man. I saw the look Tim gave you. He didn’t like you much either. I think he realized what you were before the rest of us figured it out.”

“An exorcist?” Mitch asked.

“Exactly. To a ghost, an exorcist is damn near the scariest thing you can encounter. There isn’t much that can a hurt a spirit, but you could be a real threat.”

Mitch rubbed a hand over his cheek. A light stubble growing there scratched against his palm. “Oh, man. I feel like a complete idiot. The cold hands and the fact I never heard him come into the room were hints, but the minute I saw him wearing that old uniform I should have figured it out."

"Don't beat yourself up over it. I suggest you don't rely on anything he tells you, though. He does not actually work for Dasan's Terrace. He is merely a … guest, I suppose you would say. Regarding the Dirty Bandit, however, since you've already been working the case and because it does seem to fall directly into our particular jurisdiction, you can stay on it. We would probably have to take it over as soon as I reported the more supernatural elements to the Sheriff anyway. This way, I can tell him that we're already investigating and have a few leads. You did say that you have a lead?"

"One. I need to call and set up an interview."

Mitch pulled the sheets aside and tried to climb out of the bed. Simon placed a hand on his shoulder and eased him back onto the pillow.

"Tomorrow is soon enough for all that. For today, you need to rest and heal. You can go home as soon as the doctor says it's safe for you to leave."

"Yes, sir."

"I'm glad you're feeling better, Mitch. Anything I can do for you before I go?"

"I only have one more question, sir. I noticed that Dasan's Terrace has cameras on the fences around the property."

"We do, but the majority are on the south entry gates and around the administrative buildings. There are more on the east and west perimeter walls, but there aren't any cameras further back onto the grounds. We don't have any footage of your run in with the golem, for example. The cameras we do have are all hard wired internally due to the disturbing nature of a few of our visitors, and the servers are only accessible by me and anyone I allow inside the video room. We wouldn't want certain events to be viewed by anyone in the general public."

"Makes sense," Mitch agreed. "How is the video quality?"

"Best that money can buy. I put some serious research into this system before buying it."

"Great. I was hoping you might let me review any video taken last night. Our suspect may have left the cemetery by way of the south gates and I'm hoping one of the cameras got a decent picture of him. Is that possible?"

"Of course. When do you want to review it?"

"Maybe, I could come in tonight?" Mitch suggested.

Simon laughed and wagged a scolding finger at Mitch.

"I appreciate your tenacity, but you're not leaving this bed before tomorrow morning. Come see me Monday in the afternoon and you can look through the video files."

The suite door swung open at that moment, and the petite floor nurse wandered into the room. She smiled at the chief and waved a cheery greeting to Mitch.

"Time to check on our patient," she said. "I hope I'm not interrupting anything important."

"No," said Simon. "I was just leaving. Mitch has promised to be on his best behavior today. If he gives you any problems, you have my permission to tie him down to the bed."

"Don't give him any ideas," the nurse warned Simon as she pulled down a blood pressure cuff from one of the multiple machines situated behind Mitch's bed. "Some of our patients like that sort of stuff. Actually, some of the nurses do, too." She winked at Mitch and gave him a smile that was more than merely friendly.

Mitch felt a warmth growing in his cheeks.

"I can see that you are in very capable hands," said the chief. "I'll see myself out."

CHAPTER 19

After a boring day, another bland meal of hospital food, and a fitful night's sleep, Mitch was approved to go home the next morning. The doctor went through one last round of tests on him, including syphoning off enough blood that Mitch began to worry he might pass out in the parking lot. Still, he was pronounced fit to leave the hospital. She signed his release documents with a final directive that he contact the hospital immediately if he experienced further dizziness, difficulty with his vision, or any other of an extensive list of possible symptoms. Mitch promised he would.

His uniform had been cut off of him in the cemetery where the paramedics found him, and his street clothes were still secured in his locker at the police department. Before driving to the hospital to check on Mitch's condition, Brad had taken all his partner's gear and equipment and locked it in his own locker to keep it safe. He didn't know Mitch's combination so could not gather up his street clothes for him. Fortunately, Brad had at least thought to bring the contents of Mitch's pockets to him, including his house keys, wallet, and cell phone.

While the nurses entered his release paperwork into their computers, Mitch mentally prepared himself for a ride home in a taxi while wearing the ridiculous cotton hospital gown they had provided him during his convalescence. A man in a see-through gown probably wouldn't be the strangest thing to ever crawl into the back of a taxicab, he was certain, but he wasn't looking forward to the embarrassing adventure, either.

Maybe one day, this would be an entertaining story to tell friends at a party. One day. Far, far off in the future.

To his immense surprise and relief, as the staff gave him the green light to leave the hospital, Violet arrived, bursting into his room with her usual flair for a dramatic entrance.

This morning, she wore the pale blue jeans she seemed to favor for everyday wear with a brown, yellow, and orange knit sweater. On her feet, she had opted for ankle high, suede boots, with heavy heels that clacked loudly on the polished hospital floors. He was happy to see she had skipped the black makeup and instead selected a subdued eyeliner and pale pink lipstick. Violet clumped noisily over to Mitch's bed, placed a hand on his shoulder and gave him a peck on the cheek.

She handed him a paper bag containing a shirt, sweatshirt, clean underwear, socks, jeans and a pair of sneakers. Mitch recognized all of the clothing she carried as having been in his closet or dresser drawers until recently. He thanked Violet, and pointedly did not ask the questions swirling in his head.

How do you know where I live? and *How did you get into my locked house?* were only relevant queries if the person being asked was a normal human being. Violet was not that person.

She offered him a ride home as well, and he gratefully accepted.

Mitch climbed out of his bed, reached into the bag and fished out the underwear Violet had brought. She smiled and pointed at the briefs in his hand.

"I brought you the powder blue ones," she said. "I thought they would look good on you."

"Thanks," Mitch told her. "Do you mind stepping out of the room for a moment so I can get dressed?"

Violet gave him a once over, letting her eyes trail down from his head to his bare feet, then back. "You sure I shouldn't stay here? Keep an eye on you? For your own good, of course. I could make sure you don't get dizzy and suddenly fall over."

"Very kind of you to offer, but I'm fine." He waved at her with a shooing motion.

"Spoil sport," she muttered, then walked out of the room. She paused before the door closed and peeked back in. "Sure you don't need help?"

"Go," Mitch growled.

As soon as the door clicked shut, Mitch ditched the medical gown, pulled the underwear on and slipped into his jeans. Before he could grab his shirt from the bag, Violet was already back in the room.

"Dressed yet?" she asked breezily.

"What the hell? I barely had time to get my pants on."

"Oh, stop being such a prude. What do you think I'm going to see that I haven't seen before?"

"Would you still feel the same way if it was you standing here without your shirt on?" Mitch asked her.

In response, Violet grabbed the hem of her sweater and pulled it up far enough to reveal her bare midriff and a hint of something red and lacy further up. "Should we find out?" she said. A smirk pulled at a corner of her mouth.

Mitch paused, curious how far she was going to take this dare. Then he gestured for her to put the sweater back on. "As much as I want to see more, this isn't the place for 'show me yours and I'll show you mine.' Besides, I really want to get out of this hospital and go home."

"Okay, but you're missing out." The look on Violet's face was one of genuine disappointment.

Mitched finished dressing, slipped his personal items into his pockets and gestured toward the door. "Shall we get out of here?"

A few minutes later they were in the parking lot and Mitch was climbing into the passenger seat of Violet's Toyota Tundra.

"I didn't expect a truck," he admitted as he fastened his seat belt.

"Is there a problem? Girls can't have trucks?"

"You can drive anything you want. I just hadn't pegged you as someone who drove a truck. I figured maybe you'd have … I don't know…"

"A broom?" Violet suggested, but she was laughing as she said it.

"Yes. That would have been far more appropriate. I can see me riding behind you on it, hanging onto you so I don't fall off."

"Would that be so bad?"

"What? Being behind you and wrapping my arms around your waist? No. I don't think that would be bad at all. Quite nice, actually."

Violet smiled and drove out of the parking lot.

"How did you know I was in the hospital and needed clothes?"

"Alyssandra told me you got hurt. She saw the whole thing happen."

"What?" exclaimed Mitch. "She was there and didn't even bother to help when it went sideways?"

Violet took a slow breath then blew it out. "The agreement we have with your chief is the police do not help or hinder us in any way. In return, we do the same. Favors can be obtained, but they come at a price so the balance between us stays neutral. That's why Alyssandra was so upset when she found out I had been talking to you before we had negotiated a price for helping you."

"So, if that thing had killed me, nobody would have lifted a finger to help."

Violet turned to look Mitch in the eye. The guilt in her expression was clear.

"Alyssandra would not help you for any reason. I didn't know what was happening or I would have stepped in. I like you, Mitch. I want…" she stopped before she could say what she was thinking. "If you had been killed because Alyssandra stood there and watched without helping, I would have left the coven. Trading favors is one thing, but letting someone die because you aren't directly benefitting is cowardly and evil."

Mitch let the topic drop. He was upset at learning that Alyssandra had been present and done nothing while the golem caved in his skull, but the actions of the coven leader were not Violet's fault.

"And the clothes?" he asked instead.

"Chief Jefferson called me to ask about the golem. He was hoping I could offer some insight on how to stop it. Unfortunately, I don't know anything about golems. I don't know how to make one or unmake one. While we were talking, I asked about you. He said you were being held an extra day so the doctors could be sure there was no permanent damage, and that you were getting out this morning. He also mentioned they had to cut up your uniform and you might need clothes when you checked out. I volunteered to bring you clothing and get you home."

"I hope the department is going to reimburse me for the uniform. I only have three, and they aren't cheap. I also guess I owe you a debt for coming to get me. What do you want?"

Violet shook her head solemnly. "This isn't a favor you have to pay back. This is my payment on Alyssandra's debt for letting you get hurt. We're even. Alyssandra may owe you a bit more, though. The heartless bitch sent you after the golem in the first place."

"Speaking of which, why did she help me find the golem?"

"Help you?" Violet shook her head in mild disbelief. "You're so nice. You do things to help people and you assume others' motivations are as straightforward as yours. I don't believe you're real half the time. No, she wasn't helping you, Mitch. She was using you. The magician creating the golems is drawing power from the cemetery to make his monsters. He's screwing up the patterns of force in the area that our coven uses. Whenever he accesses the magic to create a golem, some of our … more delicate spells break down and we have to reestablish them. That takes time and effort. Getting rid of the golems is to the coven's benefit, and Alyssandra was trying to get you to stop him so we wouldn't need to."

Mitch sat quietly, taking in the new information. He gazed out the window to his right and watched the dirt shoulder and chain link fencing along Highway 99 blur past in a steady stream of gray and brown. Pressing his forehead against the side window, he took a moment to enjoy the coolness of the glass against his skin. The dizziness and nausea had mostly passed, but he still had a headache that wouldn't completely go away.

"If you and Alyssandra owe me a favor," he said, still leaning against the window, "would you be willing to answer a few questions to alleviate the coven's debt to me?"

"Ask away," Violet said immediately. "If I can, I'll answer."

"I have a personal issue that maybe you can help me with. As an exorcist, I mean. I have a ghost question."

"Is it about Denny?"

"How did you…?" Mitch stared in shocked surprise, unable to finish the question.

Violet glanced at him and offered a sympathetic smile. "Dot came to me. We talked about you and about your son for quite a while. I wasn't really much help. The only thing I can do is exorcise him from the cemetery, but I don't think that's what you want. Dot has another idea. Not really a plan, but a suggestion that may help. I'll let her talk to you about it since it's her idea and she's much better at these things than I am."

"You can exorcise him?" Mitch asked. "You can set him free?"

"No, Mitch!" Violet said sharply. Her expression turned hard; her jaw clenched, and she pressed her lips tightly together. "Those are not the same thing. I can't help Denny move on from this world. I'm an exorcist. All I can do is sever his ties to his body and disperse his spirit. That would destroy him. Exactly like you did with Harold, but this time it would be a human soul erased from existence and not a fading echo. I won't do that. I won't do that to Denny, and I won't do that to you."

As the meaning of the exorcism sank in, Mitch was horrified at what he had been about to ask. He might have unwittingly been responsible for the death of his own son if Violet had agreed. A true death this time, with no hope of an afterlife. The complete removal of his child's presence from the universe.

"No. That's not what I want, either. I didn't understand what it is that you do. What *we* do."

"I know. That's why I'm here. To guide you not only in how to use your gift, but to understand exactly what it means."

Mitch pressed his head to the window again. Several minutes passed in silence as he thought about Denny, and Dot, and Violet. Violet drove on, giving Mitch his privacy and waiting for him to be ready to talk again. She seemed content to let him have the space he needed right now. Finally, he sat up and looked at her.

"You and Dot talked about me?"

"She needed some guidance and wanted someone to bounce off a few ideas. She feels guilty that she didn't realize sooner who your son is."

Mitch nodded. "I see. You know, for someone I only met a month ago, you seem to know everything there is to know about me, and I know next to nothing about you. That doesn't seem quite fair, does it?"

"What would you like to know? My life is an open book."

"Where did you grow up? What is your family like? Do you have kids? Are you married? What do you do for a living when you aren't haunting my cemetery? Things like that."

"So, you want the life story in a nutshell," Violet said. "Okay. Down and dirty, here it is. I was born on the east coast.

Oriskany, in New York. Middle class family. My parents were still married, and I had two brothers, both younger than me."

Mitch closed his mouth, and his heart began to race. He heard the hollow emptiness in her words and was all too familiar with what it meant. He had heard people speak like this before, usually people recounting loss while trying not to let old emotions overtake them. Violet's tone was too calm and too matter of fact, not like the happy reminiscence of family her words sounded like they should be. He also didn't like the past tense terms she used while mentioning her parents and brothers. It spoke of trouble that Violet might not want to relive. Trouble that Mitch might not have any business digging into.

Despite his reservations, Mitch remained silent as Violet continued talking.

"I met my first boyfriend when I was fifteen. I fell hard for him. We dated for about a year and a half. When I turned seventeen, I met my first ghost. Some friends and I went out drinking in a cute little wooded area near our school. I didn't know it at the time, but we picked a location that happened to be the site of a violent ambush during the American Revolutionary War. A lot of soldiers died there on both sides, and many of the bodies were never properly collected or buried. They were left to the scavengers and to rot in the sun.

"I was young and inexperienced so I'm not really sure if it was a full spirit or a poltergeist. I didn't know what to look for back then. Without fully understanding what I was doing, I ripped it apart when it approached us. Others saw me do it. Or rather, they saw my actions in the woods, although they couldn't see the spirit for themselves. Afterward, none of my friends wanted to believe we had actually run into a ghost, or that I had dispatched it with my bare hands, but it still made for a wonderful story. At school, they talked about the crazy girl running through the trees and fighting with imaginary monsters."

Violet smiled ruefully, but Mitch did not see any sign of amusement in her expression.

"They shared it like a campfire horror tale."

Violet's eyes had gone distant. She was no longer seeing the roadway in front of her. She was staring back at a moment in her youth, a time she clearly had not enjoyed.

"Someone must have heard the story, second-hand, third-hand, or on the millionth telling, but it reached the wrong ears. Someone understood what had happened, what I had done. They realized what it meant. Even if I didn't."

Violet glanced at Mitch. "I was seventeen," she repeated.

"I was at home one night. Liam, my boyfriend, was over at the house for dinner. Three witches broke in while we were sitting around the dining table. They slaughtered everyone in the house. Everyone except me. My brothers, my parents, and Liam, all killed while I watched. Then the three women grabbed me.

"That was when I met Alyssandra. She appeared in the house from out of nowhere and stopped the other three from taking me. She killed them with a spell before they could organize and turn their powers on her. She saved me. She later told me that she had been watching me for a couple of weeks, trying to find a way to approach me that wouldn't scare me off. When the witches broke into my house, she didn't realize what was happening until it was too late to help my family. She was only able to rescue me."

"Oh, my God. I'm so sorry, Violet. I'm sorry that happened to you. You were only a kid."

Violet shrugged, attempting to appear nonchalant, but the tightness in her jaw and the tension of her shoulders ruined the act.

"It happened a long time ago. Alyssandra saved me, not only from the other witches, but from myself. She gave me the knowledge I needed to keep me from self-destructing. She introduced me to her coven – she was only a member then – and petitioned them to allow me to join. She also introduced me to a warlock that understood what an exorcist was and could help me learn to properly use my powers. I owe her a great deal for that. Since I lost my real family, she has been the closest thing to a mother I have."

She reached across the cab of the truck and lightly rested a hand on Mitch's knee. The touch only lasted a moment before she placed her hand back on the steering wheel, but the warmth lingered on Mitch's leg for much longer.

"I want you to know how important Alyssandra is to me, so you understand what I mean when I say that I would have left the coven if she allowed you to be killed."

Mitch didn't speak. He was afraid anything he might say would be stupid or childish, and it would only serve to break the fragile link that had formed between them. He remained silent and hoped she did not interpret his reticence as a rebuff to her statement.

"I stayed on the east coast, living with Alyssandra for another five years learning to use magic. Then, about seven years ago, we moved out here to California. With my help, Alyssandra formed a new coven and has been running it ever since."

Violet tapped the steering wheel a few times with her fingertips, drumming out a little pattern. "That's me. The highlights anyway. Did I leave anything out that you want to know about?"

Mitch pursed his lips and shook his head. "Nope. I don't think so."

"I'm really glad you didn't die, Mitch." The comment was delivered lightly, but Mitch heard a depth in her voice that convinced him there was much more emotion in the sentiment than intended.

"Me, too. If I had, I never would have realized how fortunate I was to have met you."

"So tell me, what does the rest of your day look like, Officer Loman?" Violet asked, attempting to shake away the serious mood that had descended upon them.

"I have an appointment to meet with the chief this afternoon to review surveillance video. After that, I need to get my notes out of my locker and make a phone call. There's a professor I want to arrange an interview with that may help us get a handle on this golem thing."

"Nothing before that?" Violet asked. "You have a free morning?"

"I'm starving, so when I get home, I want to get something to eat, but that's it until I go meet with the chief."

"Would you like some company for breakfast?"

"You?" asked Mitch, then mentally kicked himself for such a stupid question. "I mean, of course."

"Good. Because I think we have some unfinished business to take care of."

"Magic lessons?" asked Mitch.

"No, those can wait. I'm talking about earlier today. I believe you called it, 'I'll show you mine if you show me yours.'"

CHAPTER 20

The morning and early afternoon hours passed too quickly in Violet's company. At three thirty, Mitch reluctantly forced himself to call for a ride and head to the police department. He was already later than he had planned, and he needed to get to the chief's office before Simon left for the day. Still, it was an incredibly difficult choice to leave. It was almost a herculean task to walk out the front door while Violet lounged on his couch wearing only an oversized t-shirt she had stolen from his closet.

Mitch's car was still at the department where he had left it at the beginning of Saturday's shift. Violet offered to drive him to the cemetery, but he told her she had already chauffeured him around enough for one day. As he left the house, he told her she should keep the shirt. It looked better on her than it ever had on him.

Mitch arrived at the police administrative building and caught the chief as he was packing up to leave.

"You made it," said Solomon. "I was beginning to wonder if you had decided to stay home. Are you still feeling dizzy?"

"No. I'm fine."

Simon nodded and a wry smile pulled at one corner of his mouth. "Then it was something else keeping you occupied," he said. As it was a statement, not a question, Mitch did not respond.

The chief took pity on Mitch and did not pry any further into the matter. He removed a keyring with two keys from his desk and gestured for Mitch to follow him downstairs. The video viewing room was on the bottom floor of the building, behind one of three permanently locked doors, the other two being the equipment and supply room, which Mitch had a key for, and the property storage room, which he did not.

Simon opened the video room door and ushered Mitch inside. The room was barely bigger than a broom closet, with bare plaster walls and a desk pushed into the far corner. The desk held two, side by side monitors and a desktop computer. In front of the desk, next to the computer's keyboard and mouse, was a single chair.

The chief ignored the chair as he leaned over the keyboard and typed in a login command and password.

"The system is pretty self-explanatory. The files are logged by date and can be rewound or fast forwarded using the controls on the command bar at the bottom of the screen. Active cameras can be accessed on the right monitor, and recordings are viewed on the left. Questions?"

"Um, I don't think so," replied Mitch. He hoped Simon's comment about "self-explanatory," was accurate.

"I'm headed home. Close the door when you leave and it will lock behind you. The computer will log itself off after fifteen minutes of inactivity, so you don't need to do anything to shut it off. Good luck."

Simon raised a hand in farewell and exited the room, leaving Mitch alone to search the video records.

Settling into the chair, Mitch grabbed the computer mouse and began his search. Fortunately, he only needed to search a limited time window. Unfortunately, he had multiple camera angles to check.

After two hours of viewing surveillance video, checking camera footage from all available cameras on the perimeter walls, rewinding and fast forwarding through recordings of absolutely nothing, he finally received his first bit of good news since beginning his investigation into the cemetery vandalisms. With a rare feeling of accomplishment and a new file on his thumb drive, he collected his investigation notes from his locker, as well as his clothes from Saturday, and headed out of the building. He located his personal vehicle, still parked where he had placed it Saturday night, and drove home.

When Mitch arrived at his house, he was disappointed to see Violet's truck was no longer in the driveway. Inside, on the kitchen counter, he found a handwritten note scrawled onto a sheet of typing paper she must have found in his den. It read: "Best breakfast ever! Better call me. No ghosting." The words were followed by a happy face, a phone number, and Violet's name signed with a heart over the "i." An anatomically correct heart, which Mitch wasn't sure he should find endearing or threatening. He opted for the former.

He decided he would call her later that night, but first, before he could relax and enjoy the remainder of his weekend, he had another phone call he wanted to make.

Professor Solomon Schick did not pick up the first time Mitch called. He didn't answer on the second or third attempts either. Each time, Mitch declined to leave a message, not wanting to attempt to explain why he was calling in a ten second comment. He was also hesitant to leave a recording of himself mentioning a golem tearing up gravesites in the cemetery. He felt a recording like that might come back and cause problems for him later if it was heard by someone who thought he might be losing his mind. Or perhaps worse, someone who didn't. Violet's story of unwanted attention finding her and her family weighed heavily on his mind.

After the fourth failed attempt at reaching the professor, Mitch dialed Violet's number. When she picked up after the first ring, all thoughts of golems, investigations, and murders were gone for the rest of the evening.

The following morning, Mitch attempted once again to call Professor Schick and the man finally answered his phone after several long seconds of ringing. Mitch half expected it to roll over to his answering machine again when a deep male voice answered.

"Hello?"

Mitch identified himself and explained he was calling to follow up on the burglary that had occurred at the professor's home in early January. "There are several elements to this investigation that I desperately do not wish to discuss over the phone," he admitted, after the professor asked about the Dirty Bandit murder. "Would you be willing to meet with me and answer some questions about the … items … taken from the house?"

The professor agreed but advised that he was going to be lecturing for most of the day today at the college and would not be available before Wednesday. They set an appointment for the following morning at the Dasan's Terrace Police Department.

With no further plans to get in his way, and an investigation that was effectively stalled until he could get into a room with Professor Schick, Mitch decided to call Violet again. She answered on the first ring as she had the night before.

"Hey, Violet. What are you up to today?"

"Good morning, Mitch," she purred. "Two calls in under twelve hours. Aren't you worried you're going to come across as too eager? Or desperate, maybe?"

"I am eager," he admitted. "And probably a little desperate, too. I was thinking that I didn't get my magic lesson yesterday. We were, um, otherwise occupied."

"I don't know," Violet demurred. "I thought yesterday was pretty magical."

Mitch laughed. "No arguments from me on that, but what do you say? I've got a free day. Let's go get something to eat, then we can come back to my place for a few lessons."

"You weren't that bad. Sure, you could stand some improvement, but I wouldn't say you need lessons."

"*Magic* lessons," Mitch clarified, exasperated. "Not … that kind of lessons."

Violet laughed, her tone high and musical. Mitch loved it when she laughed. She was so often careful and reserved when she was with him, it was nice to hear moments of genuine joy in her voice.

"I can move a few things around today. Sure, let's do that. I'll text you my address. Give me some time before you come over, though. I'm still in bed and want to get a little bit more sleep. Late night last night."

Mitch suddenly recalled that it had been a full moon last night. After leaving Mitch's house, Violet would have been with her coven at the cemetery until early this morning. "I forgot. Sorry. We can do this another time."

"No, no. I want to. Come pick me up in a couple hours and we'll get some lunch. Then I'll see if I can show you a few things you've never seen before. Oh, and Mitch?"

"Yes?"

"I might end up stealing another one of your shirts."

"I was very much hoping you would," Mitch admitted, grinning ear to ear.

Mitch sat at a table in one of the second-floor meeting rooms. Professor Solomon Schick sat across the table, wringing his hands and fidgeting nervously in his chair. The professor was of average height and weight, maybe a little on the thin side, with dark brown skin, watery brown eyes, and a fringe of snowy white hair around his temples. Heavy bags were visible under his eyes. They were the dark color of deep bruising, and they appeared magnified under the round rimless glasses he wore low on the bridge of his nose. Deep lines creased his face on either cheek, accenting loose jowls that hung below his jawline. Well defined crow's feet and permanent wrinkles around his mouth testified that he was a man used to smiling, but he was not smiling now. His expression revealed only anxiety and guilt.

Mitch selected one of the casual meeting rooms to talk to Professor Schick rather than the stale, intimidating interview room downstairs. The interview room was nothing more than four bare walls, a camera, and a table fitted with metal rings for handcuffs, with a bench on one side and two wobbly plastic chairs on the other. It was designed for maximum discomfort to assist suspect interrogations. Solomon Schick was not a suspect in this mess and Mitch wanted a more comfortable setting for his interview. The professor appeared to be in enough distress without adding unnecessary pressure. There was no need to treat him like he had done something wrong.

"Thank you for coming in to see me, Professor Schick," said Mitch, gesturing to several water bottles at the edge of the table. "Help yourself to water if you want it. We also have coffee or sodas available if you would prefer."

The professor picked up a water bottle and raised it briefly toward Mitch to indicate it would be sufficient.

"I've been wanting to talk to you for the past couple days, but I didn't want to do it on the phone. I like to be able to see who I'm talking to so I can gauge how serious or honest they are. It is much harder to tell if someone is lying to you if you can't look them in the eyes."

Professor Schick began to bristle. His shoulders hunched forward defensively, and his eyes flashed with anger. Mitch waved a hand placatingly in an attempt to calm the professor's ire.

"That goes both ways, of course," he continued. "I want you to be able to look me in the eyes and know that I am deadly serious when I tell you that I was attacked by a golem on Saturday and it damn near killed me. I think you might know something about it, and I would like your help."

Professor Schick deflated immediately at Mitch's mention of the golem. He nodded sadly. "Yes," he said, "I … am familiar with this creature. I am sorry you were hurt, but I am also glad you have seen it with your own eyes as it will perhaps be a little easier for you to believe what I tell you. Most would think me crazy or attention seeking for what I have to say."

"Did you create it, Professor?"

"No. I did not. Please Detective, call me Solomon. My students call me Professor, and I prefer to be on a more equal footing here."

"Okay, Solomon. Then please call me Mitch. And I'm not a detective, I'm just an officer."

"No, I did not create the golem. I do, however, feel responsible for allowing it to escape. The golem stones were entrusted to me by a dear friend who asked me to keep them safe. I have let him down terribly."

"Golem stones?" asked Mitch. "I think we're already jumping too far ahead. Let's get to those later. First, can you tell me why you believe your burglary is connected to the Dirty Bandit?"

Solomon took a sip from his water bottle, then recounted his memory of the night that a burglar had entered his home. He explained the crash of glass breaking and his rush downstairs to discover that one of the display cases in his library had been broken open and the contents stolen.

"Inside the case, I kept a gift, given into my care by a dear friend of my family's. He was a rabbi, living for most of his life in Yemen. Not an easy life, mind you, as the Jews in Yemen have been under almost constant persecution since the late 19th century. I believe most, if not all, have exited the country in more recent years due to renewed hostilities against their communities. The time I am referring to, however, was more than thirty years ago."

"This gift, it was the golem stones?" asked Mitch.

"The stones, yes. That was part of it, but there was also a book. A very old journal, written over six hundred years ago by another rabbi, Rabbi Shem Tov, who had discovered the secret to raising a golem to life. My friend was in failing health, and he was very concerned about what might happen to these possessions after he died. They were valuable items, but more importantly they could be extremely dangerous if they fell into the wrong hands. I am only now beginning to see the full extent of his concerns."

"Tell me about the book," Mitch said. "Does it explain how to raise a golem?"

"It does," agreed Solomon. "It details the process, the rituals needed, and the prayers necessary to bring clay to life. I believe that the rabbi who wrote the journal was a very powerful magician, with gifts most of us do not possess. Many people have attempted to use the book to create golems, but I am unaware of anyone who claims to have been successful. Most historians who have seen this journal believe it to be no more than superstition since there doesn't seem to be anyone capable of replicating the rabbi's experiments."

"You don't, though. Do you?"

"I don't what?"

"You don't think it's superstition."

Solomon shook his head solemnly. "I believe the book is real. I think we have been fortunate that a magician with sufficient ability has never come into possession of it."

"Until now," stated Mitch.

"Oh, no," insisted Solomon, emphatically. "The thief, this Dirty Bandit, is no magician. If he was, he would have no need to use a golem to commit petty burglaries. I believe he is simply a believer who was fortunate enough to discover a location to use the stones."

"I suppose that's a little bit of good news. So, all we need to do is recover these stones and the problem should solve itself. Tell me about them, Solomon. What are the stones, and what do they do?"

"The stones were also created by Shem Tov as a sort of short cut for his creations. By using the golem stones, he did not need to expend his own magic and he did not need to perform the full rituals. All the rabbi had to do was lay the stones on the ground, recite a brief spell and command the golem to rise. The stones were effective, but also extremely limited as they had no magic of their own. To function properly, they required a location with easy access to magical energy. The soil also had to be, as the book put it, 'a mixture of vibrant life and ancient death.' Most who have seen the book interpret that phrase to mean an older cemetery where wildlife has reclaimed the area."

"Like Dasan's Terrace," muttered Mitch. "The gated area is almost completely wild."

"Yes," Solomon agreed. "There are few places in the world that meet the criteria. Most cemeteries do not possess the requisite amount of magic, and most magic focal points don't land on cemeteries old enough to meet the needs of the stones. Until recently, I was only aware of a handful of locations where the stones might work. One was Rabbi Tov's home in northern Africa, which explains why he created the stones to behave like they do. He had ready access to a location that fit the necessary conditions."

"Why did you bring the stones to Sacramento?" asked Mitch. "Did you intend to use them?"

Solomon looked stricken by the accusation. "Never! I came to Sacramento when I was offered a position teaching at Sacramento State University. I had no idea Dasan's Terrace was here, or that it would meet the requirements to use the stones. I assure you that was a disastrous coincidence. That was why I did not try to explain what the stones could do when I reported the initial burglary. I simply told the officers they were historical artifacts. When reports of the Dirty Bandit began to emerge, I realized what must have happened, but even then, I did not recontact the police because it was only property being taken. After the murder, I knew I couldn't stay quiet any longer."

"I understand, and I'm sorry about the careless phrasing of my question. I wasn't accusing you of anything," said Mitch, although he had meant the question exactly as he had worded it. He had been curious to see the professor's reaction. "Let's talk about the stones, now. What are they, and how do they work?"

"The golem stones are actually three large sapphires," Solomon explained. "They are cut into multi-faceted spheres, each about two inches in diameter. Each stone is a different color and serves a separate purpose. The blue sapphire shapes the golem into the rough form of a man. The green sapphire animates the creature, allowing it to move. The yellow gem is the most important. This is the stone that allows the creature to be controlled."

"Blue, green, and yellow," said Mitch, scribbling into his notebook as Professor Schick spoke. "Do the stones work if only one or two are used?"

"Yes, and no. Without the blue stone, the golem cannot shape itself into anything useful and is reduced to a quivering mound of dirt. If the green stone is missing, the creature will form but it will not move. The yellow sapphire is the dangerous one to leave out. If the yellow stone is missing, the person summoning the golem is unable to control it. Its behavior will be unpredictable. It may simply choose to fall apart, or it could go on a rampage that will last until the sun rises the next morning."

"Sunrise?" asked Mitch, surprised. "Does a golem only function at night?"

"A golem? No. A true golem can move about freely during the day or night. It remains animate until its creator is either killed or commands it to stop. It can also be made of any substance. Clay, wood, stone, etcetera. Creatures created by the stones, however, are as I said, limited. The stones only work in grave dirt, as we discussed, and they only function at night. The downside is once the stones are activated, the golem will not stop if the summoner dies. The stones will continue to animate the creature until the golem completes its purpose or the sun rises."

"That's helpful. The Dirty Bandit can only use the golem for a limited time period. That could come in handy. What are the creature's other weaknesses, Professor? If I end up facing off with another one of these things, how can I stop it? Preferably without getting myself killed."

"Golems can only be stopped using the control word implanted into them by their creator. If you know the proper word, you can stop the golem. Unfortunately, a golem raised with the golem stones doesn't have a control word. The green sapphire serves as the animating force for the golem rather than the will of the magician who created it. If you can find the green sapphire and remove it, that would work."

"And what are the odds of that?"

"Not high," admitted Solomon. "You would have a better chance at trying to destroy the creature outright. Golems can be destroyed with the correct tools. An ice golem can be melted. A wood golem can be burned."

"And a dirt golem?" asked Mitch, already knowing the answer.

"A dirt golem has to be broken apart, piece by piece."

"I tried that. It didn't go so well."

"What did you use?" asked Solomon?

"My hands," said Mitch sheepishly. "And a few bullets," he amended after a moment.

"You would need a pick or a sledgehammer to do anything effective against a dirt golem. The magic binding it together is significant."

Mitch nodded, remembering the slick, black shell of force he had felt around the creature. He hadn't been able to so much as scratch the surface of that magical shield.

"My best suggestion for you," continued Solomon, "is capture the person using the stones before they are able to construct their next golem."

"I would love to be able to do that, but we don't know who the person is. Do you have any ideas? Who knew you had the stones and understood what they could do?"

Solomon sat quietly for a long moment. He drank from his water bottle as he pondered the question. "I have been thinking about that myself quite a bit over the past few weeks. I have colleagues that knew about the stones, but they are skeptics. They believe them to be historical relics with no real power. I have also discussed the stones with students in my classes. I teach religious mythology, and the golem stones are part of my curriculum. I don't bring them into the classroom, but I do show photographs of the sapphires and the journal. I suppose it is possible that one of my students had more faith in my lectures than I expected and wanted the stones for himself. Or herself."

"Okay. So, probably not another teacher. Maybe a student. That doesn't narrow it down a lot, but speaking of photographs, I would like to show you something," said Mitch. He pulled a sheet of paper from under his notepad. "I briefly saw the person who created the golem when I fought with it last weekend. I've never seen him before that I can remember. I didn't recognize him when I saw him, anyway. I'm hoping you can."

Mitch slid the paper across the table toward Solomon.

"Our surveillance cameras caught him while entering the cemetery Saturday night, climbing over the east wall. He did a pretty good job of not looking directly into any of our cameras, but we did get one profile shot that might help us. Do you know this man, Solomon?"

The picture was a still-frame from the videos Mitch had reviewed. The subject in question had walked past a pathway light that illuminated the left side of his face as he was recorded by the camera. It was nighttime, so any colors in the photo were washed out to shades of gray, but the picture was clear and detailed.

"The kid has red hair, if that helps," said Mitch.

"I recognize him," said Solomon.

Mitch's heart kicked into high gear. Finally, he had a solid lead on his suspect. "What's his name?"

"I don't know," admitted Solomon. Mitch's excitement was immediately dampened like a struggling flame drowned by a deluge of cold water.

"But you said you recognized him," Mitch said, hoping this new lead wasn't already another dead end.

"He's a student in one of my current classes. He attends Tuesday and Thursday evenings from five o'clock to seven. I would need to consult my roll sheets to get his name. I can do that when I go to work tomorrow night and then call you when I get home. Would that work?"

"Can you also get me a current address for the guy?" asked Mitch. "School records would show that information, right?"

"They would," said Solomon. "But I don't normally have access to that information about my students. Can't you get a warrant for that information once you have his name?"

"Ordinarily, yes. But I can't exactly go to a judge and request a warrant based on getting my ass kicked by an animated pile of dirt. Sorry about the language."

Solomon waved the apology away. "I hadn't thought of that. The judge would treat you exactly as the other detective treated me when I tried to explain about the golem. I see the dilemma. Yes, I think I can get his home information from the campus registrar's office. I'll just tell them I need it to mail him a makeup assignment. They probably won't have an issue with that. It will take a little longer to get you the information, though. Can you wait until Friday morning?"

"I think so. He's only burglarizing homes once every fourteen or fifteen days, so I think we have time before the next break in. Friday morning should still give us plenty of time to follow up. Although, that makes me think of another question. How often can the stones be used? Do they need to recharge, or is there a particular phase of the moon that makes them most effective?"

"There aren't any limits in my understanding," said Solomon. "The stones can be used once a night if someone wished to. Since they hold no magic internally, they do not need to be recharged after each use, and I have not read of any restrictions based on times of the month or year that would be a problem."

"So, this kid's pattern is determined by something personal rather than a requirement imposed by the sapphires."

"Based on what I know, I would say that's correct."

"Thank you, Solomon. I appreciate your help. Is there anything else about the stones or the book you think I should know? Can you tell me anything that might be helpful in stopping this thing?"

"No. I'm sorry. I can't think of anything else. I'm pretty sure you now know everything I do about the golem stones. As I said before, if you can, I would recommend catching this person before they make another golem. Once the creature is animated, very little will stop it before it fulfills its mission. I can offer one more piece of advice, though. If your suspect manages to create the golem but has not yet given it directions, shoot him."

"The golem?" asked Mitch. "I tried that already."

"No, not the golem. Your suspect. If he's dead, he cannot direct the golem. With no orders, the creature will stand in place and wait for the sun to rise."

Mitch smiled, keeping his expression as friendly as possible, although the professor's ominous advice had left him with an icy chill in his spine.

"Let's hope it doesn't come to that."

Mitch stood and escorted Solomon from the meeting room. The professor held up the half empty water bottle and Mitch advised him to keep it and help himself to another if he wished. The older man declined the offer.

"Thank you again, Professor. You've been a big help. You have my cell phone number, so please call me Friday morning with that information we discussed. Would you like me to walk you out?"

"No, thank you," replied Solomon. He waved a friendly farewell to Dot as he and Mitch walked past her desk. "I think I can find my way. If you have any more questions, don't hesitate to call me. I'm sorry I wasn't more help."

"You helped plenty. We have our first real lead on a suspect because of you. That's more than I had a few minutes ago."

Solomon waved again and disappeared through the door leading to the stairwell. Mitch watched the door close, then glanced toward Dot. The chief's administrative assistant was staring at Mitch intently.

"Good news?" she asked.

"I think we might have a suspect in custody by the end of the week. Yeah, I'd call that good news."

"I'm glad to hear that. Should I let the chief know?"

"Sure. I can write up what I learned and put it on his desk tomorrow morning. I should also call Ali, the homicide detective on this case. That's going to be a little more tricky, though. I need to figure out how to share what I found without mentioning anything about golems or magic."

Dot nodded encouragingly and directed her attention back to her computer screen. Mitch stood beside her desk and watched her type. After a few moments, when Dot realized that her observer did not appear to be leaving anytime soon, she glanced back up.

"Something else?" she asked.

"Yeah. I understand that you've been talking to Violet quite a bit about me. Are you two BFFs or something?"

"If you're asking if we sit around in our nightgowns like schoolgirls, braiding each other's hair and talking about boys, then no. Violet is the most knowledgeable witch on the west coast when it comes to ghosts, however, so I have discussed your situation with her on several occasions, trying to figure out how we can send your son on from this plane. Violet is a talented exorcist…"

"No!" interrupted Mitch. "No exorcism! Not for Denny."

Dot smiled sympathetically. "Of course, not, Mitch. I would never suggest that. I don't want to hurt your son any more than you do. I want to set him free. I was going to say that Violet is very talented in her field, but when it comes to figuring out why a ghost has become stuck, she and I are still novices. We can only speculate."

"So, you don't have any idea how to help him?"

"I didn't say that. Some spirits have obvious unfinished business. Lieutenant Delaney is a good example."

Dot's face twitched, and she appeared to be suppressing a grin. Mitch figured the chief must have informed her of their talk at the hospital. He ignored her amusement and waited for her to continue.

"He was murdered, and his killer was never caught. As a law enforcement officer that was unacceptable to him, and he stayed around hoping to see his murderer brought to justice. Although we know why he stays, we can't help him because the case has gone totally cold. With Denny, it is something completely different. I think we can help him if we can only figure out why he stayed. He is a child, and he thinks like a child, so his reasons will be something that is of great importance to a four-year old."

"And that would be what?" Mitch could hear the helplessness in his own voice. It frustrated him that he could not help his own son when he most needed him. "I give him a new bear every year. That's what he wishes for every time he sees me. Is that a mistake? Should I not give it to him?"

"Mitch, did you get Denny a new bear after he destroyed the last one?"

"I did. He tore it up, too. That one and the next one."

Dot pressed her lips together in thought. Her eyes went distant. "I think the bear is important, but clearly if Denny is destroying them, then it isn't the key we're looking for. I think we need to search a bit deeper. Denny only appears on Christmas

Eve. I think that is relevant. If we are to help him move on, we have to do it when he comes to see you."

Mitch's heart sank into his stomach. His chest felt tight, and a burning bitter taste touched the back of his throat. "We can't do anything for him until then? We have to just sit around and let him suffer for another nine months?"

"If it helps, I don't think he is actually suffering. I think he is mostly in a state of limbo during the rest of the year. Think of it as sleeping. He wakes up occasionally if someone steals his bear – or he used to, anyway – but the rest of the time he is merely waiting for Christmas."

Mitch nodded. The image did help, but not much.

"Mitch, I'm going to keep working on this. I really think I can help but I don't want to give you any false hopes by telling you what I'm thinking until I'm ready to share it. I need to process it through my head a few more times. I'm also going to keep talking to Violet. She's been a big help with this. She really likes you, by the way."

"What?" asked Mitch, caught off guard by the sudden topic change.

"What?" repeated Dot.

"Violet likes me? She told you that?"

Dot chuckled and shook her head. "Now who's going all schoolgirl? Do you want me to pass her a note for you after lunch?"

Mitch scowled, but he was more embarrassed than upset at Dot. "Okay, enough. I like her, too, so maybe that reaction was a little over the top."

"Not at all. It was nice. I like the color of your aura when you talk about Violet. It turns a very bright orange. It's pretty."

"Stop staring at my aura," Mitch snapped with mock anger. Then, in a more serious tone, "Thank you, Dot. For helping me with Denny."

"Of course. I'm going to do everything I can to solve this, Mitch. I promise."

He nodded. "I know you will. Alright. I have to work tonight, so I better head home and try to get some sleep before then."

Mitch headed toward the stairs, following the path Professor Schick had taken earlier. He did plan to go home and crawl into bed, but with all the things swirling in his head – golems, murders, ghosts, Violet – he wasn't very hopeful about getting any actual sleep.

CHAPTER 21

As he had anticipated, Mitch slept little that day after returning home. He endured a few fitful hours of tossing and turning in bed before he finally gave up, showered, and headed in to work for his evening shift. To his surprise, Sergeant Smythe took one look at him in briefing and ordered him to go back home.

"I've got things I need to do tonight," Mitch had protested, but Jorge would not be swayed.

"The chief called and told me you worked this morning. That counts as your shift time today. Even if he hadn't told me, frankly you look like hell, and I'd send you home anyway. Go on. Get some sleep. Come back tomorrow rested and ready to work. We'll be okay without you for one night. Tink and Brad handled this shift alone for two months before you were hired, I think we'll manage for the next twelve hours."

Grudgingly, Mitch left. He went home and crawled back into bed. Although he didn't expect results any different from this morning, he surprised himself by falling asleep almost immediately and sleeping through the entire night. The next morning, he awoke refreshed, energetic, and with no sign of the headache that had been lingering with him since his run-in with the golem the previous weekend. Jorge and the chief had been right, he realized. He had needed an extra night off more than he wanted to admit. As he prepared to go to work that Thursday night, he felt better than he had in weeks.

Before leaving his house and driving to the Dasan's Terrace police department, he called Violet asking if she would meet him later in the evening at Dead Town.

"It's not our night, Mitch" she had demurred. "We can only be in the cemetery sixteen nights each year."

"I'm not asking for the coven to show up. Just you. Our agreement includes you helping me whenever I need it, right? Well, I need your help. If anyone sees us or complains, I'll explain to the chief that this was my request, and it shouldn't count as one of your nights. Please. This is important."

Violet agreed to see him, but not before extracting a promise that he would take her out for dinner during his weekend as repayment. Mitch happily agreed to the stipulation.

Briefing concluded quickly that evening, as on most evenings, and Jorge announced the movie selections for their weekly viewing.

"I've got a seventies theme going tonight," Jorge told them. "We'll start with Logan's Run, then follow that up with Death Wish, the Charles Bronson version, not that bullshit they released a couple years ago with Bruce Willis. After that, I thought we'd end our night with a personal favorite, The Warriors."

"Sounds good," said Mitch, "but I'm going to be a little late joining you tonight. I need to spend some time checking out the vandalized gravesites in Northwest."

"Do you want us to wait to start?"

"No. Thanks, but it might take a while. I'll probably miss at least the first couple films, so go ahead and start without me."

"Do you want some company?" asked Tink. "Maybe I can help with whatever you're working on. Another set of eyes might be useful."

"Thanks, Tink, but no. I'm fine. Um, actually, Violet agreed to meet me out there later tonight. We have some things to work on that would probably go easier if it was just the two of us.

"I get it," said Tink with an overly understanding nod. "Having me around would cramp your style. Well, don't let me stand in the way of a budding romance. You go do what you gotta do."

"It's not like that," said Mitch, his cheeks feeling hot.

"Sure, it's not. Come on. Don't be embarrassed. Dot told us all about you two."

"Dot told you…? Jesus! Does Dot blab about everybody's business around here, or just mine?"

Jorge gave Mitch a puzzled stare. "Nothing happens in Dead Town that Dot doesn't know about, and if you want to stay in the loop, you keep in touch with her. Are you only now figuring that out?"

An hour later, still muttering under his breath about administrative assistants that didn't know how to keep their mouths shut, Mitch paced through the northwest corner of the cemetery practicing his ability to gather magic. He waved his hands through the air, pulling energy toward himself and manipulating the wisps of power as though they were physical objects he could touch and shape. After gathering a significant amount of the raw force, he shaped the magic into a ball. When it was complete, he cast the glowing sphere over his shoulder, away into the darkness where it broke apart and dissipated even as he began the process of collecting new magic all over again. The repetitive act quieted his mind and calmed him.

Letting his anger and frustration ebb one magic globe at a time, Mitch realized that Dot had meant no harm in talking to others about his growing relationship with Violet. Nothing she had shared with his partners was actually a secret. He admitted to himself that the real problem he was having was he didn't like other people talking about them as a couple when Mitch himself wasn't quite sure what he and Violet meant to each other.

Mitch gathered another ball of energy, making it flare a bright red this time before he tossed it over his shoulder.

"You're getting better. I'm glad to see you've been practicing."

He spun to find Violet standing behind him, holding the discarded sphere. In the red illumination of the magic, he could see she was wearing a brown leather bomber jacket that hung past her waist to mid-thigh. Beneath the jacket she had on skin-tight, dark leggings and heavy biker boots. Before coming to the cemetery, she had also applied her goth makeup and waist-length, black wig.

"Why the makeup?" he asked, slightly disappointed by her appearance.

"You asked me for my help, so this is a business meeting, correct?"

Mitch nodded, and Violet gestured toward his badge and gun.

"You are wearing your uniform, and I am wearing mine. Is there a problem with that?"

"No," Mitch conceded. "No, of course not. I guess I assumed since we had been seeing each other and you weren't wearing the wig before, that... You know what? It doesn't matter. Thanks for meeting me."

Violet smiled, then closed her fist, extinguishing the magic in her hand.

"You're lucky I was free," she told him. "I can't make a living solely by being your teacher. I have a real job that I can't always ignore whenever you feel like pulling my string."

"I'm sorry," said Mitch, appalled at his own selfishness. He had never thought about Violet having a job. She was a witch, and that meant … well, he really hadn't thought about what it meant, but he certainly hadn't pictured her working for a living. "That was thoughtless of me. What do you do?"

"I'm a C.P.A. An accountant."

"Wow. That's great. I hope I'm not keeping you from any of your clients."

"No. Not at the moment."

"Are you working tomorrow morning?"

Violet's gaze trailed away, and she cocked her head a little sheepishly. She slipped her hands deep into the pockets of her jacket. "No. I only really have one client at the moment. I handle investments for the coven and manage their books. They pay me a monthly stipend and cover most of my expenses in return."

"How many in the coven?" asked Mitch.

"Thirteen, including myself."

"That's right. You told me that once before. So you actually have twelve clients, not one. Maybe even thirteen, if you do your own taxes. It sounds like an important job, and I imagine they rely on you quite a bit to take care of them. Do they have much in the way of assets?"

"Substantial," Violet admitted, but did not elaborate. "Did you ask me out here to quiz me about the women in my coven?"

"No. I wasn't trying to pry. I was only making conversation and I got curious. Sorry. I asked you to meet me for something totally different. I need your help, and… Is my aura orange?"

Mitch surprised himself with the question. He hadn't meant to ask it, but it had been sitting at the forefront of his mind since Violet arrived.

"Um, what?"

"My aura. Dot told me I have a bright orange aura. Is that true? And, if it is, what does it mean?"

"I don't know," said Violet. "I can't see auras."

"You can't? Why haven't you learned how to see auras?"

"It isn't a skill you can learn, Mitch," Violet told him. "I keep forgetting how recently your gifts manifested, and how little you know. You're like a toddler and I'm showing you how to run and expecting you to keep up. That's my fault. I need to keep reminding myself that you only stood up and took your first steps a few weeks ago. Let's start over with a little refresher course, a bit of Supernatural 101."

"Okay. I'm listening."

"Some people see auras. Dot is one of them. She can see from the way an aura fluctuates or changes color how a person is feeling. She can also see if they're ill, or if someone is trying to lie to her. It's a powerful gift. Other people, us for example, can see and touch souls. You can learn a lot about someone from viewing their soul, but it isn't as versatile as reading a person's aura. Souls may change slowly over time, but they don't fluctuate from moment to moment, so they can't tell you what a person is thinking or feeling."

Violet paused to make sure that Mitch was following her explanation and did not have any questions. He gestured for her to continue.

"Finally, there are people who see magic. These three gifts cannot be learned. You either have them or you don't. They are also not mutually exclusive, though it is rare to find someone with more than one. Alyssandra sees magic. She does not see souls, and she can't read auras. Dot sees auras but has no ability to see souls or magic. You and I, Mitch, are unicorns. We see souls *and* magic. I can't read auras, and I don't think you do either, although now that I think about it, I've never tested that theory. You should talk again with Dot and ask her to test you. I think it's highly unlikely because I've never met anyone with all three gifts, but you should check anyway."

"What about ghosts?" asked Mitch. "Is that the same as seeing souls?"

"Not really, no. There are many people who are sensitive enough to see ghosts. Dot is one of those, but they don't really see souls. Just like there are many people who are sensitive enough to manipulate magic, even though they can't actually see it. Dot isn't able to look inside of a living human being and see the soul that resides there."

"Neither can I," admitted Mitch.

"Yes, you can. I haven't had time to teach you how, yet, but you have the gift. That much became obvious the first time you touched the spirit of your son. You proved it again when you shook hands with the assistant chief and when you exorcised Harold. Only an exorcist could physically interact with a ghost. No, there's no question about it. Is that what you'd like to learn today? How to see a living soul?"

"No. I mean, yes, I'd love to learn that, but not tonight. Right now, I was thinking you could teach me something a little more pressing. I need to learn how to manipulate magic as a weapon so the next time I run into a golem, I'm not completely helpless. I'm hoping we can arrest the kid responsible before he raises another one, but if I fail, if I can't stop him in time, I want to be able to fight back."

"It isn't a good idea to teach you how to use magic as a weapon before you learn how to defend yourself. You could injure yourself by accident. I could teach you how to build a shield, then when you master that, we can talk about weapons."

"Will a shield stop a golem that's trying to cave in my skull?"

Violet took a deep breath and blew it out. Mitch could see the mist forming from her breath in the cooling evening air. "No," she admitted. "It would take months of practice to learn how to build and maintain a shield strong enough to protect you from that kind of power."

"I need something I can do effectively by next week at the latest. Are there any attacks you can teach me that might have an impact on a creature like that?"

"The two most basic skills in magic are fire and brute force. I don't think fire will do much good against a walking mound of earth."

"What about force?" asked Mitch.

In response, Violet stepped closer to Mitch and placed her palm on his chest. Mitch only had time to notice the magical energies swirling around her hand before an explosive impact struck him in the ribs. His ballistic vest absorbed most of the impact, but what remained was enough to lift him off his feet and knock him flat on his back, taking the air completely out of his lungs. It felt like he had been punched in the chest by a heavyweight boxer.

Mitch remained on the ground for several seconds, wheezing in short gasps as he tried to regain his breath. Violet knelt beside him and stroked his cheek. "That was force," she said. "The strength of any attack is based on how much magic you can draw and how focused your will is when you release it. Is that what you want to learn?"

Mitch nodded. He coughed a few times as his chest loosened and breathing became a little easier. Violet bent over and pressed her lips to his, stealing his breath away for the second time in two minutes. Pulling away too soon for Mitch's liking, she rose to her feet and extended a hand to help him to his feet.

"I still think you should learn defensive tactics first, but I understand your concern and your sense of urgency. I'll teach you how to use a force spell, and I hope I'm not making a mistake."

Back on his feet, Mitch used his hands to brush the dirt off the seat of his pants. Violet's bright blue eyes watched him closely. "Are you hurt?" she asked.

"No, just impressed. That looked effortless and you totally knocked me on my ass."

"Good. Okay, first part of the lesson: pull energy into your hand."

Mitch waved his hand through the wisps of magic in the air around him, gathering enough to fill his palm.

"No. Not like that." Violet gave a small wave of her fingers and the energy in Mitch's hand evaporated like fog in a hard wind. "I want you to try something a little different. When I first taught you to gather magic, I showed you how to use your hands. Hand motions help focus the mind on what you are trying to accomplish, but they aren't necessary. When you wave your hands around, shaping a spell, others can see what you're doing and act to prevent it. If you use only your mind, unless you're facing a witch who can see the magic, your opponent will have no idea what you're doing until it's too late."

Violet held out her right hand, palm up. Surrounding wisps of power swirled and eddied, rushing to her hand and forming into a shapeless mass above her spread fingers. "Make the magic come to you instead of swatting around like a kid with a butterfly net."

Mitch imitated the position of Violet's hand and willed the magic to come to him. Nothing happened.

"You can do it," insisted Violet. "You've already done it a hundred times. You don't need your hands to help you, they're only a crutch. Imagine the power coming to you. See it happen in your head, but don't try to force it. The more you think about it, the harder it gets. Simply *believe* the magic will bend to your needs."

Mitch imagined all the times he had previously gathered fragments of power around him. It had gotten easier the more he practiced until he could draw from the magic almost without thinking about it. He stared at the wispy flows of force in the air and imagined them drawing to his hand, he pictured them swirl into a tiny eddy above his palm and draw together. This time, the magic near him, twitched, changing direction for a split second before resuming its previous path.

"Good. You almost had it, but you're trying to pull on it, to draw it to you. Don't force the magic, make it want to come to you."

"I'm not sure how to do that," said Mitch. "How do I make it want to come?"

"Picture it already in your hand. Don't fight with it or try to make it move. Tell it where you want it to be. Believe that it is already where you expect it to go. Don't accept any other outcome. This isn't an order that can be refused; it is an expectation."

Mitch tried again. He held out his palm, and this time instead of trying to reach out mentally toward the magic, he pictured a glowing yellow ball of power already in his hand. In his mind's eye, the image grew clearer as he thought of all the times he had gathered power and held it before. Trickles of the magic reacted, delicate wisps of energy traced the length of his arm and coalesced above his open hand, shaping themselves into the form he desired. They swirled, tightening into something more solid, more physical. A yellow ball began to glow above his curled fingers.

Violet blew out a breath as though she were dispersing a dandelion puff and the ball popped in Mitch's hand.

"Hey!" he complained.

"Good job!" said Violet. "Now do it again, and this time let's see if you can hang on to it."

CHAPTER 22

"Ali? This is Mitch Loman from Dasan's Terrace Police Department. I promised you I would keep you updated if I got any more information on our mutual suspect."

Professor Schick had called that Friday morning, waking Mitch after only a couple hours of sleep. He and Violet had spent most of the night practicing gathering magic and utilizing force attacks. By the end of it, Mitch was absolutely exhausted, physically, mentally, and emotionally. When the phone rang, he debated ignoring it, but one glance at the caller ID screen changed his mind.

The professor identified the suspect in his class as a twenty-year-old student, named Anthony Cunningham. A trip to the registrar's office this morning had netted the young man's current address and contact information. After thanking Professor Schick for the information, he hung up and crawled back under the covers.

Before sleep could claim him, Mitch sat back up and reached for his phone. He had promised Detective Minhas he would share whatever information he found as soon as possible, and his conscience would not let him return to sleep until he had kept his word. Clearly, he couldn't tell the man about the golem, Ali would think he was as crazy as the professor, but he could at least hand over the name and contact information.

"Hey, Mitch. Good to hear from you. Find out anything good?"

"I don't know. Is a name and an address for our suspect good?"

"You got a name? That's amazing. How sure are you that you have the right guy?"

"Ninety-nine plus," assured Mitch. "Everything tracks and I can almost guarantee we have the right suspect. I have a solid witness that can close the link between your burglaries and my vandalisms."

"Great!" exclaimed Ali. "Let me grab a pen." There was a short silence, and Mitch could hear Detective Minhas scrabbling around his desk. "Okay, got it. Give me the suspect info."

"He's a local kid. His name is Anthony Cunningham. Twenty years old." Mitch also gave Ali the boy's birth date and the address that Professor Schick had provided.

"Got it. And your witness?"

Mitch paused. "I … can't give you that. I promised total anonymity."

That wasn't true. Professor Schick had been willing to testify, but the story he would tell would get the entire case thrown out of any courtroom. Mitch had to proceed carefully if he wanted this investigation to stay untouched by anything that smelled of the supernatural.

"I can't get a warrant based solely on an anonymous tip. No judge is going to sign that."

"I know," said Mitch. "I'm sorry. All I can tell you is that I know almost without a doubt that I have the right guy. At least it's more than we had a day ago. Last week we were sitting on our thumbs waiting for him to hit another house and hoping he gave us something new to follow up on."

"You're right. But what am I supposed to do with this? Put twenty-four-hour surveillance on him until he breaks into another home? We don't have the resources for that. And if I scoop him up and bring him in to question him, all I'm doing is tipping him off that we know he's our suspect."

"I might have an idea," suggested Mitch. "What if we knock on his door and ask to look around. Totally consensual search of the home. If we find anything that links him to the burglaries, we can lock the place down and get our search warrant. We can get him without ever revealing our informant."

"*Your* informant," stressed Ali. "I still don't know who he is. And I don't think it will work. The kid could refuse to let us in, and again we'll be tipping our hand."

"We won't go when our suspect is home."

"Maybe I'm missing something, but what would be the point of that?"

"Look, Ali. The address I gave you is a house on a nice little Rancho Cordova residential street. The mortgage or rent on a place like that isn't necessarily cheap. This guy is a twenty-year-old college kid who's been breaking into houses for the past couple months and stealing cash and costume jewelry for pocket money. I'm betting he doesn't live alone in that house. He's either living with family or he has roommates to help him pay rent. Either way, he isn't alone. All we need to do is knock on the door when we know that Anthony isn't home and see if we can get somebody else living there to let us in to take a look around."

"Okay," said Ali. "There's a chance that could work. If they don't let us in, we're still screwed, though. We get nothing, and the kid knows we're onto him."

"True. But if we sit around and wait for him to make a move, somebody else could get killed."

There was another pause as Ali considered the idea.

"How do we know when he's not home?"

"He goes to Sac State. I don't know how many classes he's taking, but I know one of them. He's in class every Tuesday at five o'clock. We should hit the house then. Anthony thinks he got away with everything so far and he's going to want to keep to his normal routine. He doesn't want to deviate from his schedule and bring any suspicion on himself. There's no reason he shouldn't show up for class this Tuesday. Do me a favor, Ali, don't cut me out of this. I definitely want to be there when you go in the house."

"No worries there," the detective assured him. "If this whole thing goes sideways, I'm telling the lieutenant this was all your idea."

"You're a peach, Ali."

"Of course, you could always give up your informant and make this a lot easier."

"I'd rather take the blame if this catches fire."

"Okay. It's your funeral. Tuesday it is. I'll do a little research on the house in the meantime and let you know what I find out."

"Sounds good. Talk to you later."

"Bye."

Mitch hung up his phone, lay his head on the pillow, and fell immediately asleep.

When Tuesday arrived, Ali kept his word to include Mitch in the search. The two men agreed to meet in Anthony Cunningham's neighborhood a few minutes before five o'clock and approach the house together.

Mitch parked his car across the street and a few doors down from the suspect's home. He wore a sport coat over a white shirt and tie rather than a uniform, and he drove his personal vehicle as he didn't want anyone in the residence to see police officers coming prematurely. Ali was already there, sitting in a faded brown Chevrolet sedan that looked like every detective pool car ever manufactured. So much for not alerting the neighborhood the police were here. The homicide detective stepped out of his vehicle when he saw Mitch approaching.

It was the first time Mitch had met the detective in person since their brief introduction almost a year earlier. Ali Minhas looked to be in his late forties, with graying black hair, dark eyes, and a dark brown complexion. His long, narrow, Mediterranean features suggested he might trace his family back to anywhere from Italy to Iran. He was a shorter man, only about five feet five inches tall, but he was wide across the chest and shoulders as if he spent more time in the gym than he did behind his detective's desk. Like Mitch, he was also dressed semi-casually in a jacket and tie, with dark blue jeans underneath.

"Hey, Ali. Nice to see you again." Mitch shook the detective's hand.

"You, too. I've been watching the house. There's a car in the driveway and someone is moving around inside, but I have no idea if it's our suspect or not.

Mitch checked his watch. The digital display informed him it was four forty in the evening. "I'll let you know in about ten minutes," he said. "What were you able to dig up on the house?"

"Not much," admitted the detective. "The place is registered to a Madeline Cunningham, Anthony Cunningham's mother, so you were right about him living with family. She's forty-seven years old, divorced, and as far as I can tell, not employed. I don't know how she pays for the place. Maybe she's independently wealthy or her ex-husband is paying a hell of a lot of alimony."

"If the kid is burglarizing houses, I'm thinking they don't have a lot of extra money laying around," suggested Mitch.

"Probably true. I don't see any records that suggest there's anyone else in the house. It should only be the two of them. How are we going to know if the kid is in class tonight?"

"I'm waiting for a phone call," Mitch told him. "That will tell me if Anthony showed up for his class or skipped it. We can decide what to do from there."

"You put someone in the classroom? Isn't that a little risky? What if the kid sees some new older guy in the room that looks like a cop? He could get nervous."

"No problems there. My eyes in the room have been there the whole time. Anthony will never know we're watching him."

Ali's eyes lit up. "This is your snitch, isn't it?" he asked excitedly.

"What?"

"The guy who's going to call you. He's your informant. He's how you figured out Anthony is our suspect. Probably a student he talks to. Maybe he bragged a little bit during a break and said too much, so the kid called you. Tell me I'm wrong."

Ali was a little too close for comfort with his guess, so Mitch remained quiet, staring off toward the house and pretending he hadn't heard the detective's suppositions. Ali stared at him, waiting to see if Mitch would answer. When no response was forthcoming, he nodded knowingly.

"I'm right. It's another kid in the class. Don't know why he's not willing to testify, though. Or she? Maybe he's afraid of this Anthony guy. He did kill at least one person already. That could make a witness hesitant to speak up."

"My informant, if he is in that classroom," said Mitch carefully, "gave us the best break we've had on this case so far. Let's not look a gift horse in the mouth and wish for more than we already got. *If* he's in the classroom. Why don't we let the matter drop?"

"Right. If," agreed Ali. "And it's a he." Ali raised his hands up in surrender when Mitch gave him an exasperated look. "I'm not trying to push. Well, yeah, I am. I'm nosey, that's all. It's why I'm such a good detective."

Mitch was saved from having to say anything further when his cell phone began buzzing in his jacket pocket. He retrieved the phone and answered it. Professor Solomon's voice responded, speaking only four hushed words: "He just walked in."

"Thank you." Mitch hung up and replaced the phone in his pocket. "Green light. Let's go knock and have a chat with mom."

The two investigators returned to their cars and drove to the front of Anthony Cunningham's home. With no suspect to scare away, there was no reason to walk a few hundred feet when the vehicles were readily available, especially when they would also have to walk back to the cars again later. Mitch followed Ali to the door and stayed a step behind, letting the shorter man take lead. It was his homicide, after all. Mitch technically was only investigating a vandalism.

Ali pressed the doorbell and a series of chimes rang through the interior of the home. A few seconds later, the door swung open to reveal a tall, pale woman with graying red hair. She looked to Mitch like an older, female version of the young man he had seen in the graveyard. They were definitely in the right place.

"Yes? May I help you?" the woman asked. Her eyes were narrowed and suspicious. She clearly was not used to a pair of strange men turning up on her doorstep, which was no surprise to Mitch. Most people these days did not appreciate strangers approaching their homes uninvited. "I'm not interested in buying anything, so if that's why you're here, you're wasting your time."

"No, ma'am," said Ali. He pulled his wallet from his back pocket and let it fall open, revealing a badge and an identification card with a gold, seven-pointed star embossed on one side. "We're from the Sheriff's department and we were hoping to talk to you a little bit. Is your son Anthony Cunningham?"

The woman's eyes widened in sudden panic. "Yes, he is. Is Anthony alright? Did something happen?"

"He's fine, he's fine," Ali hastened to reassure her, at the same time slipping his wallet back into his pants. "Nothing's happened to him, but we think he may have gotten himself into a little bit of trouble. I'm hoping you can answer a few questions for us and maybe clear this matter up today."

"What kind of questions?"

Ali glanced behind him and gave an obvious look up and down the residential street. "May we come in?" he asked, turning back toward Anthony's mother. "This could take a few minutes and I don't think your neighbors need to be watching you talk to the police. It's really none of their business, don't you think?"

Mitch suppressed a smile. Ali was using a simple tactic. Most people didn't like to be seen talking to the police since curious neighbors might notice and wonder about what might have happened in the house. It made a person look suspicious when cops turned up. It made them look bad. It was an old ploy, one that had been around for decades, but it still worked more often than not. Fortunately, Madeline Cunningham was no exception.

"Of course," she said after a brief mental debate of her options. She too glanced back and forth along the street, albeit a bit more furtively than Ali had done. "Please come in. Can I get either of you something to drink? Water? I can make some coffee."

"No, thank you," said Ali, speaking for both of them.

They entered the house and followed Madeline into the kitchen. She sat down at a coffee table tucked into a nook of the kitchen where a large bay window granted a view into the backyard. She gestured that Mitch and Ali should take seats at the opposite end of the table. They pulled out chairs and sat.

"What happened?" Madeline asked as Mitch settled into his chair. "What kind of trouble is Anthony in?"

"At the moment, we don't know for certain that he is in any trouble, Ms. Cunningham. I'm hoping we're chasing a dead end, but we need to find out. That's why we're here. Do you know where your son is right now?"

"Of course. He's at school. He's a student at Sac State and he has classes on most evenings. He goes to work after class, then comes home and sleeps most of the day."

"Where does he work?"

"At the Big Block superstore. He's a night stocker."

"Excuse me?" asked Ali. "He's a what?"

"A night stocker. He stocks the shelves while the store is closed at night. He works there Sunday through Thursday nights. The poor boy works very hard to pay his school bills as they come due so he doesn't have to take too many loans."

Anthony worked Sunday through Thursday nights. That was the answer to one question, Mitch thought. All of the burglaries had occurred on Friday or Saturday night, which had at first seemed an odd pattern, particularly since Solomon had said the golem stones were not limited to what nights they could be used. It had been Anthony's work schedule dictating the consistency of his break ins.

"On the nights that Anthony has off, does he go out much, or does he stay home?"

"A bit of both, I guess. Every other Friday, we have a standing date. Anthony and I go out and have dinner at a restaurant somewhere, then we come home and watch television together. We've been doing that for years, ever since his dad ran out on us. I thought it was a nice routine for both of us to remember that we always have each other."

"That's really nice," said Ali with a genuine smile on his face. "I like that. And the other nights?"

"My son is a normal twenty-year-old boy, Officer. He has friends and occasionally goes out on dates, so yes, he is usually out of the house on the other nights. Does that mean something to you?"

"Not yet. I'm trying to figure out his schedule, that's all. You see, I'm investigating some thefts. Nothing major, but some property has gone missing, and somebody told somebody else that told me that Anthony might know something about the missing property."

"My son is not a thief, Officer," Madeline stated firmly.

"I'm not saying he is. I'm simply letting you know why we're here. We have to follow every lead we get, regardless of whether or not we think it will get us anywhere. We need to check off all the right boxes so nobody can accuse us of not doing our job. I hope you understand."

Mitch mentally applauded Ali's tact. He had completely steered clear of mentioning the murder, as the accusation might be enough to scare Madeline into freezing up and kicking them out of the house. A simple theft complaint, with third hand witnesses, wasn't quite so intimidating, and it gave her enough doubt to continue believing that her son was not involved.

Ali knew what he was doing and was handling the interview well. Mitch, knowing that Ali's focus was on Madeline, let his own attention wander around his surroundings. His gaze trailed leisurely around the kitchen, finding nothing out of the ordinary for a residential tract home probably build sometime in the 1990's. It was small, but clean. Madeline clearly took pride in her house and took care of it.

Next, he examined the window, peering out into the yard behind the house. A concrete pad had been poured to create a patio that extended about eight feet from the edge of the house into the rest of the yard. At the far end, a few trees lined the property fence. They looked like apple trees to Mitch. He had no idea what type of apples they might be, and he acknowledged he could be totally wrong about them being apples at all. Still, they were nice to look at with their small pink flowers and new leaves just beginning to form in the mostly bare branches. Between the trees and the concrete was a patch of brown and green that may have once been a lawn but now consisted of more weeds and dirt than grass. As he stared out into the tiny yard, at that mottled stretch of ground, Mitch's heart skipped a beat and began to race.

"So, what can I tell you that would help you prove Anthony has nothing to do with your thefts?"

"Ms. Cunningham, does Anthony have his own room here?"

She nodded. "Yes."

"Is there a lock on his door? Do you ever go in there, or do you stay out of it?"

"I give him his privacy, but there's no lock, and I do go in occasionally. I do his laundry for him, and I usually have to collect it off his floor." She gave the men a look that Mitch recognized from his own mother when she used to complain to him about not picking up his room.

"Would it be okay with you if we took a look in his room? Our witness said that Anthony might have some of the items we're looking for."

Madeline looked skeptical, but before she could say no, Ali continued.

"Even if we find something, that doesn't mean Anthony stole it. He might have been holding it for someone else. It's possible the only thing he's guilty of is hanging around the wrong friends. We can talk to him about that later if we need to. If we don't find anything, we can put that in our reports and move on to the next lead."

The chance that this ordeal could be over in the next few minutes if the police found nothing in Anthony's room was the carrot that Madeline needed to push her in the direction Mitch and Ali wanted. Mitch could see in her eyes her determination to prove her son's innocence once and for all. She stood up.

"Okay. Of course. Let's see if we can clear this up for you. I'll show you gentlemen his room."

As Ali rose to follow, Mitch stood and tapped the detective on the hip with the back of his hand. When he had Ali's attention, he jerked his head toward the window.

"Yard," he whispered.

"I know," Ali whispered back. "It's a wreck."

"No. Look at the lawn. At the dirt. It's heaped up in five different piles."

"Five?" Ali jerked his gaze to the window, understanding the significance of what Mitch was telling him and wanting to confirm the observation for himself. "Five," he said after a moment. "Shit."

They hurried to catch up to Madeline who had disappeared down a hallway. They found her standing beside an open bedroom door, gesturing inside with one hand. "This is his. Feel free to look around, but please don't break anything or make a mess."

"Of course, not," Mitch promised. "We'll just take a quick look around, and I promise we will put back anything we move."

"Are you sure you don't want any coffee? I'm going to put on a pot for myself and I can make extra."

"Actually, coffee sounds wonderful," said Mitch, seeing an opportunity to get Madeline away from the bedroom while they searched. "I would love a cup."

She stepped back into the kitchen with assurances that she would only be a moment. Mitch and Ali watched her disappear from the hallway, then went to work.

Initially, the two men avoided digging through any drawers or typical hiding places such as behind furniture or under the bed mattress. This was not a warranted search that would permit them to hunt through any and all potential hiding places. They wanted to find something that was more or less in plain view. All they needed was one object that could definitively link Anthony to any of the burglaries. That would be enough to get a judge to sign the warrant they needed to properly tear this place apart.

On the far wall furthest from the door, Anthony had a four-shelf bookcase. The bottom three shelves held colorful textbooks of various heights and thicknesses, while the top shelf had become a discard pile for sundry items of personal property. Mitch found pocket change, matchbooks, gift cards to a selection of stores, pens, a pair of sunglasses, and two watches. He pointed the watches out to Ali.

"What kid has more than one wristwatch? Do you recognize these as any of the missing stuff?"

"Hard to tell," admitted Ali. "They probably are stolen, but I can't tell by looking at them."

"So, we keep searching."

Ali nodded in agreement.

Mitch checked the other shelves for any other items that may have been slipped in among the books. He found a couple of paper bookmarks and some more loose change, but nothing significant. Ali moved over to the boy's desk located beside the bed. He rummaged through the clutter of papers and notebooks he found spread over the surface of the desk, careful to stick to only the areas that were visible to casual observation.

"What the hell?" Ali asked, holding up a worn notebook bound in faded tan leather. He had opened the journal and was flipping through the yellowed pages inside. The open book was barely larger than a sheet of typing paper held sideways. "What's the kid doing with a book written in Yiddish?"

"Yiddish?" asked Mitch, moving closer to peer over Ali's shoulder. The text in the book appeared to be handwritten. The unfamiliar characters were drawn in a meticulous scrawl, tiny, but neatly and carefully done. To Mitch, the writing looked more like the notes on a musical scoresheet than letters, and he had no idea how to read what he was looking at. The boxy figures depicted on the pages did vaguely remind him of something he might have seen in a museum, perhaps imprinted into a clay tablet unearthed during an archaeological dig. "That's Yiddish? You read Yiddish?"

"No," admitted Ali. "I can't read it, but I recognize it. At least, I think it's Yiddish. It looks a little like Arabic, but the characters are much more rigid and isolated." He pointed at a line in the book. "See how the letters don't touch? Arabic usually flows together, like cursive."

"May I?" asked Mitch, holding out his hand. Ali obliged and passed him the notebook.

Mitch flipped through the pages blindly, not knowing exactly what he was looking for. The notebook was clearly old, the binding cracked and worn, and the outer leather rubbed smooth from years of casual handling. The book was thin, probably not more than fifty or so pages, each of them filled with notes front and back. Most of the pages were covered with the tight boxy writing, the ink faded but legible, but a few had sketches and drawings between the written notes and along the margins. Mitch found several drawings of man-shaped figures, the head, arms and legs rounded into caricature proportions. They looked like a series of gingerbread men to him, with blunt heads and no feet or hands.

When he got to the end of the book, he turned back to the first page and began leafing through more carefully. On page four he found the proof he had hoped for. The entire page was an illustration of one of the roughly manlike figures. Next to the figure, the artist drew three faceted spheres that appeared to be gems.

Or sapphires.

Each sphere had a line connecting it to the creature beside it. One line pointed to the head, one to the chest, and one to the stomach.

"Control, form, and movement," Mitch muttered.

"That makes sense to you?" asked Ali, still standing beside him.

Mitch was interrupted by the buzz of his phone. Someone had sent him a text. He thought about ignoring it considering the importance of this recent find, but his curiosity won out. He pulled out the phone and found a text from Solomon. It read: "He just left."

There was no name, but Mitch didn't need a name to know exactly to whom Solomon was referring. Anthony had left the classroom. Before Mitch could say anything to warn Ali about their suspect's movements, Madeline returned.

"I'm sorry gentlemen, but I'm going to have to ask you to stop what you're doing and leave my house."

"You called Anthony, didn't you?" asked Mitch.

Madeline looked guilty for moment, but then her features hardened. Mitch guessed she was probably telling herself that she had done the right thing warning her son and these men had no right to make her think otherwise.

"My son does not want you in his room any longer. I think you should leave."

Ali stepped forward. Mitch was unsure if he was leaving or about to attempt to change Madeline's mind about throwing them out, but he stopped the detective with a hand on his arm. He held up the notebook where Ali could see it.

"This is enough," he said. "Lock it down and call the judge."

Ali's eyes narrowed. "You sure? I don't know what that book is."

"I do." Mitch took a deep breath. So much for confidential informants. "This came from the Dirty Bandit's first burglary."

"I don't remember seeing a notebook in the property list."

"That's because his first burglary didn't follow your M.O. so it isn't in your packet."

"You two need to leave my house. Now!" Insisted Madeline Cunningham, interrupting the investigators' conversation.

Ali turned to her, his expression twisted into one of impatient irritation. "Wait your damn turn," he snapped. "Keep your mouth shut, and we'll leave when we're ready to leave."

The sudden transition from the quiet, friendly little detective who had seemed so concerned about her son into this aggressive man in her house telling her to shut up shocked Madeline into silence.

Ali faced Mitch once more. "What first burglary are you telling me about? Be quick, and you'd better be right."

"Remember the tip line callers?" When Ali nodded, Mitch continued. "There was a Professor Schick that called. He was the one who told you...," Mitch paused. He leaned closer toward Ali and spoke softly, trying not to be overheard by Madeline. "He told you a monster committed your murder. A golem."

"The nut job?" blurted Ali. "You're talking about the psycho with the Lord of the Rings fetish?"

"Actually, it's a golem, not Gollum. Look, it's not important. Whether the guy's nuts or not, his house was broken into and stuff was taken. It's in his report. This," and Mitch tapped the notebook, "was one of the items stolen from his house. One hundred percent guarantee it. Between the notebook, the stone fragment linking the Dirty Bandit to the cemetery, and the piles of dirt outside, you've got enough for the judge."

Ali paused, thinking. He mentally walked himself through the evidence Mitch had laid out for him. Reaching a decision, he pulled out his cell phone.

Thirty minutes later, Ali had two uniformed Sheriff's deputies sitting with Madeline in the kitchen while he and Mitch rooted through every square inch of Anthony's bedroom. Drawers were pulled and dumped, the closet ransacked, and every book in the bookcase leafed through. Additional jewelry was discovered in the desk drawers, some of it matching descriptions in the Dirty Bandit reports, and a bundle of cash totaling a little over four hundred dollars was found in a shoe box in the closet. The money was collected to be fingerprinted and compared to the victims' prints.

Dirt was also collected from the piles in the yard to be soil tested and compared to the vandalized graves in Dasan's Terrace. Mitch had little doubt in his mind they would be a perfect match. The final nail in the coffin for Anthony, however, was a cellphone stuffed between the mattress and box springs of his bed. When Ali powered it on, the screen picture showed a young girl playing with a Labrador Retriever in the driveway of a home. Ali had met the girl in the picture.

She was the daughter of the Dirty Bandit's fifth victim.

Unfortunately, despite a thorough ransacking of Anthony's possessions, one critical piece of evidence did not reveal itself. The golem stones were not in the room. Mitch wandered outside into the backyard looking for hiding places before the last of the daylight faded. He even sifted through the piles of grave dirt after the tech was done taking samples, hoping to turn up the stones. He came away empty. Either Anthony had the sapphires with him or he had them secreted away in a location safely away from the home.

At the beginning of the search, after obtaining a conditional warrant from the afterhours judge, Ali requested an additional uniformed deputy to wait outside in a patrol car to pick up Anthony Cunningham when he showed up at the house. The deputies in the kitchen had been instructed not to let Madeline make or answer any phone calls while law enforcement was still inside the residence. Anthony still had not made an appearance when the search concluded a couple hours later.

When all potential evidence had been collected, bagged, and tagged, Ali gathered up several of the items to carry out to his car. Mitch collected the notebook from the pile of evidence. After Jorge had been briefed on the existence of the golem stones the previous week, he had pulled Mitch aside. The shift sergeant had given him a direct order that if he ever managed to get the stones or the notebook in his possession, he was to bring it back to DTPD and log it into their property room. The items were dangerous in the wrong hands and must be kept out of circulation. The Dead Town property room was the only place with sufficient physical and magical security measures in place to make sure that happened.

"I'm keeping this, if you don't mind," he said to the detective.

"That's evidence," Ali told him. "It stays with the rest of the stuff."

"Listen, there's something you should know. Professor Schick, the 'nut job' as you called him, is my informant. He's the one that gave me Anthony's name. He's my witness. But remember, he's a witness to a grave vandalism, not the murder.

This is actually two cases tied together, yours and mine. Technically, this burglary isn't connected to your murder investigation; it's part of mine. I would like to log this into our property room at the DTPD and list it in my report."

Ali looked skeptical. "I'm not sure that holds up, Mitch. I don't want to poison this case. We finally have a suspect, and I don't want the search warrant to go bad because I let you keep that book."

"It won't. I was here when the book was found, and I identified its significance to our case. I recognized it because I was the one that researched where it came from. It only makes sense that it stay attached to *my* investigation. When it's time to testify on the warrant, make sure I get a subpoena, and I'll testify to make it stick."

Ali nodded. "Okay. You broke this case wide open. I don't imagine you're going to let it fall apart on me now. Keep the book."

The two men shook hands and Mitch headed for his car. He was happy at the outcome of this evening, but not overly so. This was only a partial victory. They had enough evidence now to arrest and convict Anthony Cunningham for murder without having to reveal the golem's part in the burglaries to the general population, and the book on how to raise living piles of rock and dirt would soon be safely locked away in the property room at DTPD.

Their murderer, however, along with the three golem stones, was still in the wind.

CHAPTER 23

Mitch sat on a low headstone, his jacket pulled tight around his torso and his hands stuffed deep into the pockets. The weather had begun to warm over the past couple of weeks, but a sudden cold snap had pushed nighttime temperatures back into the mid-thirties. The cold, coupled with the low hanging fog covering the cemetery grounds, left Mitch wet, cold, miserable, and in a foul mood.

The waning moon overhead was half full, casting enough light to see his surroundings. In order not to be visible himself, Mitch had selected a position under three young oak trees growing close together. Their shadows kept him hidden, but the occasional large drops of condensation rolling from the branches and striking his exposed head and neck had him second guessing his choice of locations.

"This sucks," said a voice to his left. Mitch heard a series of sniffles followed by the sound of someone spitting out a wad of phlegm. Tink was huddled on another grave marker a few feet away, just as cold and unhappy as Mitch. “Do you really think he’s going to show?”

After Mitch and Ali left Anthony Cunningham’s home, a uniformed deputy had remained to watch the house for the remainder of the night. Anthony never showed. Mitch figured his mother must have warned him away, or else he simply went to ground from his own personal sense of fear and self-preservation. Whatever the reason, Anthony must know by now he was wanted for murder, and he would not risk going back to the house for any reason. He would instead, hide somewhere until he could calm himself enough to figure out his next move.

With a murder charge hanging over his head, and every cop within a hundred-mile radius carrying a copy of his picture from the wanted BOLO, the kid probably decided he needed to get out of town and lie low for a while. He needed to find a place where no one recognized him or could potentially report him to authorities. That wasn’t an easy thing to do for someone whose credit cards and bank statements were being monitored and with nothing more than pocket change in his possession. He would need an infusion of quick cash in order to get far enough away to feel safe.

Ali believed Anthony had already fled the state. Unfortunately, Sergeant Smythe agreed with the detective, believing the kid probably hopped a bus for Nevada or Oregon the moment his mom told him the police were at the house.

Mitch didn’t think Anthony was gone. Not yet. Anthony had the golem stones, and he knew of only one place on this planet for certain that they would work. The history behind the golem stones stressed that finding locations where they could function was exceptionally difficult. As soon as he left Sacramento, Anthony might never find another cemetery with all the necessary requirements to raise a new golem. Because of this, Mitch expected he would attempt one more big score before finally going on the run.

And it would have to be *really* big.

The fact he would break into another house was bad enough, but with the paltry amounts of cash and loot their suspect had managed to obtain previously, Mitch was concerned about the target the boy might choose for his last burglary. Anthony needed serious money if he was going to fund his escape and stay flush long enough to search out another cemetery as old and powerful as Dasan's Terrace. Before, it seemed the boy had targeted houses where he believed the owners would not be home, choosing to accept smaller gains in order to avoid confrontations. This time, the target would most likely be the home of a wealthy family regardless of whether they were home or not. Money had become more important than any hesitation over harming another human being.

Mitch did not want to see anyone else hurt. He also knew if Anthony managed to get his hands on some cash, he would leave the city and be permanently out of his reach within hours. For both of these reasons, he was freezing his ass off, hiding in the northwest corner of Dead Town for the second night in a row.

Wednesday night, his first shift after serving the search warrant at Anthony Cunningham's home, Mitch had convinced the entire shift to assist with the stakeout. Despite the sergeant's reservations about Anthony already being a thousand miles away, Jorge, Brad, and Tink had joined him in the cold and damp, and hunkered down throughout most of the night waiting for a murder suspect that never came. When the stakeout proved unsuccessful, Jorge had taken it as a sign that his assumption was correct.

Mitch had begged the shift to watch Northwest one more night, but Jorge and Brad had demurred.

"It's movie night," said Brad. "I'd rather be warm and enjoying a movie than freezing in the damp grass again for a kid that's too smart to show up anyway. I think you need to let this one go, Mitch."

"We have our radios," said Jorge. "If you want to spend another night out there, I won't stop you. If you need us, call and we'll come running. Otherwise, I'm sorry, but I think it's a waste of time."

Tonight, only Tink was willing to go through the discomfort and boredom a second time, though his enthusiasm for this duty was clearly flagging. Mitch appreciated the man's support. His presence here tonight made the lonely hours pass a little easier.

"Hey, Mitch. Did you hear me? I asked if you think he's really going to show."

"I don't know," admitted Mitch. "What I do know is that if he doesn't come tonight, he's probably long gone and I'm not going to get another shot at him. This is my only hope of getting my hands on him and the golem stones, so as long as there's the slightest chance he might turn up, I'm going to be here waiting."

"This sucks," Tink muttered again.

"I know. If you want to head in and watch movies with Brad, go ahead. I understand."

"Nope," said Tink, then he spat again, wiping at his nose unhappily. "I'm here for you. I don't know if you're right, but I'm not letting you tackle this guy alone if he does come. That golem thing sounds like a really nasty character."

Mitch's legs were numb and beginning to tingle. He shifted his weight on the headstone, trying to get the blood in his feet circulating. Reaching along the side of the grave marker, he touched the handle of a sledgehammer he had brought with him from home. He felt the smooth length of the wooden handle, cold and solid under his fingertips. Reassured the eight-pound maul was right where he had put it, he straightened again.

Mitch had taken Solomon's advice and brought the heavy hammer just in case he was unable to stop Anthony from raising a new golem. He knew he couldn't stop the creature with his hands or any of the equipment on his belt, so he had brought along something a bit more substantial. Tink was similarly prepared, having lifted a pickaxe from the cemetery's gardening supply shed.

"You told me you used to talk to your grandfather," Mitch said.

Tink's silhouette nodded in the shadows. "Yup. Long time ago."

"I wish he was still here."

"Why is that?"

"Because we could be inside where it's warm and he could be patrolling the cemetery for Cunningham. If the kid showed up, he could pop into the building and let us know. It would make this stake out thing a lot easier."

"Yeah, it would," agreed Tink. "But I haven't seen gramps in a lot of years. I miss having him around sometimes. Especially when I'm playing poker. It would be nice having someone telling me what everyone else was holding. I'd clean up."

Mitch snorted a quiet laugh. "Good plan. Why don't you see if Chief Delaney would help you out with that? Maybe he'd like to get out once in a while."

"Nah. Delaney never leaves the PD. I haven't seen him anywhere outside the building the whole time I've been here. He doesn't even go out to visit his grave."

"He's buried out here?" asked Mitch, surprised.

"Of course. Why do you think he's here? We're nowhere near the store where he was killed. That's all the way out on Mather Field Road. No, he's stuck in the cemetery because he's still attached to his body, and his body is buried here."

"Attached? What do you mean attached?"

"Spirits that stay in this world have to attach themselves to something. At least, that's what Dot told me. Otherwise, they would move on without any problems. Sometimes a soul gets attached to a place, a house or building or something. Sometimes they attach to an object, like their own body, for example. When that happens, wherever the object goes, so do they."

"What about Denny? He doesn't stay in the cemetery. What's he attached to?"

"Dot thinks he's attached to his body, just like Delaney. She also thinks that the reason he's still here is somehow linked to you and your house. That's why he visits every Christmas. He's looking for something."

"Quiet!" snapped Mitch.

"I'm sorry," said Tink, sounding hurt. "I didn't mean to upset…"

"No," said Mitch in a sharp whisper. "Not that. Something's wrong. Shhh."

Tink stopped talking and listened hard into the sudden silence. Mitch also scanned the darkness, straining his ears for any sounds. The hairs on the back of his neck rose and his skin began to prickle. Something was happening, but he didn't see or hear anything out of the ordinary. On a hunch, he let his vision go slightly blurry, letting his mind sift through all the sensory information around him as Violet had taught him. The magic forces surrounding Dead Town became fully visible.

The pale wisps of power that normally floated through the air and permeated the ground were all there, but there was something odd about them tonight, something that didn't look quite right to Mitch. In all the times he had observed and even used the magic, it had always hovered and flowed without noticeable purpose, meandering in no particular direction. It had reminded him of smoke drifting in the air on a windless day.

Tonight, the magic was not still. It shifted as a cohesive unit, not quickly, but inexorably, as if it had suddenly developed a sense of purpose. Stranger still, all visible lines of power seemed to flow in the same direction. The streams of force moved toward the southeast. Something was drawing magic toward itself, something that required such enormous supplies of energy that it impacted the flow of magic all around the cemetery. In an instant, Mitch knew what was happening.

Violet once told him about the disruption to the flow of magic in Dead Town whenever Anthony had raised a golem. Right now, he was seeing what she had described firsthand. The magic was being drawn toward the stones as they activated and brought the inanimate ground to life.

Mitch kicked himself mentally. He had assumed that Anthony would come back to the same spot to raise his final golem. That was why he and Tink had set up their stakeout here in the northwest corner. He realized how stupid he had been to expect Anthony to stick to his old habits, especially when the kid knew the police were hunting for him. Of course, he was going to change his routine. Mitch should have anticipated that.

"Anthony is in the cemetery," Mitch told Tink. "I fucked up. He's south of us."

Mitch leapt to his feet, grabbed the sledgehammer propped against the headstone and ran for the security fence. Tink grabbed his pick and followed right behind him. As he bolted through the gate, not bothering to pause long enough to resecure the lock, Mitch keyed the radio microphone hooked to his shoulder lapel and shouted into it.

"This is Loman. We have an active nine-oh-one south of our location. Requesting back up."

A moment later, Jorge's voice crackled on the radio asking for a more specific location. Mitch had no idea yet where Anthony was located, so he did not respond. He kept his eyes on the magic and followed the flow of power through the cemetery. As luck would have it, Mitch and Tink did not have far to go. After only about a minute of racing through Back Half, they stumbled across the would-be magician. He was standing beside one of the older graves in the area with his hands out to his sides in a dramatic flourish. The magic spiraled around the grave, swirling in from all directions throughout the cemetery, feeding the golem stones as they did their work.

In the middle of the magic maelstrom, a mound of dark earth rose from the ground, bursting upward and forming into the rough shape of a man. Arms and legs extended from the rubble, and the mass of dirt and rock rose to stand on its blunt, blocky feet. Behind the creature, Mitch could see a deep, concave depression in the earth from which the monster's physical substance had been stolen. The roughly formed head at the top of the mountainous heap swiveled right to left as though trying to orient itself in unfamiliar surroundings.

Mitch shifted his sledgehammer to his left hand and reached for his pistol. Solomon's words came back to him then, reminding him that once the golem had received its instructions, it would be next to impossible to stop it. The professor had made it quite clear if Anthony managed to raise the golem, Mitch should shoot the kid before he gave the creature any orders. If the golem had no direction, it would remain motionless until sunrise.

If it moved, there would be no stopping it.

Mitch hesitated. He snapped open the retaining strap on his holster, but he did not draw his weapon. He paused only a second, but it was one second too long. Anthony turned to see Mitch and Tink approaching.

"Kill them!" he yelled at the golem. "Kill the cops."

Mitch snapped his holster closed over the pistol. His opportunity to prevent a disaster had passed, and the gun would be useless in the coming showdown with the golem. Although frightened at having to face this lumbering beast again, he was also relieved. Mitch did not think he could have shot Anthony in cold blood, even knowing his failure to do so would lead to a confrontation he did not think he could win. His greatest regret however, was that his decision might lead to Tink's death as well as his own.

Mitch lifted the sledgehammer, holding the handle with both hands defensively across his chest while at the same time preparing to swing the unwieldy weapon. He forced himself to put aside any ideas of death or losing, those thoughts were counterproductive. Instead, he needed to figure out how to beat this monster.

The golem turned toward Mitch first, the shallow depressions in its face that served as eyes oriented on his stationary form. The paired pits of black shadow reminded Mitch uncomfortably of the dual barrels of a shotgun, and currently both of those barrels were aimed squarely at him. The creature toppled forward, appearing to lose its balance, then using the momentum of its fall, it hurtled at Mitch on unsteady legs.

Mitch hoped this new creation would behave like the last one, running at him with clumsy attacks that he could dodge at the last moment. Fortunately, at least so far, that appeared to be the case.

As the golem stumbled within reach, Mitch stepped to his right to avoid the outstretched arms. It lumbered awkwardly past him, and he swung the sledgehammer at the creature's retreating back. He missed. His counterattack with the weighted hammer had been delivered too slowly. Worse, the momentum of his swing overbalanced him and almost pitched him to the ground.

"Shit," he breathed, staggering to keep on his feet.

Luckily for Mitch, the golem took more time than he had to adjust to its own unsuccessful attack. It slowed to a full stop before turning around to reassess its intended target. Before it could begin a second charge, Tink rushed in from behind and buried the point of his pick in the monster's back. The point sunk deep and lodged in place. The golem turned to look for the source of the new assault, and the motion jerked the handle of the pick from Tink's hands, slinging the surprised man off his feet into the damp cemetery grass.

The golem took a step toward the fallen officer's prone figure, but before it could get any closer, Tink scrambled upright and scuttled several steps away. The creature paused as if considering its next move. Mitch decided this was his opportunity to repeat Tink's maneuver. He rushed forward, raising the hammer to strike the creature in the back. He swung, feeling the shudder of the handle in his hands as the weighted mallet struck home. It sent out a spray of dirt and debris from the impact point, causing small shards of rock and damp soil to pelt against Mitch's face.

Mitch tried to raise the sledgehammer for another quick strike before the golem could recover, but the flat soles of his boots slid in the wet grass and his feet slipped out from underneath him.

The fall, though jarring, probably saved his life.

As he went down, the golem spun, flailing with one massive arm. The solid appendage of dirt and rock sailed over Mitch, through the space his head had been occupying only a moment before. The fall took the wind from his lungs, but he did not have time to lie on the ground and recover. The golem was already moving, raising a massive foot to stomp and crush its fallen prey.

Mitch rolled to the side, dragging the hammer with him. When he felt he was far enough away to be safe, he climbed to his feet and took a moment to catch his breath. A movement in his peripheral vision caught his attention. The vicious giant was already charging toward him, and the creature was much closer than he had anticipated.

With no time to aim his strike, in desperation, Mitch swung the sledgehammer in the direction of the threat. The head of the hammer collided with the creature's hand as it tried to slap Mitch into oblivion. He felt more dirt pelt his face and neck as the golem's hand exploded from the impact with his weapon.

The damage was significant this time, it might even cripple the creature to some extent, Mitch thought, but he had no time to celebrate the minor victory. The impact with the golem's arm had also wrenched the hammer from his hands and sent it flying at least twenty feet away. Mitch stood empty handed in front of the injured golem, the hulking beast now positioned between him and his dropped hammer.

A blur moved in the shadows to his left. Tink appeared out of the darkness behind the golem and grabbed the handle of his pick, still buried in the monster's back. He wrenched at the wood handle, but the stuck tool did not budge. The golem must have felt the pull, however, and it flailed with its remaining good hand. Mitch heard the dull impact as the creature struck Tink and sent him flying through the fog.

Tink hit the ground like a ragdoll, all loose limbs and awkward angles. This time, he did not immediately climb to his feet. He remained unmoving in the grass.

"Tink? Are you okay, buddy?"

There was no response. That was bad.

Reluctantly, Mitch decided it was time for Plan B. He did not have much confidence in his abilities to manipulate magic as he had only been practicing the powered attacks for a few days, but his options at the moment were limited. Tink did not have time for him to try to come up with any other ideas. Even now, the golem moved to take the unconscious officer out of the fight permanently. Mitch reached out his hand, drawing from the surrounding streams of magic power exactly as he had practiced under Violet's tutelage. When a small vortex of magic hovered obediently over his palm, he focused his will and launched it toward the golem.

The magic struck the monster's torso, exploding on contact. Despite the visually dramatic results of the magical detonation, the golem seemed undamaged where the explosion occurred. The act did however have the unintended consequence of drawing the creature's full attention toward Mitch. Though mostly unhurt, the golem apparently decided that with this latest display, Mitch was now the more dangerous opponent and deserved its undivided attention.

Mitch repeated the motions, pulling power and launching another attack. The second explosion was an exact repeat of the first. Plenty of pyrotechnics and promise, but little to no actual damage. Mitch understood the problem immediately, but he had no idea how to fix it. The force of the magic was being expended in all directions when he released it, so the impact radiated outward from the creature instead of inward. Mitch needed the explosion to aim toward the golem to do maximum injury. Easier said than done. He had no idea how to make that happen. During his time practicing force attacks with Violet, this particular physics puzzle had not been addressed.

The golem rushed forward. As Mitch mentally debated how to redirect his attacks to make them more effective, the golem opted for a more direct approach to battle. Mitch held his ground and pulled power toward himself. He had an idea. It wasn't a great idea, but it was all he had left.

The golem rumbled closer, but Mitch still did not step out of the way. He waited, drawing more and more from the magic around him. The golem, perhaps surprised by his failure to move, slowed. It did not stop its charge, but its progress was noticeably delayed. Mitch took full advantage of the creature's hesitancy. He leaped forward, meeting the golem's stalled rush and slamming his open palms into the monster's belly.

Mitch expended the power he had gathered in a single, massive release. Earth exploded under his hands, flying out in all directions around him and leaving a divot in the golem's torso deep enough for Mitch to sink his hands in to the elbows. His left cheek stung where a sharp chip of rock had cut him during the blast, but he barely noticed it. It was nothing compared to the damage the golem received.

He had done it! He had actually hurt the beast.

The fight wasn't hopeless after all, he realized, elated at the results of his effort. Mitch had a real chance. Now, he only needed to regroup and try again. A few more explosions like the last one and he might be able to destroy the golem, or at least disable it sufficiently to negate any threat it posed.

Mitch attempted to fall backward and roll out of the way. He pushed away from the golem's torso, but something struck him in the back, preventing his escape. He had been too slow. While he was in contact with it, the creature had managed to get its good hand behind him and hold him in place. As he realized his mistake, the second, damaged arm closed around him, trapping him in an unbreakable embrace.

The golem squeezed, enfolding Mitch with its branch-sized appendages and lifting him off the ground. Mitch's right hand was free, but his left arm was pinned, pressed to his side by the golem's unwelcome bear hug. He wriggled helplessly, trying to free himself from the powerful arms. The pressure around his chest increased as the creature doubled its efforts to crush the life from him. Mitch's left arm, trapped between the golem and his own body, remarkably was the only thing keeping the monster from collapsing his ribcage and killing him instantly. Although briefly delayed, that final outcome was still very much on the horizon if Mitch couldn't figure a way out of his current predicament in a hurry.

In desperation, Mitch pulled at the magic around him with his free hand.

The wisps of amorphous power gathered slowly. Too slowly, Mitch thought, his heart racing as his panic to escape increased. He rushed the attack, failing to take proper time to shape the magic in his hand. Mitch slammed the mostly unformed spell against the golem's head. It erupted, creating another shower of golem debris. The damage this time was not as dramatic. Where the shallow eye holes of the creature had been, there was a single larger depression now visible.

This new injury did not slow the golem at all.

Mitch panted shallowly, unable to draw a deep breath. The creature was not fast, but it was relentless as it continued the crushing force of its hold. Something cracked deep inside Mitch and a sharp, stabbing pain radiated out from his right side. A rib had broken. More would follow soon. The broken shards would then collapse inward, piercing through lung tissue and heart muscle. Mitch exhaled but could not draw air back into his body. The outside pressure did not allow him to pull in another breath. Even if the golem stopped moving right now, if Mitch could not free himself, he would suffocate in a matter of minutes. The golem did not stop however, and Mitch figured his lifespan was currently more accurately measured in seconds.

He reached for the magic one last time, pulling everything he could hold into one bright, focused point in his right palm. He imagined a magnifying glass, orienting the dispersed light of the sun to a single, focused, burning pinpoint. He grunted weakly as he slapped his hand against the monster's head and released the power in a final, last-ditch explosive burst.

Mitch's hand punched through the golem's head, finding open space on the other side of the rough dirt oval.

The golem did not so much as flinch at the damage. Instead, it squeezed again. Another rib snapped, causing Mitch to cry out. Another lost breath he could not get back. The fight was over. Mitch had opened a hole from one side of the beast's head to the other and he had not even slowed it down. He probably could have removed the head entirely and it wouldn't have made any difference, he realized. This animated pile of earth would only stop if he completely destroyed it. Something he knew now he could not accomplish on his own. Certainly not while pinned in the behemoth's merciless embrace.

He was going to die.

Mitch stared through the hole he had created, finding black sky and the polite twinkle of stars on the other side. It was like peering through a narrow window into a world of quiet and calm; a world he could never reach. Light from the partial moon overhead cascaded through the opening, illuminating the cavern in the creature's head and casting tiny shadows over the jagged terrain of the hole.

One irregular slope in the uneven opening caught his attention. It was oddly shaped, seeming to be all edges and tiny flat surfaces, unlike the area around it. As he stared, a glint of moonlight reflected from one of the smooth planes.

The edges of Mitch's vision began to close in. Without oxygen, his body was shutting down and his thinking became sluggish. He reached his hand into the opening, unsure what he was searching for yet somehow, still desperate to reach it. He was dying, he knew that, but something inside of him, a last remaining flicker of his desire to survive was telling him to reach for the object he had spied in that hole.

His fingertips grazed the surface. The object was solid and surprisingly smooth. He dug his fingers deeper into the soil around it until he clutched the thing in his fist. It fit neatly under his palm. Mitch wrenched his hand back, pulling his prize free from its imprisonment in the golem's head. As it came out into unfiltered moonlight, Mitch could see it was some sort of gemstone.

A sapphire, his addled, oxygen-starved mind told him. It was yellow.

The crushing force around his chest eased, then released. Mitch landed on his feet, but injured and semi-conscious as he was, his legs refused to support him, and he immediately collapsed into a heap on the ground. He sucked in a deep breath, rejoicing in the sweet taste of the air as it filled his chest. It rejuvenated him, but it also hurt like hell. Mitch screamed, a short hitching cry as his broken ribs reminded him he was still badly hurt by his ordeal with the golem.

He curled into a ball on the ground and panted, trying to find the happy medium between breathing normally and not moving his injured ribcage. While he lay on the ground, helpless, a shadow passed over him. In too much pain to move his body, Mitch turned his head slightly to seek the cause of the shadow. The golem peered down at him. At least, he assumed it was looking at him. Its head was little more than a ball with a massive hole excavated through it, so there was no way to gauge exactly where it might be staring.

The golem turned and moved off, heading toward the east.

Mitch held up the gemstone in his hand, gazing into the multiple yellow facets of the sapphire. He took several more breaths, breathing in slow and shallow, then blowing the air out in a long careful exhale. He tried to remember what Solomon had told him about the yellow gem. The golem was still moving, so he hadn't removed the stone responsible for motion. It was still partially shaped like a man, so it also wasn't the stone for maintaining its form. He must have removed the control stone, he realized. The golem had dropped him because it no longer cared about him. It was now free to behave as it wished.

This could be very bad. It was good for Mitch who was, thankfully, still alive, but this could be disastrous for anyone else with whom the monster came into contact.

As if in answer to his thoughts, a scream echoed through the cemetery. Carried by the low fog and bouncing off the stone and marble of the nearby tombs and mausoleums, it was difficult to tell which direction the cry came from. Mitch guessed it was somewhere east of him, in the direction the golem had disappeared.

"Are you okay?" asked a voice nearby. A form knelt beside Mitch, and it took him a moment to recognize Jorge.

"Hey, Sarge," Mitch panted. "Tink. Find Tink. He got hit pretty hard."

"He's fine," said someone else from further away. Mitch recognized Brad's voice. "He got his bell rung, but he looks like he's going to be okay. What happened here?"

"Jorge," said Mitch, wincing at another sharp pain in his chest. He waited until it had passed. "The golem, it went east. Somebody screamed. Please, go check. Don't confront it, though. Dangerous."

"I heard it. Are you going to be okay here if I leave you?"

Mitch nodded. "Fine. Go. Please check."

Jorge rose to his feet and took off at a slow jog. He immediately disappeared from sight, melting into the fog.

"Hey, Mitch." It was Tink's voice this time. "Did it kill you?"

"No," Mitch managed to choke out.

"Hmph. Me, neither. We must have scared it away. What a pussy."

Mitch laughed, but it was quickly replaced by a groan of pain as his crushed ribs insisted that laughing was a really bad idea. He curled onto his right side, using the weight of his body to immobilize the broken bones as much as possible, then focusing back on his breathing. Air in. Air out. He heard Brad using his cellphone to call for an ambulance.

When the call ended, Mitch heard Tink and Brad move closer to his location. The two men sat next to him, settling in until Jorge could return and relay what he had found. Mitch remained where he was on the ground, not wanting to cause any more discomfort to himself than absolutely necessary.

"Ambulance is coming to get you and Tink," said Brad. "Just relax and try to take it easy."

"Tink?" Mitch asked. "Are you hurt?"

"Nah. My arm is probably broke, but I'm fine. You're the one that looks like roadkill."

Mitch coughed out another short-lived laugh. "Kind of feel like it, too," he admitted.

The three men waited, Tink and Brad chatting amiably while Mitch remained still and quiet, hugging his injured chest. After several minutes passed, Jorge's form resolved out of the gloom.

"What did you see?" asked Brad, alerting Mitch to the sergeant's return.

"I found our suspect."

"Anthony?" asked Mitch. "Where is he? Did he get away?"

Jorge shook his head. "Nope. He's dead. The golem went after him after it left you guys. I found him with his head cracked open about a hundred yards from here."

"We have to find the golem and stop it before it kills anyone else," said Mitch, pushing up to his hands and knees. Jorge grabbed him and eased him back to the ground.

"No need for that. The golem is done. When I found the kid, he was half buried in a mound of dirt. After the golem killed him, I think it decided it had finished its task and let itself fall apart. I called the Sheriff's dispatch center and asked for a couple deputies to set up a perimeter around our scene. I also put in a request for Homicide to come out."

"The stones…," began Mitch.

"Easy, Mitch," Jorge told him. "I was in briefing when you told the shift about the stones, remember? I dug through the dirt after I checked to see if the kid might still be alive. That's why I was gone so long." He reached into his pants pocket and removed two spherical gemstones. "I could only find two, though. I'll need to go back in the morning when there's more light and do a better search."

Mitch held out his hand, palm up, revealing the missing stone. "Here," he offered.

Jorge took the proffered sapphire.

"Wow. You really did it," said Tink, admiration in his voice. "You punched a couple holes in that thing and pulled out one of the stones. I wondered why it dropped you and ran off. Now I know. You kicked its ass, buddy!"

"I wouldn't go that far," said Mitch. "If this is kicking its ass, I would hate to find out what losing feels like." He coughed and choked back another groan of pain.

The four officers went silent. They could hear sirens in the distance as deputies and paramedics responded to their location.

"Okay, listen up," said Jorge. Before anybody gets here, we need to get our stories straight."

CHAPTER 24

Mitch reclined in his hospital bed, enjoying the hazy relaxed feeling from the pain killers the doctors had prescribed for his broken ribs. He was back in the same hospital where he had been treated after his concussion. The department had paid for another private room, possibly even the exact some room he had occupied previously. He couldn't be sure, though. Hospital rooms all looked depressingly alike.

Tink had been checked in with Mitch the night before, but after a couple X-rays and a temporary cast fitted on his left arm, he had been sent home to recuperate on his own. A minor concussion, bruises and scrapes, and a clean break of the left radius and a fracture of the ulna was not serious enough to keep him around.

Mitch's injuries had proved a little more complex. The golem broke two of his ribs and caused a lung puncture which had resulted in his difficulty breathing the night before. The emergency staff at the hospital had inserted a long, unpleasant needle into Mitch's side to draw pockets of blood and trapped air from his chest and allow his lung to fully reinflate. The relief was almost instantaneous as Mitch took his first full breath in almost two hours.

After several X-rays and hushed conversations, his doctor advised him that surgery did not seem to be necessary to repair the ribs. He was not cleared to go home, however. They wanted to keep him around a couple more days to make sure the broken bones remained in place and he did not develop pneumonia from the lung trauma. The doctor placed him on intravenous infusions of saline occasionally mixed with antibiotics and small doses of morphine. After the first hit of morphine, Mitch had gone out like a light with faulty wiring.

At least he didn't feel dizzy and nauseated this time, he consoled himself. The injury was painful, but it hadn't left him feeling like his brain was wrapped in cotton and wanting to throw up every five minutes. Between the broken ribs and a concussion, Mitch decided he would take busted ribs every time.

The company was better this time around as well. Instead of Brad sitting vigil over him, upon awakening, Mitch had discovered Violet curled up in one of the visitor chairs. Her legs tucked under her, and her head resting on her arm where she had propped it on the backrest, she was asleep when Mitch first noticed her. He watched her for several long minutes, grateful for her presence but not wanting to disturb her.

One bright blue eye popped open and peered back at him.

"Hey," he said softly, in case she wasn't fully awake.

"Hey," she answered back.

Violet sat upright and stretched. She wore a baggy gray sweatshirt and white jeans instead of the blue ones she typically favored. She did not have on any makeup and her hair looked as if she had come to the hospital immediately after leaping out of bed. Her blond mane was loose and a bit unruly, definitely in need of a good brushing.

All in all, she looked absolutely beautiful.

"What time is it?"

Violet glanced at her wrist but realized she wasn't wearing a watch. Glancing around the room, she finally pointed at the wall behind Mitch's head. He turned to find a rectangular wall clock displaying the current time as 10:42.

"Morning or night?" Mitch asked, as there were no windows in his room to offer a clue.

"It better be morning," said Violet. "Otherwise, I just slept fourteen hours in this chair."

She stood, yawned and stretched again. Running fingers through her hair to comb out the worst of the tangles, Violet crossed the room and sat on the edge of Mitch's bed. She laid a hand on his arm and stroked it lightly.

"Doctor told me he thinks you're going to be fine. You need to take it easy for a few weeks until the ribs heal, but otherwise you got really lucky when that car hit you."

"What? Oh, right. The car."

Mitch rubbed a hand over his face, trying to clear away the cobwebs in his head from the drugs in his system. Before he had been carried off by the ambulance last night, Jorge had made sure everyone on the shift told the same cover story when doctors and arriving deputies began asking questions.

The official report would claim Anthony Cunningham had not been working alone when committing the burglaries. He and his partner must have had a falling out when Anthony became a suspect, and Anthony was murdered to protect the identity of his accomplice. The unknown partner brought Anthony to the cemetery and attempted to bury him but was interrupted by the appearance of Tink and Mitch walking through their nightly rounds.

The suspect was chased into the parking lot where he jumped into a car with the engine already running, then he struck both officers with the vehicle during his escape. Because it was so dark and the incident happened so quickly, there was no useful suspect description, and no license plate was seen on the car.

The cover was flimsy and would never hold up under scrutiny, but as there would never be any accomplice located who could challenge the validity of the claims, and the officers involved were united in the story they told, nobody would be trying to pick it apart. The golem stones and notebook were locked away for good in the Dead Town property room, and everyone who knew the truth of what had happened understood that there was nothing to gain by sharing that information.

Detective Minhas was frustrated at finding out there was still an accomplice running around who would likely never be found, but he was also satisfied that Anthony's death afforded some resolution to the case.

"Yes, the car," continued Violet. "I talked to Alyssandra while you were still asleep. I told her that she owes you a huge favor for dealing with that car." Violet held up her hands, curling her fingers in air quotes around the word, "car."

"She doesn't owe me anything," Mitch protested.

Violet touched a finger to his lips to quiet him. "She does," the blond witch insisted, "and you are going to hold it over her head until she pays it back. It will make dealing with her much easier in the future having an advantage like that. Don't throw it away on false modesty."

Mitch nodded. Accepting his concession, Violet removed the finger from his lips and lightly tapped his nose.

"Good boy. Now, what the hell were you thinking going up against that thing again without telling me?"

Mitch shrugged. The motion caused a jolt of pain through his side even through the numbing protection of the medication. "Ugh," he grunted. "I was thinking that I was doing my job. I was trying to catch a killer."

"You should have told me so I could help."

"What happened to not offering any 'help or hinderance?'" Mitch asked. "I thought you were supposed to stay neutral."

"Not anymore. I agreed to help you learn how to use your gifts. That agreement includes making sure you stay alive long enough to learn something. You should have told me."

"I didn't want you there. It wasn't safe."

"Wasn't...?" Violet made an exasperated noise. "Of course, it wasn't safe. That's why I should have been..."

The floor nurse chose that moment to enter the room and Violet quickly composed herself, pasting on a friendly smile for the intruder. Mitch recognized the nurse as the same petite, bleached-blond who had taken care of him two weeks ago. She apparently remembered him as well.

"Hello there, Mitch," she said, standing at the foot of his bed. She grinned and wiggled her fingers in his direction. "I guess you couldn't stand being away from me and all of this." She gestured around the room at the bare walls and various medical equipment.

"Hi, Amanda. Nice to see you."

"You know you don't have to almost kill yourself whenever you want to see me. I would be happy to give you my phone number, and you could just call me."

"Careful how you talk to my boyfriend," interrupted Violet. "I've never knocked out an overly friendly nurse before, but I don't mind ticking that one off my bucket list."

The smile fell away from Amanda's expression. "Sorry. I didn't know he was spoken for. I'm not trying to get in the middle of anything."

"Then let's keep things professional, shall we?" suggested Violet.

Amanda agreed, her cheeks and ears turning slightly pink from embarrassment. She proceeded to check Mitch's vitals and question him about his current pain levels. Mitch noticed her gaze flicking toward Violet from time to time as though making sure she didn't step over any other perceived lines of etiquette. When she had updated his chart, she advised she would be back later in the day to check on him, but if he needed anything, he could always use the call button beside his bed.

"He won't need anything," Violet told her. "I'll be here to take care of him."

Amanda gave a short, apologetic nod and hustled out the door.

"Okay, I admit I didn't expect that," said Mitch after the nurse exited.

"Was that too aggressive?" asked Violet. "Should I apologize to her?"

"Not that. I meant the, uh, boyfriend part. I didn't expect that. Is that what I am now? Your boyfriend?"

Violet's features went carefully neutral. "I didn't mean to make an assumption. I mean, we never talked about it, but I thought we were … I don't know. I like when we spend time together. I thought you did, too. What would you call it, then?"

Mitch took Violet's hand in his. He interlaced his fingers with hers and squeezed gently.

"I think I like having a girlfriend," he said.

EPILOGUE

Mitch Loman sprawled on his tattered brown couch. With his head resting on a pillow propped up on an arm of the sofa, he watched *It's a Wonderful Life* for the third time that day; reciting lines along with Jimmy Stewart as characters in black and white ran and cavorted on the television set in front of him.

The toilet in the guest bathroom gurgled and flushed. A moment later, he heard the sound of the faucet running, so he dropped his feet to the floor and sat up. The bathroom door swung open and a tall woman with long brown hair emerged, wiping her hands on the pair of gray slacks she wore as she approached him.

"You still haven't bought towels for that bathroom," she chastised.

Mitch ignored the complaint.

"It's almost time," he told her.

Mitch's ex-wife, Linda, simply nodded. Her expression was tight and pinched, a combination of anxiety and fear.

"It's going to be okay. Thank you again for agreeing to come this year. I know how hard this is for you."

"Do you?" she asked, anger tinting her voice. Her shoulders suddenly slumped. "I'm sorry, Mitch. I don't understand any of this. I don't even know why I'm here."

"Yes, you do," he said. "You're here because you love Denny as much as I do, and because you're a good person. A good mother."

Mitch stood and gestured toward the couch, indicating Linda should sit.

"I'm going into the kitchen. Do you want anything?"

Linda shook her head. She let herself drop onto the couch as Mitch exited the living room.

Mitch walked into the kitchen and glanced around at the people gathered in his home. Dot and Tink sat at the kitchen table next to one another. Tink sipped from an open beer can, while Dot held a glass of water between her hands on the table. Violet, who had been leaning against the far counter, crossed the space between them quickly, raised up on her tiptoes and kissed his cheek. She wrapped her arms around his chest and hugged him.

Mitch glanced toward the wall clock.

"It's almost time," he said. "Any last-minute things I should know, Dot?"

"No. Do it exactly like we talked about. Give him the Christmas he missed out on. If this doesn't work, we won't get another chance until next year."

"Please let this work," said Mitch under his breath. He was afraid tonight might be the last time he would ever see his baby boy in this lifetime. He was also terrified it might not be.

He pressed his lips to Violet's forehead, then released her. She stepped back, gazing up at him. Her eyes were glassy with unshed tears, but she held herself together knowing that

Mitch did not need her feelings to add to his own worries tonight. His focus needed to be on Denny.

"Thank you, all of you, for being here."

Tink raised his beer. "I wouldn't be anywhere else. When this is over, you and I are going to get drunk. Whether we're celebrating or commiserating, I'm not going anywhere until one of us passes out."

Mitch smiled, a brief expression of thanks and appreciation. He met Violet's gaze one more time before returning to the living room and joining Linda on the couch.

Linda leaned forward, perched on the edge of one of the cushions. Her right knee was bouncing with nervous, unexpressed emotion. Mitch sat beside her, picking up the remote control and switching the television off. When silence claimed the room, he took Linda's hand in his and held it lightly. Although Linda was no longer his wife, she was still the mother of his child and that bond between them could never be broken. Not even by the loss of that very child.

"It'll be okay," he told her.

Tears tracked down Linda's face, but she said nothing.

"Daddy?" a voice called from the stairs behind them. Mitch heard Linda gasp as she tried to muffle a sob.

Mitch turned and spotted his little boy wearing the same blue, footed pajamas, and peering at them through the wooden railing of the stairs. His hair was damp with sweat and mussed from his pillow. He had one fist squeezed tight and was rubbing at his eyes to clear away the sleep.

"Did Santa come?" Denny asked.

"He did, buddy," said Mitch. "You just missed him. Mommy and I told him he should put your gift under the tree so you could find it when you got up. Do you want to go see what he brought you?"

Denny, now fully awake, nodded excitedly at his daddy. His eyes were wide in childlike amazement. "He came?!"

"He sure did. Come on downstairs and you can unwrap it."

The boy padded down the stairs as fast as he could manage, one hand raised high to steady himself against the guide rail. When he reached the last two stairs, he jumped the remaining distance, falling to his hands and knees as he landed. He was on his feet again in an instant, hurrying toward the flashing lights of the Christmas tree.

Denny found his gift. It was the only package under the tree. He picked it up, then turned to face his parents on the couch. "Can I open it?" he asked.

"Of course, you can. Merry Christmas, buddy."

Linda forced a smile even as she wiped a tissue under her eyes. "Merry Christmas, baby," she said.

Denny tore the paper away revealing a brown teddy bear with a furry, yellow stomach. He threw his arms around the bear and hugged it tightly. "Santa found it!" he exclaimed. "It's the one we saw in the store, Daddy."

"It is," agreed Mitch.

Denny ran across the room, the bear squeezed under one arm, and leapt into Mitch's lap. With his free arm he hugged his father's neck. Mitch returned the hug, pressing one cheek to the top of Denny's head. Linda reached out a hand to stroke the boy's hair, but her fingertips passed through without making contact. She jerked her hand back, beginning to cry again.

Mitch realized at that moment why it had been so hard for Linda to be around when Denny returned each year. He had thought her reluctance to get close to her son was from fear and an inability to understand why he had come back. It wasn't. It was the fact that Mitch could still touch the boy when she could not. She wanted so desperately to hold her baby again but could only watch from a distance while Mitch could pick him up and hug him with no physical restrictions. He suddenly felt guilty for the horrible thoughts he had harbored about her running away. He probably would have reacted the same way had their roles been reversed.

Denny pushed away from his father, still cuddling the teddy bear. He looked into Mitch's eyes with a sadness no four-year-old should have known.

"I'm sorry, Daddy," he said.

"Why are you sorry, buddy? You haven't done anything wrong."

"I'm sorry I didn't go to bed like you told me. I'm sorry I opened the window. I just wanted to see Santa."

Mitch and Linda froze. Denny did not sound like a child as he spoke these words. His voice had not changed, but the tone of it held years of experience beyond what any four-year-old boy should have. This wasn't the apology of a child caught misbehaving, it was much more. It was an expression of hard-won knowledge gained from suffering and long reflection.

"I'm sorry I died and made you and Mommy sad," he said solemnly.

"You didn't do anything wrong," Mitch told him again, speaking around a jagged lump in the back of his throat. "It was an accident. We love you. We miss you."

"Don't be sorry," Linda urged. "It's our fault. We should have nailed that damned window shut."

"I was scared you might be mad at me," Denny confessed, crawling off Mitch's lap. "I didn't want you mad at me."

"Nobody's mad at you, Denny." Mitch's vision blurred and it grew more difficult for him to talk. "You're our little boy. You'll always be our little boy."

Denny nodded, his expression too serious for such soft, delicate features.

"I have to go, now," he said.

"Go?" asked Linda. "Where are you going, Denny?"

"It's bedtime," insisted Denny, smiling now like the child Linda and Mitch remembered. All signs of the somber, pensive soul fled as he hugged his bear tight around the neck. "I love my teddy," he told them before fleeing toward the stairs.

"Goodnight, baby boy. I love you," Linda called after the running child.

"Love you, Mama."

Denny scrambled up the stairs using one hand to maneuver the climb, while the other clutched one of his teddy bear's feet, dragging the hapless stuffed animal behind him. His blue-clad form disappeared as he reached the second-floor landing.

Mitch and Linda sat on the couch, tense, expectant, as they waited for … whatever came next. Dot, Tink and Violet stepped quietly from out of the kitchen and joined them in the living room. Violet moved directly over to Mitch, sat in his lap, and wrapped her arms around his neck. She held him tightly, feeling the slight hitching of his chest as he fought the urge to break down.

"Forty-five minutes?" asked Dot, speaking softly as though loathe to break the fragile silence in the room.

"Ten thirty-two, and eighteen seconds," said Mitch, numbly. "Exactly."

"Then we wait," said Dot, taking a seat on the arm of the couch closest to Linda.

And they did.

As the five men and women counted the seconds ticking past, no one spoke. The only sound in that span of time was when Tink went into the kitchen and returned with two more beers. He set one on the coffee table in front of Mitch and kept the second for himself. Violet picked up the beer a few times and took small sips, but Mitch did not touch it.

"Ten thirty-two," said Dot, watching the second-hand trace circles around the clock face on her phone. "Ten seconds. Twenty. Thirty."

Mitch closed his eyes. He cocked an ear, trying to listen for a sound he desperately did not want to hear. He found only silence.

"Forty," said Dot. Then, "Fifty."

They all waited as an additional five minutes ticked by. Still no scream split the air. No sickening thud resonated from the patio. The pressure around Mitch's heart at last began to ease the tiniest fraction.

"Should we…?" he began.

In answer, everyone stood. Tink, Dot and Violet each took a step back, allowing Mitch and Linda to lead the way. Without further comment, Mitch headed for the stairs. They climbed single file: Mitch with Linda directly behind him, Violet next, and Dot and Tink following at the rear.

The procession moved to the second floor, turning right at the upstairs landing and moving toward Denny's bedroom. Mitch led them along at the pace of a funeral march, drawn to the bedroom, but dreading what he might find there. The boy's door was open, and Mitch reluctantly stepped inside, moving forward far enough to allow everyone else to pass through the doorway to see.

There was no sign of Denny in the room. The window was firmly shut, exactly as Mitch had left it earlier that night. The only indication that there had been a child in the room was Denny's bed. The teddy bear, Denny's Christmas present, was under the covers, tucked beneath a down comforter with its head resting peacefully on a pillow. Beside the bear, the bed covers lay rumpled in a pattern overly familiar to Mitch. The pillow also had a circular depression next to the resting teddy bear, as though a child's head had been pressed against it only a moment earlier.

Mitch approached the bed and placed a hand on the rumpled sheets.

"It's warm," he said.

For the first time that night, Linda allowed herself to cry openly. Dot wrapped her arms around her and tried to console the grieving woman. Linda gratefully accepted the gesture. Violet followed the cue and slipped her hands around Mitch from behind him.

"He's gone," she whispered in his ear.

"Is he gone, gone? Or is this just until next year?"

"He's gone," Violet assured him.

"How can you tell?" he asked, still staring at the bed.

"You broke the pattern, Mitch. Denny got the Christmas he's waited all these years to have, so there is nothing holding him here any longer. Trust me," she said, squeezing Mitch tighter. "He's moved on. He's at peace."

"I'm glad," said Mitch. "I'm glad he's found peace. I hope I can, too."

"You will," Violet said. She pressed her cheek to the back of his shoulder. "I'll be here to make sure of it."

About the Author

G. Allen Wilbanks, an Amazon internationally best-selling author, was born and raised in northern California. For twenty-five years he worked in law enforcement to pay the bills while writing horror and fantasy fiction during his free time to keep himself sane. In 2016 he decided to retire from real life and live in a fantasy world of his own making full time. For additional information about G. Allen, including where you can find more of his writing, please visit his website at www.gallenwilbanks.com.

www.ingramcontent.com/pod-product-compliance
Lightning Source LLC
Chambersburg PA
CBHW031547240626
47153CB00002B/408